# What Reviewers S
# Jesse J. Thoma

**The Chase**

"The primary couple's initial meeting is a uniquely amusing yet action-packed scenario. I was definitely drawn into the dynamic events of this thoroughly gratifying book via an artfully droll and continuously exciting story. Spectacularly entertaining!"—*Rainbow Book Reviews*

**Seneca Falls—*Lambda Literary Award Finalist***

"Loneliness and survival are the two themes dominating Seneca King's life in Thoma's emotionally raw contemporary lesbian romance. Thoma bluntly and uncompromisingly portrays Seneca's struggles with chronic pain, emotional trauma, and uncertainty." —*Publishers Weekly*

"This was another extraordinary book that I could not put down. Magnificent!"—*Rainbow Book Reviews*

"…a deeply moving account of a young woman trying to raise herself from the ashes of a youth-gone-wrong. Thoma has given us a redemptive tale—and Seneca isn't the only one who needs saving. Told with just enough wit and humor to break the tension that arises from living with villainous ghosts from the past, this is a tale woven into a narrative tapestry of healing and wholeness." —*Lambda Literary*

**Pedal to the Metal**

"Sassy and sexy meet adventurous and slightly nerdy in Thoma's much-anticipated sequel to *The Chase*. Tongue-in-cheek wit keeps the fast-moving action from going off the rails, all balanced by richly nuanced interpersonal relationships and sweet, realistic romance."—*Publishers Weekly*

"[*Pedal to the Metal*] has a wonderful cast of characters including the two primary women from the first book in subsidiary roles and some classy good guys versus bad guys action. ...The people, the predicaments, the multi-level layers of both the storyline and the couples populating the Rhode Island landscapes once again had me glued to the pages chapter after chapter. This book works so well on so many levels and is a wonderful complement to the opening book of this series that I truly hope the author will add several additional books to the series. Mystery, action, passion, and family linked together create one amazing reading experience. Scintillating!" —*Rainbow Book Reviews*

## By the Author

**Tales of Lasher, Inc.**

The Chase

Pedal To the Metal

Data Capture

Seneca Falls

Serenity

# Serenity

*by*

Jesse J. Thoma

2020

**SERENITY**



**ISBN 13: 978-1-63555-713-8**

This Trade Paperback Original Is Published By
Bold Strokes Books, Inc.
P.O. Box 249
Valley Falls, NY 12185

First Edition: August 2020



---

**Credits**
Editors: Victoria Villasenor and Cindy Cresap
Production Design: Susan Ramundo
Cover Design By Tammy Seidick

## Acknowledgments

As always I would like to thank the entire Bold Strokes Team, from Rad and Sandy, to everyone who even glanced at an email concerning this manuscript. I appreciate all the hard work and support. A special thank you, as always, to the editing superhero Victoria Villasenor. She consistently challenges me to be better and I cannot thank her enough.

To the readers, thank you for your continued support. I love being able to share my stories with you.

Finally, to my wife, thank you for ignoring me when I can't get a scene right and I'm grumbling at the computer. Thank you for not rolling your eyes when I decide to keep working on that same scene in the middle of the night and then complain about being tired in the morning. And most of all, thank you for reminding me every morning what true, never ending, deep, long-lasting love looks like.

# Dedication

To Alexis, Goose, and Bird who make my world go round.

Grant me the serenity to accept the things I cannot change
The courage to change the things I can
And the wisdom to know the difference.

# PROLOGUE

Kit Marsden surged into the single seater public bathroom and spun on wobbly, achy legs to close the door. Her hands were shaking so badly it took a few tries to get the door locked. She startled when she turned around and caught a glimpse of the woman in the mirror, not immediately recognizing herself. She sank to the floor, relief flooding her, when she realized she was alone.

She wiped her face, ridding herself of the sweat and snot that had been collecting there, and pulled a small bag from her pocket. It had taken her so long to procure her next shot of heroin she was now in withdrawal, but this tiny Ziploc contained the cure.

Moving as quickly as she could, Kit pulled out her works and began setting up for her shot. Someone else would need this bathroom eventually, but if she rushed things, she would bleed all over the place and that would be hard to explain. She carefully laid out the water bottle, cotton swab, lighter, sterile syringe, and spoon. She'd managed to find a ladle from a kid's play kitchen a few months ago to use as her cooker. It was the perfect shape and depth and had a handle that made cooking easy. She was especially grateful today with her hands so shaky. The last thing she wanted was to slosh half her hit across the floor.

Once everything was ready, she opened the bag and stuck the tiny test strip in, coating it with the powdered heroin. She hated the extra step, but fentanyl had changed the game. Now, instead of a nice steady march to oblivion, she had to add the extra step of a test strip or a test shot to make sure her stuff wasn't laced with poison. Her life might have gone to shit, but that didn't mean she wanted to end up dead.

*Fuck.* The strip turned purple.

The sweet salvation contained in her little Ziploc would probably kill her. Although if she was being honest, all the heroin these days had fentanyl in it. She'd been playing roulette with her life for months. Today was just the day she decided to test her hit and let the proof stare right back at her like a fully loaded assault rifle. She debated whether she cared. She already felt like death. Withdrawal played her central nervous system like a coked-out symphony conductor. And she was still early. It was only going to get worse without relief.

As if on cue, a wave of nausea hit and Kit lurched to the toilet, barely making it before vomiting. When she was fairly certain she was done, at least for the moment, she sank back against the door and looked at the bag of heroin she still clutched. She considered her life, such as it was, and what she risked losing if she injected these drugs.

"God damn it," she said.

She tried to remember the chant or prayer that some of her sober friends found so much comfort in. "God, grant me…A balloon, world peace, three wishes? He's God, not a genie. Salvation? A lollipop? Fuck it."

She stood up, feeling barely strong enough to hold herself upright, and stumbled back to the toilet.

She looked at the ceiling. "How about a sign at least, Genie, God, person? Is this rock bottom?"

There was only the faint buzzing of the overhead lights.

"Fine. Thanks for nothing."

Before she lost her nerve, she dumped the contents of the baggie she had worked so hard to procure and flushed it. She scooped up her works, turned, unlocked the door, and somehow, made it out of the bathroom without falling over or bouncing off walls. At least she thought she did. She definitely didn't hit the floor. She wasn't sure she would get back up.

The public library was busy at this time of day, and right now, that was both a blessing and a huge fucking annoyance. Maybe she could blend into the crowd and no one would bother her, but navigating the crowd was a challenge in her current state.

She stumbled through the library and tried to ignore the looks from the other patrons. She'd seen what stared back at her in the mirror. She looked like what she was, a strung-out heroin user. Their stares were justified. But right now, she didn't have time to care what anyone thought of her, she only cared about getting out the door before someone called the cops. She hadn't technically done anything wrong, if you discounted bringing heroin into the library in the first place, but that didn't mean they wouldn't haul her in and make her current living hell even worse.

When Kit burst through the front doors and into the fresh morning air, she thought she might cry with relief. She still felt like shit, but at least the fresh air cooled her sweaty skin and felt like a magic potion flowing into her lungs. She felt rather than heard someone exit behind her. She looked over her shoulder and saw a library employee eyeing her. He was looking at her intently, but not unkindly. It unnerved her all the same.

The shaking was worse than it had been. The steps felt like they were playing tricks on her and moving under her feet, but staying put wasn't an option. Especially not with library dude staring at her. She started to feel light-headed halfway down. Three-quarters of the way down, her vision dimmed and she felt the heaviness in her limbs as she passed out.

Kit came to as she was rolled onto her back. She opened her eyes and immediately slammed them shut against the sun overhead. She was aware of people all around and yelling. Lots of yelling.

One voice stood out, a man shouting over the crowd. "Get Thea out here. Now. I think we have an overdose."

"I'm here."

Kit liked the sound of the woman's voice. She wanted to open her eyes and see what she looked like, but the sun was being a jerk, and she wasn't feeling all that well. Maybe she'd just lie here a minute more. She shifted a little to get more comfortable. Something jabbed her right in the ass. She was pretty sure it was a rock.

Despite the circumstance, Kit started laughing. Rock bottom. One hell of a sign.

"Hey, can you hear me?"

There was that nice voice again. Kit opened her eyes this time. The sun was blocked by the most beautiful woman she'd ever seen. She wasn't in such bad shape she couldn't notice that. That had to count for something. Her curly, shoulder length brown hair was framing her face as she leaned over, and her chestnut brown eyes were soft with concern. Kit looked hard for judgment, revulsion, or reproach but didn't find any.

Kit saw a naloxone kit in the woman's hand, poised for deployment. Good thing she got a rock to the ass. The last thing she needed was a snoot full of naloxone. Her withdrawal problems were bad enough already.

"You don't need that." Kit tried to push the naloxone away. "I'm not overdosing."

"Are you sure? When was the last time you used?"

"Given the shape I'm in right now, too long ago. I'm withdrawing, not overdosing. Save that for someone who really needs it." She felt better when the woman lowered the dose, apparently satisfied.

"Okay. I'll sit with you for a few minutes all the same."

"Suit yourself," Kit said.

She dragged herself up on the step and into a more or less upright position. The crowd had dispersed, probably after they realized she wasn't dead and there wouldn't be any lifesaving heroics taking place. The library employee who had followed her out earlier was loitering nearby. She looked more closely at the woman sitting next to her. She was a library employee too. *What is a library employee doing running around with naloxone?*

"My name's Thea. I'm happy to provide you with computer time, reading material, food, any resources you may need, but I need something from you in return."

"What's that?"

Kit couldn't remember a time in her life where she felt so sick and yet she also wanted to stick around just to sit next to this woman. She was calm and steady, and very pretty.

"You can't use drugs in my library.

"Your library?" Kit said. "I thought it was a public library."

*That's really the direction you're going here? Idiot.*

Thea smiled slightly. Kit couldn't be sure because her brain was slowly becoming consumed with the physical symptoms of withdrawal that were taking over and getting more demanding by the minute, but it looked like Thea might have been amused.

"No drugs in my library."

"For what it's worth, and I realize it's not much, I planned on using drugs in your library, but I flushed them instead." She was shaking badly now, and despite the relatively cool temperature, sweat was pouring down her face and pooling at her waist. "God, how did I get here?"

Kit didn't mean to ask the last part aloud. It was despair and sickness escaping in one outlet of breath and in front of a complete stranger, no less. To add to Kit's mortification, Thea answered her.

"If you mean how you physically ended up here, I'd be happy to get you directions home. But you sounded a bit more philosophical just then. If you are looking to make changes to your current life circumstances, I'm also happy to provide you with any resources you require to get you started on your journey. The library is a wonderful resource."

Again, Kit looked for judgment or reproach but didn't find any as she searched Thea's face. She wondered how often Thea provided those wonderful resources to lost souls like her.

*Don't feel special, she carries naloxone in her pocket. She must see sad sacks like you all the time.*

"I appreciate the offer, but I don't think a library is what I need right now," Kit said. "The hospital's around the corner. I'm going to head to the emergency room while I can still walk. I think it's time to make some changes in my life."

## CHAPTER ONE

"Kit, you asshole, are you going to help me or stand there staring at the tools all day? This drywall ain't light, you know."

"All right, don't get your nuts in a knot," Kit said. "You know I didn't get clean to listen to you yappin' all day, old man. If I'd known I had twelve months of this to look forward to…"

Kit looked at her cousin Josh laboring under the weight of the full sheet of drywall. She thought about letting him sweat it out a little longer, but it wasn't worth it.

"You get the pleasure of listening to me. That's what you meant, right? Meanwhile, I have to look at you. Twelve months and you still look like death warmed in the microwave in tin foil. You should be carrying this so we can get some muscle back on you. Now get over here and help me hang this."

Kit flipped him off. "I'm strong enough to hang you on this wall and tape your mouth shut." She didn't mind Josh's teasing. They'd grown up together and were as close as siblings.

They worked in silence for another hour, hanging sheets of drywall until the room was fully enclosed. Once that step was done, they broke for lunch. Kit would have been happy to keep working, but Josh was the boss and he insisted they stop. Usually, there was a bigger crew, but Josh and Kit were handling this part themselves.

"What are you going to do when I'm not squatting on your couch packing your lunch for you?"

"Come crash on your couch and beg you to keep feeding me." Josh shrugged.

*You'll never need the handouts. You've always had your shit together.* She just gave him a quick grin.

"Hey, you know I don't mind you staying. You always have a place with me. I'm proud of you." Josh must have read Kit's mind. He'd always been good at that.

"I appreciate it, I do, but I just want to move on. I'm happy to keep working this job with you for the rest of our lives, but eventually I need to find a place and get back on my feet. Right now, it feels like I'm stuck just trying to be sober. That's not who I am," Kit said.

"Maybe not all of who you are, but it's a part. Kit, you are who you are. All the parts. You've got the good and the bad just like the rest of us. And you can work the rest of your life if you want. But me, I'm going to retire somewhere warm and clothing optional as soon as I can."

"How am I supposed to get that image out of my head now? Are we going to get back to work or do you have more words of wisdom to pull me out of my self-pity spiral? It was cozy in there. I was enjoying the spin cycle. And now I have no pity party and thoughts of your sunburned dick to keep me company."

"Haven't you ever heard of sunscreen? Go put the music on." Josh pointed to the radio. "We have to get this room mudded so we can sand and do a second pass tomorrow. If we finish in time, you wanna grab dinner and a movie later?"

Kit shook her head. Dinner and a movie sounded like heaven actually, but she had somewhere she had to be. Josh seemed to know not to push. He headed to the joint compound and drywall tape to set up.

Mudding drywall was one of Kit's favorite tasks since she'd joined Josh's construction company. It took concentration and skill, but was also repetitive. It had a meditative effect. The scraping of the drywall taping knife, the joint compound sealing the tape and filling the joints. The rest of the workday flew by. Tomorrow they would sand this coat and apply the next. She was tired but satisfied.

After work, Kit walked along the quiet sidewalks and enjoyed the warm, still evening. It still felt foreign to not have thoughts of her next hit consuming her. Her mind wandered to the strangest places now. She'd spent longer than she cared to admit two days ago contemplating the best way to pack grocery bags to maximize space and minimize smashed strawberries. It was a welcome change.

When Kit reached her destination, she stopped short. She hadn't paid much attention to the change in venue notification for today's Narcotics Anonymous meeting, but she should have. The NA meeting was at the library where she'd chosen not to tempt fate and where she'd finally made the decision to change her life for real.

She stared up at the stone facade that most people would probably find welcoming. If it weren't for the trash cans always near capacity, the benches three years past their "best if used by" date, and the heavy feel of toxic stress and inertia, the library and park could be dropped on any Northeast college campus. It was an undeniably beautiful old building and the park had a stateliness to it, with its mature trees and rambling paths. The embodiment of human complexity that littered the park didn't take away its natural grace.

Kit's memories of this place weren't especially positive. Except for Captain Naloxone the Super Librarian. Even in the midst of miserable withdrawal, she'd made a lasting memory. Kit couldn't have banished the woman's beautiful face or kind eyes even if she'd wanted to. And she didn't. Did she still work there or had she moved on to save lost souls elsewhere? Kit's legs tingled and felt weak at the memory of their meeting. She could feel the rock poking her in the ass when she'd rolled over on that step. Why was Super Librarian carrying naloxone? Her heart rate jumped. She needed a few minutes before she walked up those steps.

Kit had time before the meeting, so she turned away from the library and wandered into the park. There were the normal assortment of park goers, kids, folks in pairs out for a stroll, the physically active, but Kit also saw those that others ignored or overlooked. She noticed two homeless men camped under a graffiti covered footbridge, a drug deal being finalized behind a tree, and two people she didn't ever expect to lay eyes on again. Before she could decide what to do, they saw her too and headed her way. *Shit.*

"Kilo!" the man said. "Haven't seen you in a couple months of weekends. What can I get you? Friends and family discount on account of you being gone for so long and one of my favorites."

"Hey, Parrot Master." She had no idea what the man's real name was. Everyone called him Parrot Master. "Nothing for me, thanks."

"Do you hear this?" Parrot Master turned to the woman with him. "Kilo turning me down? My feathers must be shooting rainbows because today is truly a unicorn."

"Can it, you crazy old bird," the woman said.

Her name was the Zookeeper. There was affection in her voice as she shooed Parrot Master away. Kit had never understood the pair, but they were devoted to each other and she respected that.

"Let me talk to Kilo alone," the Zookeeper said.

Parrot Master flew off, his arms out as if flying, and he perched on a bench not far away. Kit wasn't sure, but it looked like he struck up a conversation with a pigeon.

"You straight?" The Zookeeper looked her over.

"About a year now." Kit was proud of it, but it felt weird talking about her sobriety with one of her former drug dealers.

"Well, shit. Good for you. I guess Kilo doesn't suit you if you're not shooting a kilo in your arm anymore."

"Is that why you called me that? I always thought it had something to do with my name."

"Honestly, kid, I have no fucking clue what your name is. When you disappeared, I hoped I wasn't going to find you dead somewhere with a needle in your arm."

Kit thought about how close that had been to happening. But it wouldn't have been the Zookeeper who found her. Would it have been the pretty librarian? Or some kid who had to pee? She pushed the thought away. No use dwelling on a mistake she didn't make.

"Kit, my name's Kit. What did it matter to you where I ended up?" Kit was curious, not accusatory.

"Everything that happens in my neighborhood matters to me. And now you're back and you're straight. Is that going to matter to me?"

"What, like are we going to start sending each other Christmas cards?"

"You always had a smart mouth on you, Kit. Are you going to cause us trouble now that you've found your way to the other side? I'm a survivor, but I need to be around to look after Parrot. He was always good to you."

"Isn't he the head of the local gang around here?" Kit looked around the park and saw plenty of Parrot Master's followers on benches, huddled in small groups, or playing cards at the tables.

"A head doesn't get where it needs to go, or see what it wants to see, without a body and a neck. I told you, he needs me."

Kit had never fully appreciated this dynamic when she was using or even understood what the Zookeeper was talking about most of the time. Mostly, Parrot Master was a source of drugs. Now she wondered what else she'd missed about them.

"All I want to do is go to work and start my life over. If I could erase all this from my memory, I would. I'll leave you well enough alone."

The Zookeeper nodded and shook Kit's hand. "You can't run away from who you are, Kit. Sometimes you just have to accept it."

"Accept that I'm a drug addict and go back to using? I don't believe that."

"That's not what I said." The Zookeeper jabbed her finger in Kit's chest, then turned and walked away.

Kit watched as the Zookeeper approached Parrot Master. He looked like he was asleep on the bench. She turned before she got to him.

"If you need us, Kit, or Kilo, you know where to find us."

Kit checked the time. She was going to be late. She jogged across the park to the library and back into the place where she'd left the last remnants of her old self. However unlikely, she was a little worried she might still find a piece of that Kit hiding along with forgotten dusty tomes. She shook off the thought.

Maybe that beautiful librarian would be there. Maybe Kit could apologize. She sighed. The world was full of maybes.

## CHAPTER TWO

The library was quiet in the early evening. Libraries had a reputation of always being silent, stale places, but Thea Harris had never found that to be true. It certainly wasn't true in her library. If you were to visit the second floor children's library mid morning, it more closely resembled a house party than the silent recesses of space. With more and more community groups, events, and programming for all ages happening, Thea felt the buzz of community all day. But now, she welcomed the tranquility. She was, after all, in a library.

She made her way to the front desk to check on Walter, her right-hand man. He had thirty years on her twenty-seven, but they had clicked the moment she took over this branch. When Thea arrived at the front desk, she knew she was in for some kind of trouble. The look on Walter's face was solely reserved for mischief making.

Carrie, the children's librarian, and a few other staff members and librarians were milling about, trying out what Thea was sure was their best attempt at looking casually busy. Except Carrie should have been upstairs and she, along with many of the others, had no real business loitering at the front desk. Carrie was also one of Thea's best friends and she'd always had a terrible poker face.

"Out with it, Walter." Thea put her hands on the desk and tried to look menacing. "We've got to turn the community room over for the next group meeting at six."

"Relax, just this once." Walter never stressed about much of anything. "Do you know what day it is?"

"Of course I do. It's Tuesday. The date is—"

"No, not that. You probably know exactly what time it is without consulting your watch, too. I am referring to why this date is noteworthy."

"Oh, yes." Thea had no idea why Walter felt the need to bring up her divorce.

"Don't look so forlorn, my dear," Walter said. "It's your divorceiversary. We're celebrating."

Walter pointed to Carrie who had appeared by his side, a wide grin on her face. On Walter's cue, she pulled a string behind the desk and a sign unfurled. It read "Happy Divorceiversary!" Suddenly, a cake was on the desk and someone was trying to put a party hat on Thea's head.

"Take that down." Thea waved at the sign as if she could strike it from existence. "We can't have that in here while the library is open."

"It's not open," Walter said. "There's no one here but us. This is the perfect occasion for a bit of revelry."

"I don't think a divorce is the kind of thing you're supposed to celebrate." Her protest was a little weaker this time. The cake looked awfully good.

"It is when the cause of the divorce is a lying, cheating, no good, rotten scoundrel." Walter slid the cake closer. Carrie and a few others nodded enthusiastically.

"It wasn't really cheating. We just had a difference of opinion on whether we were in an open marriage." Thea eyed the cake. Her protest sounded ridiculous leaving her mouth. Walter wasn't usually so heated, and Thea appreciated his protectiveness. "Okay, fine, she was a lying, cheating, dirty, rotten scoundrel. Does that deserve cake?"

"I don't know, honey, you were married to her. Is cake enough?" Carrie put her arm over Thea's shoulder and kissed her cheek.

"Not hardly, but it's a start." Thea examined the floor next to her shoe feeling defeated, wishing she were standing tall, eyes forward, chest puffed out, defiant.

In truth, Thea had been thinking about Sylvia all day. Getting divorced would have been bad enough, but being cheated on had rocked her foundation. Thea craved, no, *needed*, stability and predictability in her life. But the person who supposedly knew her best, who was supposed to love her forever and have her best interests in mind, had trampled all over her needs and desires, not to mention their marriage. Her parents hadn't been the safe harbor she'd needed either. Was it something she'd ever find? So much for revelry.

After Thea had eaten her fill of cake and all signs of the surprise celebration were cleaned up, Thea and Walter set up the community room for the six o'clock NA meeting. The group hadn't met in the library before. Walter had some reservations, but Thea had convinced him it was a good idea.

For a while, the library had been immune from the drug problems, especially opioids, impacting so many communities across the country. But slowly, the encroachment reached a critical mass and active drug use cropped up in the library. Thea wasn't sure how to stop it, but she was sure she needed to. She wanted the library to be a safe place for everyone. Needles in bathrooms and the threat of overdose endangered the emotional and physical safety of everyone. Thea felt the danger acutely. She grew up afraid to open her front door, never knowing what she'd find inside. That wasn't what she wanted for the patrons who opened her library door. They needed safety and so did she.

Walter had raised concerns with inviting the NA group to meet since Thea was working so hard to keep the library free of drugs. As far as Thea was concerned, anyone bothering to show up to an NA meeting, even if they were still actively using, should be encouraged. If she could help that by hosting the meeting, she was willing.

After setting up, Thea returned to the desk. Technically, she was off the clock, but since it was the first meeting for this new group, she wanted to stick around in case they had questions, or any problems arose. She didn't have anything pressing left over from the day, and getting started on the staff schedule for the next week, or worse, the quarterly budget, wasn't appealing. Instead she pulled up a favorite task. She searched a few new 3D printer templates to add to the approved folder for the teen sessions while she waited for the NA meeting to begin. She loved working with the adolescents as they picked a project, planned, and saw it through to the end. They usually worked with tools and materials they'd never used before. She was constantly amazed by the creativity and ingenuity of the young people who passed through the library.

A few minutes after six, a woman burst through the front doors and headed straight for the desk. She was slightly breathless as she asked for directions to the NA meeting. Thea pointed her in the right direction and watched her walk quickly down the hall. The woman had short cropped hair and was tall and slim, skinny even. Thea couldn't shake the feeling she knew her from somewhere.

*I know those eyes. Is it against divorcisversary rules to notice if someone's really attractive? Because she was and I did.*

"She looks familiar." Walter had a habit of sneaking up on Thea, which she hated. "Do you know her?"

"Not that I know of," Thea said, though it didn't feel true. It was her eyes, sapphire blue and searching. Those eyes were unforgettable.

For the next hour, Thea tried to remember where she'd seen the woman before. A lot of people came through the library, but for some reason this felt different than one of the nameless patrons she saw daily. It felt like it was just on the edge of her memory, but when she'd try to reach out and grab it, it would skitter further into the shadows.

Thea was surprised the hour was already gone when a large group of people passed her heading for the exit. She'd sent Walter home, so cleanup would take a little longer. It could technically wait until the morning, but she didn't like to leave things to hold over another day.

As she walked down the hall to the community room, the woman from earlier exited the bathroom. She looked guilty, and when Thea looked more closely, she could see why. In her right hand, she had a used syringe sticking out of a paper towel. She wasn't doing a very good job of concealing it, if that's what she was trying to do.

Suddenly, Thea remembered the woman. She remembered her stumbling out of the library and falling down the front steps. She remembered Walter yelling for her to bring the overdose reversal kit. Mostly, she remembered how ill this woman looked then, how ill and how lost. She looked better now, much better. And if Thea weren't so angry, she'd have been more willing to take a better look. As it was, however, she was strolling out of Thea's bathroom, after an NA meeting, with a used syringe, and an only mildly guilty look. This was what Walter had been worried about.

"You can't do that in here." Thea pointed at the syringe.

"You need sharps containers in the bathrooms." The woman turned slightly and gestured to the bathroom.

"I wouldn't need them if you didn't use drugs in my library. Especially if we're hosting NA meetings, I'm sure you understand why drug use in the library isn't okay."

The woman didn't say anything.

"Look, I don't care what you do on your own time. I hope the NA meetings help and you can get clean. I really do. But when you're in the library, there is no drug use. None. If I see anything like this again, or suspect you've been using, I'm going to have to ask you to leave and if it comes to it, you'll be banned from the library. I don't ban people lightly, so please don't make it come to that."

"Are you done?" The woman started to move past Thea. "I have to be up early and I need to find a sharps container before I go home."

Thea wanted to continue lecturing the woman strolling through her library with a dirty needle, but she'd said what she needed to say. Her sobriety really wasn't her business. And piling on after she'd used following an NA meeting was just mean and useless. The woman would change when she was ready. Thea could be angry solo. After she left.

Thea held up her hand and stopped her. "Follow me."

"Is this the part where you bury me behind a long-forgotten bookcase and they find my body in ten years while doing renovations?"

"Don't be ridiculous," Thea said. "They'd never find you."

"Oh damn." The woman held out her hand. The one that wasn't full of syringe. "Well, before I meet my grisly end, my name's Kit."

"Thea."

When they arrived at Thea's office she pointed at the wall opposite the door. Kit dutifully stood while Thea unlocked the door and retrieved the sharps container she kept locked in her desk drawer.

"Here, put the syringe in here. No more deposits though, okay? This was your one and only get out of jail free card."

Thea couldn't tell what emotion rolled through Kit's eyes. Whatever it was, it was gone quickly.

"So, no murder today then?"

"Afraid not," Thea said.

Thea wasn't sure how, but some of the anger from just a few minutes ago seemed to have lost its bite. Kit was rather charming if Thea didn't think about what she had been up to in the bathroom fifteen minutes prior.

"Well, then I'll get going." Kit started down the hall, then stopped and turned. "I hope to see you around the next meeting. Every time we meet you add to your mystique. First naloxone, now a sharps container. I'll admit, I'm intrigued."

Thea watched Kit walk away without another word. The entire encounter left her confused. Kit wasn't behaving as if she were high, but she had walked out of the bathroom with the syringe. Thea wasn't ready to analyze her reaction to their conversation. That was a cliffhanger she'd leave for another day. But one thing was certain, Kit remembered her too.

## CHAPTER THREE

Kit stared into the half empty coffee cup she had been slowly spinning on the Formica diner tabletop for the past fifteen minutes. She could feel her sponsor, Ethel, watching her. She swore the woman was a CIA interrogator in a former life. She just sat there like a statue staring at you, never blinking, never shifting, never needing to take care of basic human bodily needs, until your innermost thoughts and feelings spilled out.

She'd been resisting the power of Ethel for two and a half cups of coffee, which was a new record, but she was going to have to give in soon, since she really had to pee.

*Damn it, next time I'm going to have to wear diapers.* "Fine, you win." She leapt out of the booth and headed for the bathroom. "Order me something to eat if you're going to torture me."

When Kit returned eggs, pancakes, hash browns, and bacon were waiting for her. Her coffee cup was also full.

Ethel was already eating.

"Come on, champ. Your food's getting cold. I told the waitress to bring it all over thirty minutes after we arrived. Your bladder is surprisingly predictable."

"You know I hate you, right?" Kit said.

"Yeah, yeah. You going to finally tell me what's going on?"

Even Kit wasn't sure what was going on. She'd been out of sorts since the NA meeting at the library and her interaction with Thea. Dealing with emotions now that she was clean was a pain in the ass. Sitting with them, sorting through them. But if anyone could help, it was Ethel. If she let her.

"I ran into the librarian after the NA meeting."

"*The* librarian? Your librarian? Captain Naloxone the Super Librarian? No wonder you don't know your tits from your ass right now. Is she as hot as you remember? Is she not? Is that why you're such a grump?"

Ethel looked more excited than anyone had a right to this early in the morning.

"She's not *my* librarian, and I ran into her carrying a used syringe. Pretty sure based on the two interactions we've had, I might never be allowed back in the library."

"Kit." Ethel's expression was all business. "You should have called me. We've talked a lot about slips and relapses. They're a natural part of the recovery process, but I'm here for you, and I want to be here for you. You don't have to do this by yourself."

"The syringe wasn't mine. I would have called you if I was struggling that much, Ethel. I found it in the bathroom, just sitting on the sink. Anyone could have found it. I wrapped it in a paper towel and was going to bring it out and get rid of it, but then Thea caught me."

"And that bothers you?"

"Of course, it bothers me." Kit threw up her hands. "She's hot as fuck and it's her damn library. And for some reason she carries naloxone and has a sharps container in her office. And both times she thought I was a massive screwup, she was still kind to me."

"That does sound like a lot of bother, sport."

"Don't mock me, Ethel."

"Wouldn't dream of it. Perhaps we could talk about why you're most bothered by Thea's reaction?"

"What do you mean?" Kit was confused. She just told Ethel why she was bothered.

"A hot woman, who you're intrigued by, caught you with a syringe. Now it's almost a week later and you're still bent out of shape about it. Why? Specifically?"

Kit thought about her reaction. A lot had bothered her about Thea catching her with that syringe, including the fact that carrying it made her incredibly uncomfortable to begin with. But it was more than that. She wanted Thea to see a different picture than that syringe painted.

"Will people ever stop seeing me as a recovering addict?" Kit drummed her fingers on the table.

"Ah," Ethel said, rubbing her hands together. "Now we're getting somewhere. Tell me more."

"That's it, that's my question. Is this who I am for the rest of my life? Is this how people are going to see me?"

"It's part of who you are. You can't change that." Ethel took another bite of pancake. She didn't look like she had more to add.

"Why do people keep saying that?" Anger started to bubble.

"I'll let you reflect on that yourself, ace. Kit, people look hardest for things hidden just below the surface. You're trying so hard to cover up this part of yourself, it's like a big flashing neon sign everyone turns to look at."

"How could I possibly hide it? I go to meetings, I meet with you, I take my buprenorphine. It feels like all I do is work on staying clean."

"And it's tedious?"

"Yes. I just want to start my life again. When do I get to do that?"

"Kit, this *is* your life." Ethel put her fork down. "You need to build your life with these things in it. It will get easier with time, but it's always going to be important. Look at me. I've got twenty years under my belt and I'm still going to meetings. I've got to work at it every day because you just never know."

"What I know is it sucks," Kit said.

"It absolutely does," Ethel said. "But it would be easier if you embraced this part of yourself and stopped warring with it. Like you said, you come to meetings, but you're just warming a seat. Maybe try participating?"

"You've got some wild ideas." Some of the weight of the past week slipped away. Kit picked up her fork. "The earliest part of sobriety was energizing. It was new and exciting. This part is a little bit of a slog."

"It's why having a community is so important, kiddo. Don't discount that. Now, the most important questions. Are you going to eat that bacon, and what are we going to do about your librarian?"

# CHAPTER FOUR

"Jayden, I don't care how you try to hide what you're doing over there, I can still tell you're trying to use my 3D printer to make a penis." Thea arched an eyebrow at the offender.

The room full of teenagers erupted in laughter.

"Actually, I was trying to figure out how to make some really big balls," Jayden said with a big goofy grin. "I hadn't gotten to the junk yet."

"I'm going to have to veto the testicles too. I'm sure you can think of a more appropriate use of my printer? Or perhaps I can reassign your time to someone else for a while?"

"Whoa, whoa, I got it, I got it. I'm going to print you a big ol' bouquet of your favorite flowers. What are your favorite flowers?"

"Jayden?"

"Yes, ma'am?"

"Get back to work," Thea said.

Jayden kept smiling and returned to the computer to work on his designs. Thea saw him trash the anatomical sketches and open a few designs that would have a chance of being approved for printing.

This was probably Thea's favorite part of any day. The schedule officially set aside time for teenage "makers" to come and build robots, Legos, use the 3D printer, work on coding, or other projects. But kids also came to work on homework, surf the internet, and hang out with friends. Some of the kids only stopped in during the structured time every now and then, others she saw every day for hours. The teen librarians staffed the majority of the teen activities and the entirety of the teen library, but Thea still loved spending time with the kids whenever possible. She only officially worked with them during this twice a week block of time, but she was in and out of the teen section of the library regularly.

Regardless of how often they came, she tried to greet all of them by name and make a welcome space for each kid. It was important to her to be a consistent, reliable presence. She knew from her own childhood experiences how important that could be. She'd used a library similar to this one, and the generous adults there, to fill the gaping hole left by parents unable to care for her.

"Thea, you're a librarian."

Thea turned to the young woman working on homework at one of the tables across the room. Her name was Frankie. She was a regular and Thea had a soft spot for her.

"That's what everyone keeps telling me," Thea said.

"Is it your kind that is responsible for labeling this monstrosity a 'classic' and forcing it on unsuspecting high school students?"

Thea would have laughed, but Frankie was waving the offensive piece of classic literature so vigorously in her direction Thea thought better of it.

"Uh, no. I didn't personally have a role in designating any book a classic. You can stop threatening me with fourteen hundred pages of Russian literature."

"Okay, well, then can you help me? All I have figured out about this book is that it's the best sleep medicine in the world. Like the minute I look at it, I'm asleep. Doctors should prescribe this instead of pills."

Thea pulled up a chair next to Frankie. A few other kids who were also working on homework joined them with their own questions. If she was down here, this was always part of the routine. The predictability was comforting, as was knowing she was making a difference to these kids. Although she was going to have to brush up on her geometry. One homework assignment had stumped everyone there until Frankie finally stepped in and helped solve the problem.

After most of the kids left, Thea cleaned up the space. Frankie's backpack was still there, but that wasn't unusual. She was almost always the last to leave the library. Thea found her all over the place. She wasn't one to limit herself to the teen area. She was curious and seemed interested in what Thea was doing. Enough that she would sometimes just follow her around asking questions until it was time for one of them to head home. Thea didn't mind her young shadow. Frankie reminded her of herself at Frankie's age.

Just as Thea was finishing up, Frankie ran into the room.

"You've gotta come to the bathroom. Someone left their works there and a big mess. I didn't want to leave it, but I didn't know what else to do," Frankie said, looking understandably upset.

Thea dropped her armful of books and headed after Frankie.

When they arrived at the bathroom door, Thea nudged it open carefully. She stuck her head around and found exactly what Frankie had described. On the floor was a small black bag with everything needed to shoot heroin, and surrounding it was quite a mess. Paper towels and ribbons of toilet paper were strewn all over the floor. Some of them appeared to be bloody, but it was hard to tell exactly what had soiled them from the doorway. Thea could see one dirty syringe under one of the paper towels.

"Okay." Thea took a deep breath. She was disheartened. Seeing Kit carrying a syringe out of the bathroom had been hard enough. This was altogether different. She texted Walter to bring her supplies from her office.

"Must have gotten spooked." Frankie poked her head over Thea's shoulder. "Probably why there's blood all over and why they left their works behind."

Thea had forgotten she was still there. "How do you know so much about this?"

"School and the library aren't the only place to get an education." Her face was dark and her expression closed.

"I'm sorry the library too closely resembled some of your other learning environments." Thea turned and put her hand on Frankie's shoulder. "I'm trying hard to keep this outside the walls of the library."

"I like coming here because it's safe and predictable. I know you'll help me with all the 'classics' somebody thinks are important for me to read. That doesn't mean I don't know what's right outside the door. I live in this neighborhood, remember? You can't change who else lives here. They come to the library too."

"You're right. But do I have to like this part?" Thea waved at the chaos in front of her.

"You better not," Frankie said.

Walter arrived with the supplies Thea asked for. Cleaners would be through overnight, but this wasn't something they could or should handle. Besides, the library wasn't closed for the day. She couldn't leave the bathroom like this.

"Thanks, Walter. Can you make sure Frankie gets to wherever she needs to go?"

"You okay here? I can do the cleanup if you want."

Thea waved him off. She watched him lead Frankie down the hall. She wished she could have protected Frankie from this. She wished she could protect all the kids from this, in the library and out.

She grabbed the biohazard bag, sharps container, latex gloves, and TurtleSkin gloves Walter brought. She slipped on the latex gloves followed by the TurtleSkin. They were puncture proof so even if she missed something in the debris, she was protected. She never would have imagined this set of items being part of her librarian toolkit.

*The things they should have taught you in grad school. Dr. Schroeder would be passed out by now if he had to slip into TurtleSkins.*

After the bathroom was tidy and sterile once again, Thea swung by the front desk. It was past six, and once again, she should have gone home, but the quiet evening hours at the library were a part of her routine she enjoyed. And tonight, she had a specific reason for staying.

A little past seven, folks filed by the desk on their way out. Thea watched them leave, looking for Kit. She didn't know if Kit had come to the NA meeting tonight since she had been ass deep in aborted drug injection when it started.

When the last of the group filed out, Thea was surprised at her disappointment.

Was she disappointed that a not at all recovered woman didn't come to an NA meeting or that she didn't get to talk to her? Thea wanted no part of answering that question.

She scooted around the desk and headed back to the community room as if she could outrun any wandering thoughts that might dare follow her.

Her mind was still elsewhere when she flung open the door to the community room and almost knocked Kit over.

"What are you doing here?" It sounded more accusatory than she meant.

"Well, the past hour I'm not really supposed to say. You know, the anonymous thing, but since you already know about it, I was here for a meeting. If you're curious, it was a step meeting tonight. Step ten, if you're extra curious. What I was doing before you attacked me with the door was cleaning up terrible coffee and donuts that I'm pretty sure were baked last year. Wait, did you leave these for me? Was this how you planned on offing me?"

Thea managed not to laugh, but barely. "I have no intention of offing you. I'd never get the smell out of the books and I'd never risk my job dragging a body out of here."

Kit looked amused. Thea liked the sparkle in her eyes when she appeared to be contemplating mischief.

"You love this place."

It was a statement, not a question, but Thea nodded anyway.

"I could tell when you threatened to toss me out on my ass because you thought I'd been using drugs in your library last week. You were mad about that, but you were kind to me the first time we met."

"Are you saying you didn't use drugs in my library last week?"

"I've never used drugs in your library." Kit paused her coffee mop up and looked at Thea. "Although to be fair, I intended to once."

Thea believed Kit even though there was no real reason for her to. She was relieved the scene Frankie discovered earlier wasn't Kit's handiwork.

"What's wrong?"

*I need a better poker face.*

"Why did you have the syringe last week?" Thea joined the cleanup effort so she had something to do.

"Someone left it in the bathroom. I didn't want a kid or someone else to find it."

"And is that okay, you being around syringes?"

"I don't love it, but it's not a trigger, if that's what you're asking. I associate it with using, but the association isn't a good one. It doesn't make me want to use. There are plenty of other demons I have to wrestle with in that regard. That's not one of them."

"There was another one this afternoon." Thea sighed. "Same bathroom. This time it included bloody paper towels and the entire works."

"Oh shit," Kit said. "They must have gotten interrupted."

"That's what Frankie said."

"Who's Frankie?" Kit threw the last stale donut in the trash.

"A teenager who shouldn't know all that she does. She found the mess in the bathroom and got me."

"You worried about this kid?" Kit leaned against the table and looked at Thea seriously.

"I worry about all the kids here," Thea said. "And all the community members who walk through the doors and might stumble on something like that scene in the bathroom, or something worse. I probably shouldn't be talking to you about this. I'm sorry."

Thea didn't know Kit well enough to identify the emotions Kit was trying hard to hide. Anger was easy to spot, but there was more to it than that. She felt bad for upsetting her.

"I told you last week you need sharps containers in the bathrooms." Her words were clipped and her tone had lost the softness when she asked about Thea and the library.

"Won't that be as good as a sign inviting more drug use?"

"Needle exchanges don't lead to more drug use. They just keep dirty needles off the streets and keep people healthy. But since you shouldn't be talking to an addict about any of this, I'll let you figure it out with someone who's allowed to be involved in the conversation." Kit headed for the door without looking back.

At least Thea knew where Kit's anger was coming from. She hadn't meant to offend her, but clearly had. She tried to stop Kit, to apologize, but Kit grumbled something about work in the morning and left.

Thea sat in the nearest chair and looked around the room without really seeing anything. So far, every encounter with Kit had left her feeling off balance, a feeling she detested. But seeing Kit made her feel…something else, too. She couldn't put her finger on it. It was a feeling she didn't have a lot of experience with and she wasn't entirely sure she liked. Or at least her rational, organized, routine driven brain wasn't sure about it. The tiny sliver of herself that was prone to fits of wild abandon liked the feeling quite a lot. And that was reason enough to give her pause.

# CHAPTER FIVE

"Would you rather have a skunk for a roommate for six months, or rub your dick six times with a cheese grater?"

Kit was working on a new job with Josh's crew. They were forty-five minutes into "would you rather."

"Are we talking the zester side, or the cheese grater side?" Kit paused, hammer mid swing.

"I don't know, you pick."

"She's going to pick the dick grating, asshole. Why'd you give that one to her? She doesn't have a dick," said another guy on the crew.

"Mine's a hell of a lot bigger than yours. And it never goes soft." Kit winked at Josh.

"And she's got hella big balls. Not like your tiny little twig and berries," one of the guys shouted.

All the guys turned their attention, and teasing, to the guy who'd tried to compare sizes with Kit. They were a tight-knit group, and no one would take any of the banter personally. Kit liked working with these guys. They didn't treat her differently because she was a woman, or because of her past. All they cared about was the work she did, and she more than held her own.

When Josh released them for lunch, Kit grabbed the bag she'd packed and headed out into the fresh air. She loved working with the boys, but sometimes she needed to air out the testosterone.

The new job they were working wasn't far from the park in front of the library, so she headed there. It was what middle-class folks would probably describe as a rough neighborhood. There were security bars instead of stained glass, chain link instead of picket fences, and graffiti instead of expensive public art, but it was better than most of the places Kit had called home the years she'd been using. The park was busy in the middle of the day, but Kit found an open bench.

She didn't see Parrot Master or the Zookeeper around. She wondered what they were doing. She thought about what she would have been doing on a day like today a year ago. She didn't like what she pictured. Why was everyone making it impossible for her to shove all that behind her and let her move on?

"I was going to see if you wanted company, but it looks like you're in the middle of brooding. I don't want to interrupt."

Kit looked behind her and was struck by just how beautiful Thea was. The sun was directly above her, making her hair glow.

"What good has brooding ever done anyone?" Kit moved her lunch aside. "Have a seat."

"It worked okay for Batman." Thea sat and stretched her legs in front of her. "But you don't seem like a Batman."

"I'm intrigued. Just what do I seem like? Do not say Aquaman. If you say Aquaman, get right off this bench, you're not welcome here."

Thea laughed. Kit liked being the cause.

"Aquaman's not so bad, he has his fans. As for you, I'm not sure yet. I don't know you well enough. I just know you're not a Batman."

They sat in comfortable silence eating their lunches. Kit's was shoved in a brown sack, while Thea's was organized neatly in a two-tiered bento box. Kit was startled when Thea put her hand on her shoulder. It was unexpected, but she wasn't at all opposed to the contact.

"Look, Kit, I'm sorry I upset you yesterday. I was trying to be sensitive to the fact you might not want to listen to me complain about drug use in the library when you're in recovery, but I clearly bungled it and offended you. I'm sorry"

"Thank you." Kit debated whether to say more. Why did she need to explain her reaction? "I don't use drugs anymore, but everyone still insists on seeing me as a drug user. It drives me nuts. My whole life is consumed with *not* being a drug user, but when people look at me, that's what they see. All I want to do is move on with my life and be visible for something else, something a little more useful."

"I don't see you as only a drug user. I'm sorry that's what you felt yesterday. And for what it's worth, I thought about your suggestion of putting sharps containers in the bathrooms. I'm going to install them. You're right. If people are going to be using in there, I'd rather they not leave the syringes lying around."

"That should help," Kit said. "It's good for people who have medical needs who require syringes, too. Are you going to start patrolling outside the bathrooms with a drug sniffing dog?"

"Do you think that would help?"

Kit was pretty sure she was joking. "You would probably save a lot on toilet paper, but a few little kids might pee their pants in your nice chairs. Are you trying to keep drug users out, or lower the risk of overdose?"

"I'm concerned about safety. Do you know that two people have died in this park this year from overdoses? What if someone died in the library?"

Kit could hear the fear and pain in Thea's voice. She thought about how close she had come to being Thea's worst nightmare realized. She shuddered.

"Is this hard to talk about?"

"Yes, but maybe not for the reasons you think." Kit dropped what was left of her sandwich back in the bag, no longer hungry. "Do you remember the day you first met me? When I was in withdrawal and you were ready to shoot naloxone up my nose?"

"You did leave an impression," Thea said.

*What a first impression. I wonder if she'll ever be able to see me any other way?* "I could have been that someone you're scared of. My heroin was laced with fentanyl. I knew it and almost used it anyway."

"I'm really glad you didn't die in my library. I'm really glad you didn't die, full stop." Her expression was serious, but her eyes were still kind. They were always kind.

"Me too." Kit's shoulders were tensed up around her ears. With effort, she slowly relaxed them.

"So how do we keep the next you from dying in there too?" Thea turned to face Kit and looked at her expectantly.

"Why are you asking me?" Kit leaned back, away from Thea's expectations, but the arm of the bench held her in place.

"Who better to ask?"

"I think you missed the part about my wanting to move on with my life," Kit said.

"Just think about it." Thea turned back to face the park. "Now enough talking. My lunch break is almost done and I'm trying to be caught sitting with a hot woman I met at the library."

Kit looked around before realizing Thea was talking about her. That was an unexpected twist to her lunch break.

"And what if that woman wanted to learn more about you? Would talking be allowed then?"

Thea hesitated, and Kit wasn't sure what she'd said wrong. It seemed to take some effort on Thea's part to acquiesce to Kit's request. Kit had no idea if it was because of her, or something that had nothing to do with her. But she wanted to find out.

"Tell me about the library. I can tell you care about it."

"I don't have enough time to tell you everything about the library." Thea looked up at the library, love written all over her face. "But I love my job. I love the familiarity, the comfort, the reliability, the possibility that a library represents. You can go to any library in the world and the books may be different, but when you walk in the doors, you have a general sense of what to expect. How many other things are there like that in the world? Things that aren't trying to sell you something?"

"NA meetings are like that." Kit leaned her head back and looked up at the trees.

"Really? I didn't know that," Thea said.

"Knowing I could be anywhere in the world and find an NA meeting to hold as a reliable, steady, source of strength is extremely comforting."

"I imagine it is. I feel the same way about the library. I find comfort in the rules of the library. I don't mean rules like 'talk quietly,' but the order and rules of how the library is set up and runs."

"There's nothing more rock solid than the Dewey decimal system." Kit stole a glance at Thea.

"I knew I liked you." Thea smiled when she caught Kit looking.

"Don't go spreading that around," Kit said. "It will ruin my reputation as a brooder if people think I'm likable."

"I already told you, brooding doesn't suit you."

"You did mention that. But no final verdict of what does suit me."

"When I figure it out, I'll let you know. These things take time."

"Promises, promises."

Thea laughed. Once again, Kit was happy to be the source.

"That smile certainly suits you," Kit said before she could censor.

"Then I guess you should come around more often." Thea stood and picked up her lunch. "I seem to do more of it when you're around."

Before Kit could wrap her head around what Thea had said, Thea was heading back to the library. She looked back once and waved. Thankfully, Kit had pulled herself together enough to pull her jaw off the grass and manage the socially appropriate thing and waved back.

It was time for Kit to head back too, but she sat a few minutes longer.

*Thea was flirting with me, right?*

Kit had women hit on her when she was using, but they almost always wanted something from her. Usually drugs. What could Thea want from her?

Suddenly, Kit felt her good mood evaporate. The thought of Thea flirting with her had made her feel on top of the world, but now, blaring like a ten-thousand-piece, out of tune marching band, was the all-important question.

*You live with your cousin and sleep on his couch. What could a prize like you ever have to offer Thea?* She smashed her lunch sack and threw it into the garbage bin with more force than it deserved. On her walk back to the job site, she wondered if Thea would agree she was brooding now. She felt like she was brooding.

Kit decided it didn't much matter what she had to offer Thea. Thea seemed to like spending time with Kit and Kit liked spending time with Thea.

Nothing complicated about that, right? Right.

# CHAPTER SIX

Thea leaned against the counter in her kitchen and stared into space. She thought, not for the first time, that it was past time to hang something on the walls. She'd moved in six months ago, after selling the house she'd purchased with Sylvia. The white walls didn't bother her. They felt neat and orderly. Sylvia had been all about color and flash. It made Thea twitch. Especially the bright yellow Sylvia had insisted on painting the kitchen. Thea loved to cook, but that kitchen had felt like chaos come to life. She was always afraid of chopping off a finger from the frenetic energy of the place.

She wondered what her apartment would look like through an outsider's eyes. She knew what Carrie, who in addition to being a co-worker was also one of her closest friends, thought. She wasn't shy with her opinions. They were mostly along the theme that Thea was too controlled, and boring, and careful. What would Frankie think? Did anyone know what a teenager was thinking? Unbidden, the thought of Kit and her opinion popped into her head. How would Kit view her home?

Thea was annoyed at the thought, just as she was annoyed at her flirting and invitation for Kit to spend more time with her. Or was she annoyed that it had been weeks and Kit hadn't taken her up on it aside from a few rushed conversations on the way to meetings? No, she was most annoyed at herself. Kit was straddling two worlds, one of which Thea wanted nothing to do with ever again. She could admit the attraction; Kit was gorgeous, a walking, talking wet dream of butch sex appeal, but she was also off limits. Kit had the potential to be the bright yellow kitchen of women, and Thea wasn't willing to paint in such bright colors. Kit screamed excitement, unpredictability, and chaos. Thea craved stability, predictability, and routine.

It was getting dark in the apartment by the time she pulled herself out of her musings. She wasn't sure how long she'd been indulging in her wanderings. She made dinner and pulled out her laptop to get a jump-start on the quarterly budget waiting for her in the morning.

While she waited for the spreadsheets to load, she thought about the first time she met Kit, if that's how it could be described. She'd been so scared that Kit was going to be the first person to die from a drug overdose in the library, even if she'd technically been on the steps. Walter had called for her and she'd run, praying she would be fast enough to reverse the effects of the overdose.

When Kit got up and walked away, Thea didn't expect to ever see her again. Truth be told, she also didn't expect her to get clean, or even survive much past the time they briefly interacted. But now, Kit was, well, Kit. An unexpected surprise in her life. Maybe for once, she would just let that be enough, for now. In the meantime, she could still get a hold of herself and knock off the flirting. No matter how good-looking Kit was, it didn't do anyone any good for Thea to lose her head.

She worked for a couple of hours until she started to doze in her seat. She checked her email one last time before heading to bed. There was an email from Frankie. Thea read the email twice. There wasn't anything in it especially weird or alarming, but something didn't feel right. Frankie was asking if she could have a job at the library, offering to do any odds jobs or work to help out. That wasn't all that unusual, but she'd sent it late at night and Frankie had never emailed her before.

Thea wrote back asking Frankie to find her as soon as she could the next day.

❖

Despite Thea's invitation to spend more time with her, Kit hadn't had the time to make it happen. Josh had asked her to work extra hours on a job that had fallen behind schedule. It felt like the last few weeks all she'd done was work, go to meetings, and sleep. She'd barely had the chance to say more than a few words to Thea as she darted into the NA meeting each week, and Thea was gone when the meetings ended.

Now, the job was finally done and although she was exhausted from the punishing schedule, she felt immensely satisfied. She knew Josh was happy, which she was proud of. It had been a long time since someone could count on her.

Her long work hours might have given the wrong impression to Thea, though. Last week when Kit was running five minutes late to the meeting, she thought she saw disappointment on Thea's face as she rushed past. Today she had the day off and planned on rectifying her lack of attention. She was armed with time and a plan.

Kit walked into the library and headed for the front desk. Thea wasn't there. The man Kit recognized from her first inglorious visit to the library and a woman she didn't recognize were chatting behind the desk.

"Excuse me," Kit said. "I'm looking for Thea."

The man appraised Kit without answering. It wasn't exactly unfriendly, but there was no warmth in his gaze either. The woman, on the other hand, was all smile and open evaluation.

"Begs the question, is Thea looking for you?" The woman leaned over the desk just enough to be suggestive.

"I don't follow." Kit looked to the man for assistance.

"Oh, leave her alone, Carrie," he said. "Is that for Thea?" He pointed at one of the coffee cups in Kit's hands.

"Yes, sir."

"Well, far be it from me to stand between that woman and a cup of coffee. She's in the community room. My name's Walter."

She introduced herself to both of them. It was nice to meet some of Thea's people.

Kit walked quickly down to the community room. She wanted a few minutes with Thea before everyone arrived for the meeting.

Maybe she should have come earlier. When she pushed her way through the door, it was a letdown to see Thea wasn't alone.

Thea and the teenager with her didn't notice Kit right away. Thea seemed to be instructing the girl on setting up the room. Thea said something that made the teen groan and turn toward the door. Her hesitation at seeing Kit made Thea look as well.

"Oh, hi." Thea didn't look overly excited to see her. "You're early. We're almost done here."

Suddenly, Kit felt awkward standing there holding two coffee cups and not really knowing how to explain them or her presence. The teen seemed to know what was up and looked like she was settling in for a good show. All she was missing was popcorn.

"Uh, right." Kit started to put the coffee cups down but stopped. She wanted to have something to do with her hands. "I actually came by to see you. To apologize for running in and out of here the last few weeks. My boss had me working some crazy hours. Normally, it wouldn't be a problem to skip out or say I was sick or something, but my boss is my cousin and I live with him, so…"

"So now you're here," the teen said.

Kit thought she looked like she was having way too much fun at her expense.

"Frankie, don't you have literally anywhere else to be right now?" Thea shot Frankie a look.

"You're my new boss and you told me to be here." Frankie didn't move.

"Wait, you're the Frankie who found the bathroom a mess and knew what happened?" Kit asked.

Frankie looked at her shoes. Kit had definitely killed her good mood.

"Yeah, that's me."

"I don't know why you knew what you knew." Kit put the coffees down this time and moved into Frankie's line of sight. "But for what it's worth, I used to be someone who left messes like that. And now I'm not."

"Really?" Frankie looked up. "This is probably a dumb question, but was it hard?"

Kit thought about how to answer. Getting clean was the hardest thing she'd ever done, but also once she finally made the decision, one thing that was easy to fight for. It was getting to the point of making the decision to really, truly, absolutely go for it that had taken a long time.

"Yes," Kit said. "It took a lot of work to be ready and then a lot of really hard work to make it happen. I had a few false starts, but I've come a long way. I'm still working hard."

Frankie looked pensive. Kit offered her one of the coffees and the other one to Thea. She would make do with NA meeting sludge again.

"I brought this for you." Kit handed Thea her coffee. "I notice you always have coffee when I come in for the meeting. You seem like an unsweetened latte kind of woman. I'm trying not to hold it against you. I brought ginger cardamom syrup and golden turmeric if you decide you want to live a little and try one."

Thea looked horrified when Frankie dumped half of the golden turmeric Kit brought into her latte. Kit hadn't seen anyone look that suspicious of any substance since someone she knew from the streets was high and hallucinating and thought a sugar packet was an obstinate, militaristic grasshopper.

"You really should try this," Frankie said.

"I'll stick with what I know." Thea wrinkled her nose. "Thank you for the coffee. That was very sweet of you. Frankie, Kit is responsible for the new sharps containers in the bathrooms."

"Wicked good idea." Frankie tipped her coffee cup in Kit's direction.

"If you have any ideas or more questions, Thea can always get in touch with me." Kit wasn't sure what possessed her to offer, but when she was talking with Frankie, she didn't mind questions about her past. Something about teenagers asking questions felt more honest, less judgmental.

"Thanks." Frankie looked shy and young. "I don't really know anyone like you. Someone who stopped, I mean. Obviously, I know people do, but I thought maybe only rich people, or other kinds of people. No one from around here."

"There are lots of us," Kit said. "I'm kinda new to the game, but my sponsor's been clean forever. She's not rich and she grew up in this neighborhood."

Frankie spontaneously hugged Kit, which seemed to surprise her as much as it surprised Kit, and then she practically ran out the door.

When she left, Kit found Thea staring at her.

"Thank you," Thea said.

"It's just coffee." Kit shrugged. "And I am sorry I didn't make it around. You were really nice to ask me to come by more often, and then it probably seemed like I was avoiding you. I wasn't."

"I wasn't talking about the coffee, but thank you for that too. I didn't think you were avoiding me. No one could look as frazzled as you did every week and have a master plan to blow me off. And at least a few times you were covered in sawdust."

"Damn, I tried to clean up before I came in here, but it gets everywhere."

"If I'm being honest." Thea arched an eyebrow. "It's a look that works for you."

Thea looked like she wanted to slap her hand over her mouth and shove the words back in. The door opened and folks took their seats for the meeting. Kit cursed their timing.

"Can you tell me more about that?" Kit leaned in so only Thea could hear her.

"Nope," Thea said. "You're busy. See you after your meeting," She waved on her way out the door.

*Damn it. There are too damn many people in this damn library today.*

Kit flopped down in the nearest chair. She didn't bother with the coffee being set up. She'd given Frankie the only stuff worth drinking. Funny how she had standards now.

"You all right, skip?" Ethel slipped into the seat next to Kit and patted her knee. "You look like you've got troubles. Hard to diagnose, though. We dealing with a combo platter?"

Kit thought about her disclosures to Frankie and Frankie's spontaneous hug. Did the kid really not know anyone who was clean? That wouldn't be so discouraging except it was obvious she knew plenty of users. It had been impossible to pretend her past didn't exist with Frankie and for perhaps the first time, Kit hadn't really wanted to.

That was enough to give her pause, but then Thea said she liked Kit covered in sawdust. Kit felt like she was so far removed from normal social interactions, even after a year back in, that the intricacies of flirting still felt foreign. Not to mention she was sleeping on her cousin's couch and working on his construction crew. There was a reason Ethel had advised her to figure out her shit before hopping back in the dating game.

"Nah, it's nothing." Kit waved dismissively to Ethel. She'd figure it out.

"Don't bullshit me, kid," Ethel gave her a no-nonsense glare. "You're not very good at it, for one. For another thing, it's not going to do you any good."

"Were you put on this earth to be a pain in my ass?"

"It's my sole purpose. Now shush, the meeting's starting. Why don't you consider participating this week, huh?"

The meeting started with the comforting rhythm repeated at every meeting. The readings differed from meeting to meeting, and some of the faces came and went, but the scaffolding of the meeting was there, a foundation to build on.

This week's speaker focused on her fear of identifying as someone in recovery. Kit thought the topic was a little too on point. Ethel seemed to think so too. She jabbed Kit with her knee and looked at her pointedly. Kit tried to ignore her. Ethel upped the ante and gave her a sharp elbow jab to the ribs. Kit had to acknowledge that. She was worried the next poke would be to her eye.

Kit appreciated hearing someone else talk about the inner battle they faced moving from one identity to another. As with many things in NA, there wasn't an easy solution presented. It still helped to know she wasn't the only one struggling to figure out who she wanted to become.

After the meeting, Kit assured Ethel she really was fine and went in search of Thea. As seemed to be a frequent routine, Thea was sitting at the desk. The coffee Kit brought her was perched on a pile of books. Kit got a little thrill when she noticed the slight yellow tinge around the rim of the cup. Thea had added the turmeric.

"It changed your entire outlook on life, didn't it?" Kit pointed at the cup.

"Excuse me?"

"The turmeric. Will you ever look at a latte the same way again?"

"It was…unexpected." Thea picked up the cup and eyed it.

"Well, shit. The past heroin use didn't do it, but bringing something 'unexpected' into your coffee routine is going to be what gets me on the librarian no-fly list, isn't it?"

"And now you've got jokes," Thea said.

"I've got way better jokes than that. Would you like to hear them?"

Thea groaned and shook her head.

"I'll spare you because there's only so much mirth and frivolity one can provide in a day. I've gotta pace myself."

"Is that what is happening here?" Thea pointed between herself and Kit. "How was the meeting?"

"It was really good. Insightful. Hey, are you leaving? Can I walk you to your car?"

Thea was headed to the bus stop, which happened to be on Kit's way home. She waited for Thea to grab her things and they left together. Kit saw Walter watching them. She threw him a wave but didn't get one in return.

"Not sure your main man likes me much. I know I joked about the coffee earlier, but I know even exploring the possibility of a friendship with someone like me is probably almost as unexpected for you as the turmeric. Thanks for not writing me off just because of my past."

"You have no idea." Thea looked sad.

It was so quiet Kit almost missed it. "I'd like to," Kit said.

"I grew up in a neighborhood a lot like this one." Thea indicated the apartment buildings and urban scarred landscape.

Kit was startled by the abrupt subject change, but she accepted Thea's lead.

"Really? What's your favorite memory growing up there?"

Thea looked distressed, and Kit wished she could take back her question. Kit seemed to be making a habit of stepping in it.

"You don't have to tell me. Tell me about your day at work instead. Or something else entirely. Yell at me about turmeric. Tell me your favorite spice and I'll bring you that next time." *Stop talking.*

"It's okay." Thea touched her fingers to Kit's shoulder. "The answer is an easy one. My favorite memory is the library. I spent a lot of time there."

"No wonder you're so protective of your library now. If it was your favorite place growing up." Kit was sure there was more to the story.

"I feel strongly every community should have a safe place available for use by everyone. A place for learning, reading, research, community, and fun. At least, that's what I try to encourage."

They arrived at the bus stop a few minutes before Thea's bus.

"Thanks for the unexpected today, Kit. I don't know that I'll ever try that particular coffee combination again, but I am glad I tried it today. I don't really like things that are unpredictable, but you managed to get me to drink yellow coffee. You should be proud of yourself."

"Oh, I most certainly am." Kit puffed out her chest dramatically, which drew a laugh from Thea. "Thanks for trying something different. And for telling me about your library growing up. Just to be safe, I'll go for something less weird next week."

As she walked the rest of the way home, Kit let the contentment flow without question. For once it didn't matter how the world saw her, what her future looked like, whether she was ready to date or not. For tonight, she got to walk a beautiful woman to the bus stop and maybe, just maybe, she was making a new friend. She started grading her life on a curve a long time ago, but even without the cheat, today got top marks.

## CHAPTER SEVEN

Kit and Josh were the first to arrive at the job site, as usual. They worked in tandem preparing for the day. While Kit pulled out supplies and readied for her work, she marveled at how far she'd come. It wasn't long ago that she'd trailed along behind Josh in the mornings like an eager puppy, clueless, but willing to learn. Now, he didn't bother giving her instruction or direction. They knew the list of what needed doing and worked together to check the boxes. The fact that he trusted her, that he felt she had earned his trust, meant everything to her.

"'Bout done over there? Or are you going to daydream my money away?" Josh indicated the work she should have completed by now and pointed at his watch.

Kit flipped him off and finished what she was doing. She rejoined him when she was done. She didn't particularly like the fact that he'd caught her in a moment of reflection and idle hands.

"A couple new guys are starting today." Josh flipped through a stack of papers. "At least some of the day I need you to keep an eye on them."

Kit nodded. She could babysit a couple of newbies while they decided if this was the job for them. It usually didn't take more than a day or two for the job to separate those who came to work versus those who liked the sound of hardhats, power tools, and a hard-earned paycheck.

"Try not to let the guys ride them too hard. I'm down a couple men, so it would be nice if these two stuck around."

"Yeah, yeah. If they can't take the guys though, it's not going to work. Might as well figure that out today."

"Go easy on them, please?"

"You're the boss." Kit grabbed her tool belt.

Half an hour later, the rest of the crew began arriving. They were framing out a four-bedroom enormous monstrosity of a house. The apartment Kit was sharing with Josh felt like it could fit in any of the four bathrooms in this place.

Kit didn't have much interaction with the new guys, Micky and David, in the morning. She kept her eye on them as promised, but she didn't have a good reason to wander by and chat. What she did get was an earful from the regular crew. Micky and David weren't making many friends.

Today, instead of heading off on her own for lunch, Kit stuck around. She'd been hoping to have lunch in the park and maybe catch Thea, but the mood of the crew felt volatile and she didn't want Josh to have to deal with any flare-ups alone. She'd barely sat down when Micky struck up conversation.

"So, Kit, you don't feel out of place working here?"

"I don't follow." Kit wasn't in the mood for twenty questions.

"Being the only woman."

"Oh, Kit's not a woman," Felix, one of the usual guys, said. "She's just one of the guys."

"I don't think your wife was looking for one of the guys when she was whispering in Kit's ear last night," one of the other guys said, teasing Felix.

The whole crew laughed, except Felix. He turned to Kit.

"You weren't? With my wife? Behind my back?"

"I'd never do that to you, man." Kit shook her head. "Don't let them get to you. Your wife is crazy for you."

Felix nodded a few times and then smiled.

"Why would any man's wife be interested in someone like her?" David asked.

"Hard worker."

"Hot as hell."

"Smart as fuck."

"Makes a really good sandwich."

The guys spontaneously went around the circle listing off Kit's attributes. None of them looked happy with the question. Kit could sense the tension rising again. Micky and David looked annoyed. Kit didn't know what they were getting at, but she wasn't interested in more conversation with them if this was the direction they were heading. They, however, didn't seem to be done.

"That's not exactly what I meant," Micky said.

"I don't care what you meant." Kit stood. "Lunch time's over and so is this conversation. Back to work."

The men dispersed, but the air of barely contained powder keg did not. She switched with one of her guys so she would be the one working with Micky and David. She hoped that would help. It didn't. They started in on her again as soon as they had the chance.

"How does someone as morally bankrupt as you even find a job? I know you're not fucking the boss," David said. Apparently, it was his turn to hassle her.

"What's your deal with me?" Kit spun around to face him. She had no idea why these guys had singled her out.

"What you've done is offend every fiber of my being." David's face was red, and he took a step toward her. "The fact I have to work with you is insulting."

"No one's forcing you to stay." Kit pointed to the gate. She didn't bother telling them today was probably their last day anyway.

"I have no intention of leaving."

"Fine, then shut up and work."

Micky and David were quiet for a blessed fifteen minutes before they were overcome with the need to continue being assholes.

"Does Josh drug test you constantly?" Micky asked.

"Is that what this is about?" Kit pointed between herself and Micky. "I figured it was the gay thing, but you're hung up on the drugs? At least you're original. How do you even know about that?"

Micky ignored her. He picked up a nail gun and waved it in her direction.

"Are you high right now? Could you safely operate this tool if asked?"

"Sure as a cricket fart *you* can't. Put that down." Micky obviously had no idea how a nail gun worked and was swinging it around dangerously. Worst of all, he was holding it with his finger depressing the trigger, meaning he could discharge a nail accidently without much effort. All he had to do was bump the safety catch and a nail would fire, into the air, or his dumb self.

A couple of the guys who had been working nearby suddenly appeared. Kit figured they'd been letting her handle it until the two idiots playing dress up involved power tools.

"Hey, man, why don't you put that down before you hurt someone," Billy, one of the crew, said.

"I want to know if she could use it? Did anyone drug test her this morning? You work with a junkie and you don't know if she's capable of using the tools around you."

"She's not a junkie, you piece of shit," Billy said. "And she's capable of using that nail gun and nailing your mouth shut. When she's done, I'll shove it up your ass."

"Billy, it's okay." Kit held up her hand. "He's not worth it. I'm not high, not that I have to answer to you." She was trying to remain calm and not let Micky or David get to her, but her reserve of patience and calm was draining fast. "And I don't pick up tools I don't know how to use because that would put the rest of the guys here at risk. Something you're doing right now. Take your finger off the trigger."

Micky seemed disinclined to relinquish the nail gun. "Don't lecture me. Do you know why you used drugs? Addiction isn't a disease or a medical condition like some people try to say these days. It's a moral failing. You are weak. You are pathetic. You are a failure." He punctuated each of his points by jamming the nail gun in the air in Kit's direction.

Shell-shocked, Kit just stared at him. Even in her years using, she had never been so brazenly attacked. She stood motionless, unable to flee or fight back. Micky had a look of victory in his eyes, which infuriated her. He'd started to say something else when a fist connected with the side of his jaw. It was Felix. Kit saw Josh holding Billy back, but he was yelling at Micky at the same time. It all felt like it was happening in slow motion.

Micky lunged at her and she stepped forward. She had to get the nail gun out of his hands before someone got hurt. Kit reached for the gun as Micky raised it. It looked like he was going to take a swing at her face. She put her hand up, palm out. Kit distinctly heard the air pressure build on the nail gun and the loud pop as the nail gun bounced along her palm. The fucking idiot still had the trigger depressed and the pressure against her palm was all that was needed to shoot a nail into her hand.

Instinct overrode the need to keep her hands up against additional insult, and she doubled over, cradling her wounded hand. In her peripheral vision, she saw Micky on the ground under a pile of angry men. Josh was trying to keep them from pummeling him. David was being held against a truck. Felix and Billy were by Kit's side, although she wasn't sure when they arrived.

"Hey, tough guy, you think you can swipe away nails with your bare hands now? That's some ninja bullshit." Felix had his hand on her back and was crouched next to her, real concern in his eyes.

"I can give you this same memory, if you'd like. Go get me that fucking nail gun." Kit's hand was throbbing and bleeding heavily. "Can you go get me something, so I don't keep bleeding on my shoes?"

"Sure thing. I'll get you a glove and cut a little hole in it to accommodate your new Wolverine claw," Felix said.

"Funny man." Kit grimaced against the pain.

She appreciated that even in this situation Felix and Billy were giving her a hard time. They cared about her.

She looked at her hand for the first time. She shouldn't have looked. The nail had gone all the way through her palm, so she had a new claw palm up or down.

Once Josh had finally calmed down the scrum, he came to check on her. She had taken a seat on the big cooler of water while she waited for Felix. The pain was fierce, and her hand throbbed with every heartbeat.

"I asked you to keep an eye on the new guys. Not get shot by them and then start a brawl."

"Hate to break it to you, but after spending time with them all day, the new guys suck." Kit held up her hand to show Josh.

"That's what I hear. I had to fire them."

Felix returned with a towel. Kit wrapped it carefully around her hand, avoiding the nail sticking out of her hand.

"Felix, Billy, send everyone home for the day. Make sure everything is cleaned up first and the site is locked up tight. I'm taking Kit to the hospital. Call the police and have them deal with Micky and David. Let them know where we are so they can come by and talk to us."

"You got it, boss."

Josh started walking and Kit followed. She protested as they walked. She felt bad causing so much trouble. She knew it wasn't her fault, but she still felt guilty. Time was money for Josh, and shutting down for half a day wasn't good for business. Maybe she should have handled Micky and David differently.

"What did those guys have against you?" Josh looked over his shoulder as they walked.

"My moral failings." Kit shrugged and tugged the towel tighter.

"Gay thing?"

"No, surprisingly. Drug thing. They were really hung up on it."

"Huh, I bet if you'd asked nicely, they'd have given you an earful about the gay thing too. They seem like those kinda guys. But neither one is a moral failing." Josh yanked open the truck door and tried to help Kit inside. "Drug thing's brain chemistry."

Kit shoved him away and awkwardly got into the seat one-handed. "They would vehemently disagree. I have no idea how they even knew about my past. It's not like I wear a sign on my shirt."

"You should." Josh cranked the engine and headed to the hospital. "You should be proud of how hard you've worked. But I think a couple of the guys were talking about your recovery. The twin idiots must have overheard."

"Why were they talking about me?" Kit didn't like knowing people were talking about her behind her back. The pain in her hand was wearing on her and the hospital didn't feel close enough. Even on her best days she didn't like people in her business and today wasn't her best day.

"I think Joe's brother is struggling with an addiction to painkillers right now. Billy was telling him you've been clean over a year, so he shouldn't give up hope."

Kit thought about Frankie. She wondered if Joe knew anyone who had gotten clean aside from her. But maybe he didn't even know anyone who used aside from his brother. This was the second time someone knowing her story seemed like a good thing for them. But it didn't always feel like a good thing for her.

When they got to the hospital Josh insisted on coming in with her. She tried to tell him he didn't need to, but he wouldn't take no for an answer, and truthfully, Kit was glad for the company. She was also glad for the support. She knew she'd be offered pain medicine repeatedly. Although there wasn't any rule that said she couldn't have it if she was injured, she didn't want it. She'd fought so hard to rid her life of opioids, and she couldn't welcome them back, not now, not for any reason. She needed Josh to help her say no as many times as necessary.

In the end it wasn't so bad. They numbed her hand when they took out the nail and cleaned out the hole it left. She was up to date on her tetanus shot so she didn't have to endure that fun. By some miracle, it'd missed doing damage that required surgery or extensive bracing. She couldn't work while it healed and it hurt like hell, but overall, it was the best outcome she could ask for after tussling with a nail gun.

The real problem was all the headaches the injury was going to cause Josh. There was workman's comp, injury recording forms for Josh, the decision whether to pursue legal action against Micky for harassment and assault and battery. Not to mention now they were half a day behind and three men short.

Josh had told her not to worry about paying rent that month since she couldn't work, but she did worry. She worried a lot, which was compounded by the fact that she was still sleeping on his couch.

It felt like she was taking advantage of him. In the morning, she would figure out a way to pay the rent for the month even if she couldn't work her regular job. When she was using, she'd needed other people to help her get through her days and get her next fix. But now, she'd worked too hard getting back on her feet to feel completely dependent again.

## CHAPTER EIGHT

Thea set her coffee on her desk and pulled up a particularly challenging research request from a local business. She loved getting requests from the community to help find information that wasn't easy to track down. It made her feel like a super sleuth and she usually learned a lot about a topic she otherwise wouldn't explore.

On a few of her favorite projects she'd helped with an extensive family history research project, learned more about community zoning than she probably would ever need, and pulled models of clinician ride-along programs in police departments around the country for the local force.

While she waited for her computer to boot up, she popped the lid off her coffee and contemplated the unsweetened latte. She would never admit it to anyone, but she was having trouble looking at her morning cup of heaven and not thinking it a bit boring. There was no way she was going back to turmeric, but she had added hazelnut syrup a week ago. That felt outrageously bold. It had also been delicious.

*Kit, I just might end up cursing you or loving you. I'm not sure I want to do either.*

She put the lid back on, stuck with boring this morning, and returned to her computer. She opened the spreadsheets and documents she would need to record her findings. She labeled everything and made a list of the details she wanted to search. There was nothing more exciting than an outline and an organized plan of attack.

*I need to look for other sources of excitement in my life if this is what I count as entertainment.* Thea was about to get started when Walter knocked on her door. Thea was happy to see him. She always was, but their schedules hadn't lined up recently so she'd seen even less of him than usual.

"Walter, did you come by for a chat?"

"I do love our stimulating repartee." Walter leaned against the doorframe and tilted his head, clearly examining Thea. "And I hate to interrupt your coffee, but there's a patron upstairs who may need your attention."

Thea couldn't read Walter's expression.

"Is everything okay? Do I need the naloxone?" Thea's stomach dropped. She hurriedly locked her computer and shuffled through her drawer. Usually, she kept the naloxone on her during the day. If someone was overdosing, she wouldn't have time to run to her office, but it was early and she was still working in her office.

"No, no. Nothing like that. Just someone I think would be best handled by you personally."

There were a few patrons that Thea handled, but they were regulars and followed a predictable routine. And Walter wouldn't need to be so secretive if it was one of them. Thea followed Walter upstairs. She'd known him long enough to know he would've shared more if he were so inclined. Pestering him with questions wasn't going to do her any good. She would find out more when she got where he was leading.

Once on the main floor, Walter led her to one of the banks of computers. The stations were about half filled with early morning visitors. Walter stopped a few feet from the first row. Those using the computers had their backs to them. Walter subtly motioned at a woman hunched over one of the workstations. It was Kit.

"She seems frustrated. She's cursing under her breath." Walter leaned in close so only Thea could hear. "Not disruptive," he said quickly when Thea looked at him for clarification. "And her hand."

Thea couldn't see Kit's hands so she didn't know what he was talking about. She patted Walter's shoulder in thanks and approached Kit. She came around the front so as not to startle her. When she turned she could finally see Kit's hands.

Kit was using her left hand to hunt and peck at the keyboard. Her keystrokes were aggressive and the frustration was evident in her expression. Her right hand was resting on the desk next to the keyboard and it was heavily bandaged. Only the tips of her fingers and thumb were visible. Thea felt a flutter of anxiety in her chest. Clearly, Kit was okay since she was sitting in front of her assailing the keyboard, but she was injured. That bothered Thea in a way she didn't expect.

Thea took a quick calming breath since Kit hadn't yet seen her, and then stepped forward and knelt next to her. She leaned against the desk and caught Kit's eye.

"Who's winning?"

Kit glanced up and looked happy to see her. Thea counted it as a win.

"Not me." Kit leaned back in her chair and tried to run her hands through her hair. She put the bandaged one down and looked disgusted. "I wasn't spending my years of drug use improving my computer skills, and with one hand I can't type for shit."

"What happened?"

"I need a job." Kit waggled her right hand. "Just until this heals. I have bills to pay."

"Did it happen at work? What about workman's comp, or disability?"

"Thea, I need a job. It's not enough, okay?"

Thea swallowed her retort. Who was she to argue what Kit needed? Her argument was based on her own desire for Kit not to be hurt in the first place and for her to trust her enough to tell her what happened. Since she hadn't figured out time travel yet and Kit didn't seem to be feeling chatty, there was only one thing to do.

"Okay."

"Okay? Okay what?" Kit turned away from the computer and looked at Thea again.

"Okay, let's find you a job."

"Thea, that's not your job. I'll be nicer to your computer. Walter didn't need to call you over to tell me to behave."

"That's not why he got me. He knew I'd be worried about you, which I am. And it is my job, actually. So scoot your ass over so I don't have to watch you hunt and peck us both into old age." When Kit didn't move fast enough Thea put her hand on her hip and utilized her stern librarian face.

Kit moved over, although she looked reluctant.

"Explain to me how it's your job to find me a job? Is this charity?"

Thea sat down and opened a new browser. "Not charity at all. You are a library patron. You have a research query. I'm a librarian with the skills and resources to assist. Doesn't matter if you're looking for a specific book, the best paella recipe in the world, or the meaning of life. We're here to help."

Kit was looking at her incredulously. "That's not really how I pictured librarians."

*Do not ask her what she pictured. Do not do it. You promised no flirting.* She squelched the desire to be playful. "I get that a lot. Now, what kind of job are you looking for?"

Kit looked thoughtful, a very different posture from the tight shoulders and aggressive typing of earlier. She'd seemed angry before. Less so now.

"I guess I hadn't really gotten that far. I just needed to make some progress." Kit nodded toward the computer. "Which I was clearly doing."

"Obviously. Let's start with what you do know. You said something short-term. And you need to cover your expenses. Driving seems like it would be difficult with only one hand, so no ride share services."

"One hand, no car, and no driver's license," Kit said. "Are those important?"

Thea held her thumb and index finger up half an inch apart. "Nothing that requires your own transportation then."

"Hey, I'm very good at transporting myself on the city bus. And my own two feet. I probably still remember how to ride a bicycle. But I don't have one."

Thea stole a glance at Kit, who caught her looking and grinned. Kit was wildly attractive, but right now the best word to describe her was irresistibly adorable. Her hair was a bit of a mess, she was leaning on the desk haphazardly, and trying to convince Thea a pair of sneakers counted as viable transportation.

"There's an entire gig economy out there." Thea loved this part of her job. "Let's see if you can fit into it."

It wasn't hard to rule out anything that required a car, heavy lifting, or the use of Kit's hands, alcohol or substance use or promotion, and beauty and brand promotion. Kit had drawn a firm line at peddling any products. She also wasn't interested in being a foot model or sleeping in a research lab for two weeks, no matter how well it paid.

"Ready to get back to work and give up on this?" Kit was alternating between pacing behind the computer and being slumped against the desk.

"I already told you, this is work, and we're just getting started."

"Seriously?"

Kit didn't look like she was feeling Thea's enthusiasm. She clearly wasn't acquainted with the thrill of the chase.

Thea looked at the clock. They'd been working for longer than she thought. It was nearly lunch.

"Ten more minutes and then I'm taking you to lunch."

"You are?"

"I am," Thea said, although it sounded a bit weak, even to her.

"Hey, you can take it back. I won't be offended." Kit made sure to catch her eye.

"Absolutely not. I'm taking you to lunch. I'm not usually so impulsive. It caught me off guard. The invitation was sincere."

"Okay, but I'm not your charity case. I can pay my own way." Kit stretched and rolled her shoulders.

Thea looked her over carefully, then made sure she was paying attention. She leaned in closer.

"My charity cases are mangy dogs and stray cats. They most certainly don't look anything like you."

*Stop flirting. Stop it right now. Enough.*

She didn't give Kit a chance to answer before she turned back to the computer and began a new search. She could see from the corner of her eye that Kit looked slightly flummoxed, but not at all displeased.

*Although if you are going to flirt, that's the look you should get when you do.*

When the ten minutes were up, Thea had a promising lead. Kit was reticent but hadn't ruled it out. A local nonprofit that provided peer support and crisis services to those experiencing mental health or substance use problems needed someone to do filing and other office work for a few weeks. Kit wasn't sure about stepping into a center related to substance use. Thea understood. It was up to Kit whether she was comfortable or not. But that wasn't the work for hungry stomachs.

Walter looked surprised when Thea told him she was going out for lunch. She wasn't sure if she'd ever done it before. Sylvia had never stopped by to take her out, and she wouldn't go with Walter or Carrie because the library would be too shorthanded. She wondered if that made her as pathetic as she felt. Who hadn't ever gone out to lunch at work? Should she change that? Did she want to?

"Hey, you okay? You look like you're wrestling with something big and mean all of a sudden."

Thea lead the way out of the library, oddly liberated by leaving work in the middle of the day. "Not at all. Just realizing I haven't gone out to lunch in way too long."

"I'm happy you're making an exception for me. Just don't hold it against me when I look like a complete idiot using a fork with my left hand. My cousin Josh thought it was hilarious last night."

"I would never." Thea tried to keep a straight face.

Frankie bounded up the front steps as they walked out. "Hey, Thea. Hey, Kit. Thea, I'm almost done with all the stuff you gave me to do last time I was in. I think maybe an hour and a half and I'll be done. What do you want me to do if you're not back when I finish?"

Frankie was a bundle of frenetic teenage energy. "I'm free until the library closes today, so I can stay as late as you want me to. I'll stay until closing anyway, so if you have work for me to do, let me know. Even if you can't pay me, I don't mind helping out."

"I'm going to lunch, Frankie. Not…" Thea wasn't sure exactly how she intended to finish that sentence when she started it. "Not leaving for the day. Homework first. I will not be the reason your grades slip. You understand?"

She waited for Frankie to nod her understanding before continuing. She was happy to have Frankie onboard as a library assistant, but not if she sacrificed her future even temporarily.

"Good, if you finish early with what I gave you, check in with Walter. He probably has some things you can help out with."

"Sure thing. Have fun."

Thea watched her run up the stairs, taking two at a time. A little part of her wanted to follow. Have fun? She wasn't sure how to have fun at lunch in the middle of the workday. Was it the same as any other time? She looked at Kit, who smiled at her. Thea relaxed.

"Ready?"

*As I'll ever be.*

She pointed Kit in the direction of her favorite restaurant and an entirely new direction for herself. She wasn't the woman who went out to lunch in the middle of the day. But maybe she wanted to be. One way to find out.

# CHAPTER NINE

Kit knew Thea was uncomfortable with the idea of going to lunch with her as soon as she'd offered the invitation. She'd tried to give her a way out, but Thea hadn't accepted. Kit assumed it was because leaving the library in the middle of the day didn't seem like something Thea would do. But Kit had shown up with a bandaged hand and hot, simmering anger. Not exactly characteristics in the handbook for fifty hottest dates.

She decided it wasn't worth trying to figure out. Thea was here with her now. Kit was a little horrified to realize she had no idea what to talk about. She never seemed to have trouble striking up conversation in the library, but there seemed to be more pressure in the real world. Was this a date? Casual lunch between friends? Would Thea realize she had no idea what she was doing? What if Thea *didn't* realize she had no idea what she was doing? Why had she swallowed her tongue?

Kit took a sip of water and looked at Thea. She looked similarly tongue-tied.

"Frankie." Not particularly smooth, but at least something came out of her mouth. "Frankie's been around the library a lot."

Thea looked relieved. "She's working there now. Part-time. She asked for a job."

"She adores you." Kit had a little momentum now. "Most kids worship athletes or movie stars or people they'll never meet. Not every kid gets to talk to their hero every day. She's pretty damn lucky."

"I'm quite certain that's not at all how Frankie would describe our relationship." Thea took a sip of water and averted her gaze. "I'd say she tolerates me. At best."

Kit felt the ice break. She and Thea were themselves again. She refrained from wiping her brow or letting out an inappropriately loud sigh of relief.

"First, you're full of it. Second, I'm very good at translating teenager. I stand by my assessment."

"Okay, braggart, it's your lucky day. This place is full of teenagers. I'll point, you translate."

They worked their way around the room. Thea pointed out teenagers at random and Kit provided her assessments of their inner thoughts. Most of the time she shared what she really thought was going on in their head, but a few she just made up.

"Blue shirt, your three o'clock, face buried in his phone." Thea moved her fork on the table to point at the target.

"Wants his parents to think he's not interested but is really desperate for them to tell him to put down his phone."

Thea considered. "Not bad. I think you're right. Poor kid. Why don't you go over and have a chat with the parents?"

"Oh no." She held up her hands in defense. "I absolutely do *not* speak parent. I can provide references to that point."

"Fair. I'm not a huge fan of them either."

Before Kit could follow up, Thea moved on.

"Okay, your ten o'clock, pink shirt, blond hair."

"Regretting a sit-down restaurant for the first date. But just caught a look at you and I think made a rather significant personal discovery."

"What? You definitely made that last part up." Thea turned subtly so she could look at the blond girl.

Kit estimated her to be about nineteen. The girl winked at Thea and Kit hid her laugh behind her soda.

Thea snapped back around quickly. "How did you make her do that?"

"I'm not the only one who can recognize a beautiful woman when I see one. I just happen to be the only one sitting at her table. But I'll gladly accept the dirty looks. It's well worth it."

"Charmer," Thea said.

Kit tipped an imaginary cap.

"Oh, now here's an interesting case." Kit tapped her chin and furrowed her brow. "Mr. Captain Marvel shirt back there is thinking about French fries. That's his sole focus right now."

"You can tell that from his facial expression?" Thea leaned forward, looking skeptical.

"The little drool droplet on his chin gives it away. That and the French fry doodles on his placemat and his nonstop yammering about it."

"I think that's cheating." Thea leaned back and crossed her arms. "You said you were going to read facial expressions."

"I said no such thing. I said I would translate teenager. 'Yum, yum, French fry' is an easy translation."

"And what about librarians? Any experience translating them?"

Kit felt like her heart jumped the curb then slammed to a stop before gunning it and running a red light. What exactly was Thea asking? What was she hoping Kit said? She searched Thea's face. No Rosetta stone there. Why was she so bad at this? She answered honestly.

"I'm not fluent in librarian. But I'm enjoying getting to know the one I'm having lunch with right now."

"Good. Your librarian is enjoying it too."

When Thea smiled, Kit was sure its light would filter into the darkest places and bring warmth.

While they waited for their food, Kit asked about the library. Thea updated her on the sharps containers. Although they weren't full, a few needles were deposited every day or so. Most importantly, since the containers had been installed, no one had found a used syringe left anywhere in the library.

Kit thought it sounded like a success, but she could see Thea was hesitant.

"People are still shooting drugs in the library, Kit. Even if they clean up after themselves, the activity is still ongoing."

"And you don't want drug users in your library?"

"Yes. Wait, no. I don't want people *using* drugs in my library. I want the library to be a safe place for everyone."

"Do you know why I came to the library last year? The inauspicious day we first met?"

Thea waited for her to continue.

Kit took a deep breath. What would Thea think after she shared? It wasn't as though it could get worse. She'd seen the worst of it.

"I came to the library precisely because it was safe. I was starting to withdraw. It had taken me forever to finally get my next hit, and I felt terrible. I knew I was vulnerable. I wasn't close to any of the usual places I used or people I used with. I came to the library because I knew I would be safe. And I knew that if I overdosed, someone would find me."

It still gave Kit pause to think of how little regard she had for her own life when she was in the throes of her addiction. The cravings and physical and psychological hold the drug had on her were so powerful it was nearly enough to override the basic human instinct to stay alive. She was thankful every day she had found her way out the other side, even if the journey was a daily struggle.

"I never thought of the library as a safe haven for the people using drugs." Thea rolled her fork around and around on the table absently. "Thank you for sharing that with me. So how do I protect everyone?"

"Who says you have to? Why does it have to be your job to do that?" She wanted to reach out to take Thea's hand, but she held back. A big bandaged club hand wasn't very comforting anyway.

"I do," Thea said. "A library was there for me as a kid when I needed it. It's there for kids like Frankie and anyone else who needs it."

"Don't forget us recovering souls who grace your establishment once a week to drink bad coffee and improve ourselves."

"You are unforgettable." Thea winked.

Kit reached out this time and ran her fingers across the top of Thea's hand. Only the tops of her fingers were sticking out of the bandage, but the brief contact felt like enough.

"The problem with having us all in there, is any one of us, at any time, could be the drug user you're trying to keep out. I want nothing more than to put my past behind me and move on, but I keep showing up to meetings because I know there's always a danger of relapse. For me. My sponsor. Anyone in that room."

Thea's shoulders drooped and she scrubbed her face with her hands. So much for an enjoyable lunch with a friend.

"Hey, let's talk about something else. You came to lunch to get away from work."

"It's okay, it's not like I don't think of this at all hours of the day anyway. This way at least I'm not talking to myself. As a kid it would have shattered my sense of safety in the one place I felt any, if I had stumbled upon what Frankie did. As an adult, I can't imagine ever making you feel unwelcome, for any reason."

"Maybe there's a way it doesn't have to be one or the other," Kit said. "And before you ask, because I can see you're going to, I have no idea how. But I'm sure we can figure it out."

"Deal. But now," Thea picked up Kit's bandaged hand carefully, "will you tell me what happened?"

Kit looked down at her hand. She felt the anger roar again, as if someone had reignited coals that had never fully extinguished. But now she felt something else just as strongly. She was embarrassed. It wasn't as if Thea didn't know about her drug using past.

But this was different. This was her past refusing to take on its proper past tense and instead meddle in her present. It was embarrassing that she couldn't keep her past from popping up now in such a violent way. What the hell would Thea think of her?

"Disagreement with a nail gun." Kit pulled her hand back and put it in her lap, under the table.

"I don't really know how nail guns work. You're not left-handed, are you? Do you usually use them with your non-dominant hand?"

"I wasn't the one wielding it." She wished Thea would leave it at that, but she knew she wouldn't. Thea was curious and observant and wanted to understand things. It was one of the things Kit liked best about her.

"Someone shot you with a nail gun?"

Thea looked so offended, and Kit liked someone being outraged on her behalf. The guys at work had been furious, but this was different.

"Were they new? Were they incompetent?"

"Yes, to all three. Although, I don't think he actually meant to shoot me. But he and a friend picked a fight with me because of who they thought I am. My *moral corruption* was offensive to them. I guess I'm lucky I only got a nail through the hand, a few appointments with a physical therapist, and some time off work, and not a stake through the eye or a date with a flaming pyre." Kit saw Thea's question before she could ask it. "Drug use, not the gay thing."

"Kit, I'm so sorry."

*Damn it. I can't do this to Thea. I can't hurt her. Look what I've already done to Josh.*

Thea reached for Kit's hand, the one left on the table, again. This time Kit gently pulled it away. It hurt when she did. She knew it was the right thing to do. Telling Thea about what happened had clarified that for her. Thea was light, and beauty, and fresh sea air. Kit's life didn't have room for those things. Not yet, and maybe not ever.

"Thea, thank you for inviting me to lunch. You're amazing. Probably the most amazing woman I've ever met. But me, I'm the thing you're trying to keep out of your library. Apparently, I'm instability, and chaos, and projectiles. I'm nail guns to the palm."

"So, you're going to what?" Thea pulled her hand back and wrapped her arms around herself. "Walk out of here and not talk to me anymore? Not come to the library?"

"I don't know. I want to protect you and what you've built at the library until I can get control of my past."

"It looks to me like you have pretty good control of it, Kit. I'm not asking you to get up and leave. I don't need your protection. Not from you. Not from your past."

"I know." Kit stood and put her napkin on the table. "Thank you for lunch."

Kit kissed the top of Thea's head and walked out the door of the restaurant. She felt like a jerk for leaving her like that, but it felt like the right thing to do. Her past was still so much of her present. She couldn't pretend it wouldn't come back to hurt her or someone she cared about when she had the literal wounds to prove otherwise.

If only it didn't feel so shitty.

# CHAPTER TEN

Kit was reading and rereading the mission statement of the nonprofit organization looking for temporary office help when Josh got home.

"You better not have watched ahead on our show or I swear I will throw your clothes and then you out the window and write you out of my will." Josh kicked off his work boots and rolled his shoulders.

"That's the line?" Kit looked away from Josh shedding the last of the job site. She wanted to run and put it all on and get back to work. "I always thought it was throwing away your weird bread making science experiment from the back of the fridge."

"You wouldn't touch my mother starter." Josh looked like he wanted to run to the fridge to check on his pride and joy. "You like eating my bread too much."

"Truth," Kit said. "But I did lick the top of just one of your ridiculously overpriced tiny cartons of ice cream in there. You'll never know which one."

"You have chocolate on the side of your mouth." Josh flicked her nose as he walked by. "And you're making a huge assumption that I care."

Kit scooped food onto two plates and shoved one Josh's way. She only had one hand, but she could still be useful around the house.

"How did you fill your day of leisure? Manicure?"

Kit tried to flip him off, but the bandage prevented the satisfaction. Once he started laughing at her there was no point switching to the other hand.

"I went to the library, might have found a temp job, and had lunch with Thea, before walking out at the end like an ass. I was busy."

"Wait. What? I'm going to go in order here. I told you, you don't need to find another job or worry about the rent this month. Thea's the librarian you have the hots for, right? Why, for the love of God, would you walk out on a beautiful woman? Did the drugs mess up your brain more than it already was? Do I need to remind you how it works when you're across the table from a woman you're interested in repeating the experience with?"

"I remember how it works. I was using heroin. I wasn't dead."

"Then what's your problem now?" Josh stopped shoveling food in his mouth long enough to look at her like she had turned into a smelly, three-headed yeti while he was at work.

Kit didn't want to get into it again, but she knew Josh wouldn't let it go. He was both good like that and a total pain in her ass.

"Those two assholes who came after me, they did it because of my past. Now you're jammed up and I'm out of work for a couple weeks until this heals. Thea's trying to get away from drug use and all that comes with it. She doesn't need me around until it's further behind me."

"God, you're an idiot sometimes." Josh waved his fork at her. "You used to pull shit like this when we were kids too. Always trying to do whatever you thought was the noble thing, even when your logic was crap."

"Straighten me out then." Kit felt her anger ramping up again. She and Josh loved each other, but they also had a history of some pretty explosive fights. She had stitches to prove just how far they were willing to go to settle their disagreements.

"You think you're going to stop becoming a recovering heroin user after some number of days or years passes? You think people are suddenly just not going to know about it anymore or you just aren't going to be *that* anymore? Twenty years from now, one of those idiots could have taken offense at that part of you and picked a fight. Maybe it won't be as fresh and maybe fewer people will know about it because you'll talk about it less, but it'll still be there. There are some things you can't change, no matter how hard you wish them away."

"I'm not trying to wish it away." Kit jabbed at a chair leg with her foot.

"Well, you shouldn't," Josh said. "I'll say it until you believe me. You should be proud of yourself for changing your life. I'm sure as hell proud of you. You worked your ass off for this. You keep working your ass off every day. Maybe stop working so damn hard to forget it ever happened. And go apologize to that librarian. Walked out during lunch? What the hell were you thinking?"

"Why am I listening to you? You live with your addict cousin and bake bread in your spare time."

"I'm a catch," Josh said. "And so are you. Now what's this job you're considering taking until you can get back to doing real work?"

"It's at the mental health and substance abuse crisis center." Why did her voice sound so small and timid? What was she afraid of?

"Kit, that's fantastic. They do peer support there too, right? Is that what you'll be doing? Did you swing through there when you were first starting out?"

Josh looked far more excited than Kit was. He'd always been more excitable than her.

"Yeah. They need someone to do filing and stuff. Probably some computer work. Maybe fetch coffee. Shit I can do one-handed."

Kit wondered if anyone there would remember her. She figured they saw so many people that one in a sea of crises wasn't going to stand out. She hadn't really utilized many of the services they offered, but she had reached out and talked to a crisis counselor. It was the day she'd first met Thea.

"Does anyone actually keep enough paper copies of things that they need help filing? Is that still a thing?" Josh asked.

"Oh, for fuck's sake, I don't know. They need someone to do office work. It said something about files. I want the work, but the location freaks me out a little."

"You can be anyone you want to be locked in that office doing your filing." Josh made sure to drag out the word "filing" like it had some kind of double meaning. "But you could also find out more about what they do. You'd be a pretty amazing peer mentor."

"I'm not sure I trust your judgment. I hear you hired a couple of lunatics and let one of your employees get shot with a nail gun."

"Well, when you put it like that." Josh shrugged and took a sip of his drink. "I'm still right. Take the job. Apologize to your librarian."

"Just like that?" She knew when Josh was done talking about something because he'd settled on the solution.

"Yep. Just like that. You have a game plan, we have a show to watch, and I have pre-licked ice cream to consume."

"Fine, I guess it's settled. I'll get the spoons." Kit cleared their plates if not her worries.

"Hell no. You had your chance to actually eat some rather than just lick it. Your loss."

While Josh got his ice cream, Kit queued up the show they'd been binge-watching. She thought about the crisis center. Josh was right. It didn't have to be a big deal. She'd call about the job tomorrow.

She was less certain about her course of action with Thea. She'd felt justified leaving when she did and her logic had felt sound. But Josh had always had a way of setting her straight and making her look at multiple perspectives. Now she wasn't sure she'd done the right thing. Especially since she really hadn't given Thea much chance to have an opinion. Kit hoped she hadn't blown a chance at a friendship. She wasn't in a position for anything more, but having a beautiful friend around wasn't a bad thing.

Kit paused the show mid explosion, before she chickened out. "Hey, you still have tickets to the game in a few weeks?"

"Sure. You wanna go?"

"Uh, yeah. But not with you. You might be right that I screwed up with Thea and I want to make it up to her."

Josh cocked his eyebrow but didn't say anything. Kit glared at him.

"You would be less annoying if you just said I told you so. You know that, right?"

Josh took a big, overly exaggerated bite of ice cream, but mercifully didn't say a word.

They settled in to watch the rest of the show, but Kit was distracted. The day had been an emotional smorgasbord. She'd started off with white-hot anger, then cooled to happiness at Thea's invitation. Sadness and acceptance had ruled after lunch, and now she was left with confusion and a sprinkle of hope. No wonder she was so tired. She'd have to watch this episode again anyway, so she didn't fight the sleep when it descended. She was out before the final credits rolled.

## CHAPTER ELEVEN

Thea sat at her desk and stared at her computer. She had been staring at it for longer than she cared to admit. She was supposed to be reading reviews of new books with an eye to whether they would be a fit in the library's collection. It was something she loved. Today she couldn't seem to focus. It was late in the day and she was ready to go home, even if the clock was being stubborn and unsupportive.

True to her word, Thea hadn't seen Kit outside of the usually scheduled NA meeting time. Kit had zipped into the meeting and then left, talking to an older woman Thea had seen at a few other meetings. Kit had waved but didn't stop to talk. Thea was annoyed at how much it bothered her. After all, she didn't know Kit all that well. They'd only just begun this friendship so what did it matter? But it did matter and that was the part that stung. She wanted it to matter to Kit, too. But if it didn't, or couldn't, it was better to know that now.

"You look like you could use a pick-me-up." Walter plopped down in the guest chair and deposited two coffee mugs on Thea's desk.

"How do you always know when I'm tired and running low on caffeine?"

"I brought you coffee for that too." Walter nudged the coffee closer. "Let's have it. Why are you wallowing?"

"I most certainly am not wallowing." At least, she hoped she wasn't.

"Save an old man the time of having to argue semantics or pull it out of you. I will sit here all night if I have to, but I have a salacious book and a perfectly aged bottle of port waiting for me at home. I fully intend to give both their due."

"You're a national treasure, Walter. I'm really fine. I had lunch with Kit a few days ago. I thought we were starting to build a nice friendship. She feels differently. No one likes to feel rejected, that's all. Sorry I made you worry."

Walter didn't answer right away. Thea could tell he was weighing his words carefully, but she couldn't tell what he was thinking. She wished he wasn't working so hard to censor himself and would just spit it out already.

"Somewhere in this library is a recipe for a truth serum. Don't make me go looking," Thea said.

Walter held up his hands defensively. "I was simply wondering if with that particular woman, it wasn't rather a good thing. Especially given your history."

Thea sighed. She wanted to be mad at Walter for the suggestion, but it wasn't like she hadn't considered that herself. Being hurt by those who used drugs was an indelible part of her history. By that measure, she should run from Kit. But that was about dating Kit. This was about friendship. It felt like there was a difference.

"It seems that's everyone's argument." She didn't mean to be as short as it came out. "I'm sorry. The thought has crossed my mind. And a version of it is what Kit said when we last spoke, although she was talking about the library, not my personal history. She doesn't know about that. In the abstract, you're right, I want nothing to do with her. But we don't live in an abstract world."

Walter looked contemplative again. It was one of his greatest qualities, but sometimes Thea really needed him to get on with it. She recognized the contradiction in herself. For someone who was careful and organized about everything, she wanted more action, less thinking on his part.

"I guess the question is what are you going to do about it then?" Walter took a sip of coffee and looked ready to wait as long as needed for an answer.

Thea didn't need to ponder. "Nothing. She made it clear she's not interested in a friendship. What is there to do? There's no point in pursuing someone who doesn't want you around."

"Thea, I love you, you know that," Walter said. "But sometimes you need a good shake. I know how your parents shaped your world view, and Sylvia reinforced every instinct you've developed. But life is far more interesting and richer when you haven't already played out five moves ahead. Sometimes sacrifice the queen at the beginning of the game because it makes things more exhilarating."

"You know I don't know how to play checkers." She waited for Walter's face to turn red and the indignant sputtering to start. "Oh, chess. You were talking about chess. That's right, you like to play."

Walter snatched the coffee he'd brought with him out of Thea's hand. She was mid sip so it was an especially cruel punishment.

"Are you telling me to torpedo something in my life just to see if I can work my way out of it? Because I feel like a lot of my life has been overcoming obstacles I had nothing to do with. I don't really want to create new ones if I can help it, and I'm not sure that kind of chaos sounds *exhilarating*."

"Not at all what I'm saying." Walter returned the coffee. "I'm perhaps wondering if dipping a toe into the world of spontaneity and stepping outside your comfort zone would do you some good."

"I did go out to lunch. During work hours." Thea tilted her coffee cup at him.

"I would hardly believe it if I hadn't witnessed the event with my own eyes."

"And what, pray tell, would you have me do, spontaneously, and well outside my comfort zone, with Kit?"

Walter raised his brow. "That sounds like a question this old man has no business answering."

She started to clarify her meaning while trying hard not to blush, but Walter shushed her with a loud laugh as he got up to leave.

After he left, Thea gave up completely on reading reviews. She thought about Walter's suggestion to be bolder. There was no denying she was careful, and she'd had that instinct reinforced over and over in her life. Maybe Walter was right, though, maybe she could be a little more adventurous. Cautious was safe, but what had she gained by playing it safe? She'd never known what she was missing until Kit walked out of the restaurant. Friendship felt like something worth taking a risk for.

Thea decided. The next time she saw Kit, she wasn't going to let her walk by without talking to her.

Now all she had to do was figure out what the hell to say.

## Chapter Twelve

The longer Kit avoided Thea, the more of a coward she felt. She didn't have a good excuse for not rushing back to the library after talking to Josh and apologizing to Thea. Embarrassment, fear, inertia…take your pick.

She also wanted to go back to Thea with more than a smile and her hat in her hand. Today was the end of her second week at the substance abuse crisis center, Star Recovery. There had been very little filing, but she had done plenty of office tasks. She'd also seen how the center worked and the clients they served, and it was interesting seeing it from the other side of the sober counter. It had taken almost the full two weeks, but eventually she worked up the guts to talk to some of the peer mentors. They were pretty incredible. NA provided peer to peer support, but this was different. More professional and structured. Kit knew she would have benefited from the peer mentorship when she first started her road to recovery.

Kit bounded up the library steps, suddenly eager to see Thea. She always looked forward to seeing her, and the first glance often took her breath away, but today she also couldn't wait to finally talk to her again, too. In fact, she wasn't sure what the hell she had been thinking staying away so long.

It took her a few minutes to find Thea in the busy library. She wasn't at the desk and Kit couldn't immediately pick her out of the crowd. She considered going down to her office. Before she did something really embarrassing like standing on the front desk and scanning the crowd, she heard Thea's voice.

Thea was crouched next to an elderly man working on one of the computers. He was a worse typist than Kit, which didn't seem possible. Thea was talking to him softly, clearly providing much needed encouragement. Kit watched the interaction. It was obvious there was genuine affection between the pair.

Kit wondered what someone watching her would see. Probably a woman trying hard to convince herself she was absolutely not jealous. Not at all jealous of an old man trying not to cry after accidently turning on track changes and not knowing what the hell had happened. It's not like the computer was cheating on her. Computers fucked with her all the time. And she had no claim to Thea. Wasn't even sure she wanted one, but damn if she wasn't beautiful.

Before Kit could spend too much time wondering how long she was going to stand staring at Thea, she turned around and caught Kit staring. Not nearly the smooth entrance Kit had been hoping for, but it was what she had to work with.

Kit was about to launch into her apology and ask for forgiveness when Thea took her by the arm and pulled her over to the computer and the older man.

"Kit, sit. This is Mr. Blackman. Mr. Blackman, this is Kit. I'm not sure if she's a friend of mine, but she's a generally agreeable lady. She's going to help you with your document for a few minutes while I go and find someone I'm sure is a friend of mine. If you have any questions, she'll be happy to answer them."

"I would?" She looked at Thea. There was very clearly only one acceptable answer. "Yes, I would. I'd be very happy to help."

*Shit.* Generally agreeable was how you described an old, grumpy ass cat that left dead mice on the front porch and refused to shit in the litter box.

Thea walked away without another word. At least she hadn't kicked her out.

"She's not happy with you," Mr. Blackman said.

"Mr. Blackman, you are wise beyond your years."

"There are no years beyond mine, youngster. I don't like to see anyone suffering, but that was more fireworks than this old man's seen in two decades." Mr. Blackman pulled out a hanky and blew his nose before turning back to the computer with a scowl.

"What are we working on here?" Kit didn't particularly want to be Mr. Blackman's fireworks.

"I wrote a poem for my wife. My handwriting's not so good anymore, and her eyesight isn't either, so I wanted to put it into the computer for her. I heard you can make it as big as you like. I used to write her poems all the time. It's not so easy now."

"That's very sweet of you. How long have you been married?" Kit could tell this was a man devoted to the woman he'd married.

"Fifty-five years. The best years of my life. You figure out where you went wrong with your lady there and apologize. Trust me, it's not worth staying angry."

Kit was confused until she realized he was talking about Thea.

"Oh, Thea and I are just friends. I mean, as you said, she is mad at me and has every reason to be, but we're just friends. I came here to say sorry."

Mr. Blackman looked her over. Kit tried not to squirm as he did. She was marginally successful.

"Didn't sound like she was all that interested in being friends. You riled her. I only have one person in the world who can rile me, and it isn't any of my friends. It's okay if you two don't know it yet, time has a way of sorting these things out."

Kit wasn't convinced Thea wanted Kit to be the one who could rile her, but now that he'd brought it up, it was like a catchy song she couldn't get out of her head. It wasn't like the thought hadn't crossed her mind, her and Thea.

"Quit your daydreaming. I'm already pushing it getting this thing typed before I die. Don't need you off in the clouds when we need to focus."

"Yes, sir." Kit suppressed the urge to salute. "Let's get to work."

She and Mr. Blackman painstakingly started typing the poem he'd written for his wife. It was the sweetest thing she'd ever read. She hoped someday she'd love someone enough to want to work as hard as he was now to give this gift to his wife.

They were four lines in when Thea returned with Walter.

"Uh-oh," Kit said to Mr. Blackman. "She brought the bouncer."

"For me or you?" Mr. Blackman winked at her.

"They'd never toss a good-looking guy like you out of a fine establishment like this," Kit said. "I think this is where we part, Mr. Blackman. It was very nice to meet you. Walter, which door are you tossing me through?"

"You should be so lucky." Walter took Kit's vacated seat next to Mr. Blackman.

Thea once again took Kit by the arm and marched her through the library, past the desk, and out the front door. Kit wanted to ask questions, a lot of questions, but she felt like it was best to follow Thea's lead.

Whenever Thea stopped leading them and they got to their destination, Kit would get down on her knees and beg for forgiveness, if that's what Thea wanted.

*If a woman like Thea turns her head your direction, what kind of idiot walks away?* "This idiot," Kit said.

"What?" Thea slowed and let go of Kit's arm.

Kit wanted to offer it again. She liked the contact and the power and surety that radiated from Thea through their connected limbs. "Oh, nothing. I'm the idiot. I have a few things to apologize for." Kit looked around. "Uh, where are we going?"

"You are, you do, and we're going somewhere you can start making it up to me."

Was Thea trying to be suggestive? Was she reading into it?

"I have no idea what I said that is putting that look on your face." Thea circled her finger in the air around Kit's face. "But you are going to buy me coffee. While I drink it, you're going to tell me what the hell you were thinking walking out of lunch, why you've been gone so long, and what you're going to do about it now."

Kit was pretty sure Thea was doing it on purpose. She had to be, right? She felt like she was doing the mental equivalent of staring at Thea's chest. Why was her mind suddenly going places it hadn't previously strayed?

*Damn it, Mr. Blackman.*

When she went to the library she was ready for a big public apology if necessary, even some light public groveling. But now, Thea was in charge of the situation and was seemingly, from everything Kit knew of her, acting in a very uncharacteristic manner. It had Kit feeling so off balance her brain was doing whatever the hell it felt like, including reading innuendo where there was none. Bolting from coffee, again, wasn't an option so she was going to have to figure it out. She just had to sit there like a normal human being and try not to make things weird. Why was that suddenly a big ask?

"You don't need to look so scared," Thea said. "You made a colossal mistake and I was annoyed about it, but I really do want to get coffee so we can talk. I'm not taking you out in public so I can scream at you."

"Well, that's a relief." Kit wiped her brow jokingly, but her hands were a little shaky. "But if you change your mind and you're going to throw your coffee at me, give me a heads up. I'll ask them to pour you the dregs of the last brew. I know you're into your coffee. No need to waste a good cup."

"You're never a waste." Thea took Kit's arm again, but this time she looped hers through and they walked arm in arm.

Kit liked having Thea on her arm. It made her feel important and like someone she wanted the world to notice.

"Are you nervous leaving the library unattended in the middle of the day?" They settled into seats at the coffee shop and Kit twirled her cup.

"Did you see how many staff members were in the library when you came in? My leaving doesn't mean they have to shutter the place. I think they'll muddle through without me."

"Muddle, yes. But I don't get the sense that you leave very often for coffee jaunts in the middle of the day. I feel deeply, truly, honored, even if you hauled me out of there so that I wouldn't embarrass you with the fifteen-stanza apology poem I'd prepared. Which, by the way, I would have coupled with a gracefully awkward interpretive dance."

"Get up." Thea pulled the coffee cup from Kit's hands and jokingly began to stand. "We're going back now. What do you need? Sound system? Dance space? I'll call ahead and have it ready. Please say you need those scarves. You know the ones I mean? The little dance scarves?"

"Sorry to disappoint you. You'll have to settle for my sincere, one-on-one apology." Her smile faltered and she bit her lip. "I really am sorry, Thea. I shouldn't have walked out on you. My reasoning seemed solid in my head at the time, but even Josh told me I was an asshole, and he's the nicest man alive. Unless you mess with his mother starter. Then all bets are off."

"Thank you." Thea cocked her head. "His what? Never mind. I know what you were trying to do. I don't hold that against you. I don't need an apology, although it is nice to get. I need assurance. I need to know you aren't going to get up and walk away again the next time you get scared. You joked that I never leave the library for meals or spontaneous coffee dates. That's true. Dependability, reliability, predictability. Those are all things that are crucial to me. It's how I feel comfortable and safe. So if you have no intention of being reliable and dependable, let me know now. I'm perfectly capable of making my own decisions, so give me the benefit of the doubt that my brain is still working admirably, please?"

Kit took a moment to think about what Thea said. There was a lot to decipher. She had a lot of questions, but there was only one thing Thea needed and that was the most important thing to address right away.

"I screwed up. My intentions weren't bad, but I ended up making a mess, which is never good. The friendship we've built is important to me. If you need me to punch a timecard every night on time before I can see you, I'll do it."

"You don't have to do that." Thea tapped on the table with her fingernail. "In fact, I'd really prefer it if you didn't. Just don't walk out like that. People thought I got dumped on my lunch break."

"Is that what people thought?" Kit grinned.

"Three people offered to buy me drinks and that teenager you pointed out slipped her number in my back pocket 'in case I wanted to talk about what happened.' I'm not sure a librarian's ever been so popular."

Kit noticed Thea's cheeks turning a slight shade of pink. There seemed to be more to the story, and she couldn't help the jealousy that flared.

"Is that all she gave you? Your cheeks are a shade of red that makes me curious."

Thea's cheeks reddened significantly. Kit wasn't sure whether to continue being jealous or enjoy how cute Thea looked.

"Not that it's any of your business, but I also got a kiss on the cheek and a compliment on my ass."

Kit needed more details. Immediately. "This compliment, was it just a general observation, or was it after she slipped the note in your pocket? Did she cop a feel while kissing your cheek? I'm not sure how I feel about that."

"Whoa." Thea held up her hand, palm out. "You don't have to feel any way about it, because as it turns out, it has nothing to do with you. Except that the whole situation was of your own making. But you also have no reason to be jealous."

"Who says I'm jealous?" Kit found the bottom of her coffee cup extremely interesting.

"I do. And so would anyone else sitting in my chair right now. I'm not sure what exactly *is* making you jealous. But I think I like you a little off balance and wanting more. Maybe it will keep you from running out the door and leaving me to the wolves again."

Kit didn't tell Thea that she was always off balance when she was around her. Thea was simultaneously able to right her world and knock it off center. She'd done that the first time they'd met and Kit was at her lowest point, and it hadn't stopped since. As for the wanting more, well, Kit didn't know what to make of that.

"I told you at lunch, you are the most amazing woman I've ever met. I'll always want to spend more time with you. And just in case you think I've never noticed, the kindergartener was right, you do have a fantastic ass."

"Thank you." Thea tilted her head and played with her napkin.

"I'm your friend, but I'm not blind." Kit shrugged. "Do you have to be back right away?"

When Thea shook her head, Kit took her hand and linked their arms again. She led them out of the coffee shop and back into the park, then started down the path that looped around the outside of the central green, heading in the opposite direction of the library. It was a beautiful day, the park was quiet, and Thea was willing to spend time with her. Kit was in no hurry to return her to work.

"Your hand isn't bandaged anymore. Are you back at work?"

"Not yet." Kit held up her hand and looked at it. "I have another appointment with the doctor next week. I hope I'll be cleared to go back then. The hole in my hand is pretty much healed. It only hurts when I extend my fingers all the way and stretch out my palm or try to make a fist. Doc says that should sort itself out, but it might be stiff and sore for a while. But I took your advice and I've been working at Star Recovery. It's been incredible. The work they do there is, well, there really aren't words. But my time's up there. I'm swinging by later today to finish up a few last-minute things. You were right, it was the perfect temp job."

Thea squeezed her arm. "Kit, that's so great. I bet you're amazing there."

Kit puffed out her chest dramatically. "I'm unrivalled entering data into spreadsheets and you know how good I am delivering coffee."

"Have you considered joining the peer mentorship program? I saw how Frankie responded to you when you were talking to her. And I know how you make me feel when I talk to you. I think you'd be a real asset to that program."

"I've talked to a couple of the peer mentors, but I'm not part of that program. Strictly office lackey." Kit shoved her free hand in her pocket. "Can we go back to how you feel when you talk to me?"

"I believe we were talking about you." Thea bumped her shoulder into Kit's as they walked.

Kit was really enjoying this more intimate, casual time with Thea. Not that she didn't enjoy seeing Thea in her element in the library, but this felt different, special somehow. Whatever it was, she liked it.

"Explain to me why it took me making you so mad you had to drag me by my ear out of the library to get you to leave work in the middle of the day?"

"That's a simple question with a complicated answer." Thea sighed.

"I'm not afraid of complicated." Kit was surprised to realize that was true. Since she got clean she'd tried hard to keep things simple, but right now, she was happy to dive headfirst into any messy, complex situation Thea wanted to lay out. Mudwrestling in molasses, cannonballs into a Jell-O mold, epic food fight, she was down for any and all.

"I'll give you the two-cent version. It's too nice a day to get into all the details. My childhood was a chaotic mess. I had no structure or predictability. My parents were unreliable and high when they were present, but they were absent most of the time. I think my life was a lot like Frankie's, and like her, I'd never seen the other side."

"Your parents were users?" She couldn't believe Thea was walking arm in arm with her right now if that had been her experience during childhood.

"Yes." Thea looked lost in the past. "My father died of an overdose when I was a teenager. My mom was pretty functional until I started school. Then I guess she had too much time on her hands. When it got bad or they would disappear, a neighbor would look after me, or a friend's parents. Sometimes I'd stay with my grandmother for a few days. I'd beg everyone not to put me in the system. School and the local library were the only stable things in my life. I don't know what I would have done if I'd been pulled away from those. I know it seems crazy now, but for some reason they all agreed. No one took me in, but I had a group watching out for me as best they could. I don't think I would have done better in foster care."

"Thea, I'm so sorry. I can't imagine the suckage."

"Suckage?" There was a hint of a smile. "I don't know that one. And remember, I'm a librarian, I'm a nerd for a living. I know a lot of things."

"It's a technical term and I think you're using a librarian stereotype against me. I can't imagine the horror of growing up in that situation. It's no wonder you're so protective of the library and have taken such a shine to Frankie. I also completely understand needing dependability in your life. I'm sorry I let you down when I walked out on you. But I'm wondering if I wasn't right? Why would you want the noise that comes with my past drug use in your life when you already have enough trauma from that messiness in your own past?" It was a hard question to ask, but it was an honest one, and she didn't want to get close to someone who would run the other way if things went weird.

Thea looked thoughtful and didn't answer right away. "I've asked myself that quite a lot. Walter's asked me as well. I don't know the answer. In the abstract I'd kick you to the curb, but in the flesh and blood, I don't have any desire to get rid of you, even if it's the safer choice. But please, don't let me down."

Kit wished she knew if Thea was talking about friendship or something more. In the end it didn't matter. Thea was asking for something Kit could give. At least, she hoped she could. Her future was still foggy and her sobriety was still new, but she felt good. The buprenorphine was working to stem her cravings and she was stronger every day thanks to NA meetings and help from Ethel and others she'd met along the way. She felt optimistic for the first time in a very long time.

"I won't." It was a simple response, but Kit didn't think she needed to elaborate.

"I'll hold you to it."

"Do you still keep in touch with your mom?"

Thea stiffened next to her. "No. I haven't talked to her or kept track of her in years. I tried for a while, but she wasn't easy to follow. Then I gave up trying. I felt like I should have kept trying or I shouldn't have given up on her, but I couldn't do it anymore."

"There's nothing for you to feel guilty about." Kit squeezed Thea's hand. "She had to want to be found. You couldn't work harder than she needed to, especially in the throes of her addiction. Maybe someday you'll find your way back to each other, but it's not your job alone to make it happen."

Thea kissed Kit's cheek and wrapped both arms around Kit's, which pulled them even closer together. "Thank you."

Kit felt on top of the world with Thea's arm in hers and the kiss on her cheek. It felt like she was strutting as they walked the rest of the way back to the library, despite her best efforts not to. She couldn't help it. Anyone in her shoes would do the same.

❖

Kit was surprised at how emotional she felt walking into the office of Star Recovery for what she assumed was the last time. Her time there had been valuable for more than just monetary gain. She wished she had taken advantage of more of the programs offered at Star when she was in early recovery.

As she made her way through the office she could hear the outreach calls happening in the next room. Peer mentors and volunteers called people in the Star Recovery network to cheerlead their recovery, link them to services if needed, or encourage them to reengage with treatment if required. Kit found the calls inspiring. Even the ones that were obviously difficult, where the individual on the other end had relapsed or was no longer interested in recovery. Kit knew how powerful it was to have someone who cared whether you were alive or not. Whether you used again or not. Even if that support felt grating at the time.

"Kit, we're going to miss you around here." Luanne, Kit's supervisor, entered the office and clapped her on the back. "Don't suppose we can poach you from your glamorous gig out on the construction yard to toil here in this rundown building with us? Making no money and doing work that is chronically underappreciated by society at large?"

"Luanne, you should write greeting cards with that poetic touch," Kit said. "If it weren't familial relationships on the line, I would never be able to turn down that offer. But I was wondering if there was a way I could stay involved? I've really liked my time here and you know what you do here is relevant to me."

Luanne's face lit up. Kit was worried what she had just signed up for. Luanne was looking a bit too pleased. A little bit like a toddler who somehow scored an extra-large chocolate chip cookie without anyone calling her on it.

"Whoa, what are you plotting?" Kit backed away but bumped ass first into the break room table. "That look makes me nervous."

"Go sit in on some phone calls or help set up for the job training. Make yourself useful if you're going to stick around for a few." Luanne followed Kit's retreat and clapped her on the shoulder. "I'll be by before you know it with some paperwork for you to sign."

Kit slipped into the call center room and waved to a couple of peer mentors she'd had a few conversations with. One was finishing up a call, and when he hung up, he came over. His name was Zeke. He motioned Kit out the door.

"I hear you're leaving us," Zeke said.

"Officially, yes, but I talked to Luanne about sticking around with some volunteer work."

Zeke seemed pleased. "We'll be happy to have you. We always need more peer mentors. You'll be great. I know you're a little unsure, but we all were when we started out. Do you have more questions? I know you had some the other night. Rachelle and Jordan might have answered some of them."

"Peer mentor?" Kit didn't know what he was talking about. She wanted to laugh, but she was worried it would come out in some kind of weird panicky screech. "I just want to clean the bathrooms or something. I wasn't signing up for what you do."

"Why not? There's nothing special about what I do."

"No disrespect," Kit said. "But I'm trying to put the mess I made of my life as far behind me as I can and move forward. Talking to people every day about using…that's not going to help."

"Maybe," Zeke said, "the problem is you keep trying to slam the door in the face of your past. Have you thought of inviting it in and figuring out how to cohabitate? I mean, you're here."

Anxiety made it hard to breathe. "Maybe I wasn't as ready for this as I thought. Tell Luanne I'm sorry I put her to all the trouble. I have to go."

Kit shouldn't have run out the door without saying good-bye to Luanne, but she needed to get out of there. She couldn't hear another person telling her how to live her life. Did she have to walk around with a sign on her back saying she was a recovering heroin user for the rest of her life? Was that all people would ever see when they looked at her? She also didn't want to be the kind of person who took off every time she freaked out about something, but lately that seemed to be her MO. At what point would she stick around and not piss people off?

Josh was proud of her recovery, probably prouder than she was. And Thea didn't seem overly focused on her past use, even when she had every right to. But the rest of the world? She'd been shot with a nail gun by a couple of the world's representatives.

Kit was happy to be going back to her job with Josh the next day. When she was using, she hadn't relished physical activity, but now, she looked forward to sore muscles and a tired body, especially when her mind refused to calm.

# CHAPTER THIRTEEN

The book display wasn't coming together like Thea wanted and she was frustrated. It was her turn to highlight some of the books from the collection into an eye-catching display, but she was struggling. All the librarians brainstormed ideas for themes, but it was up to the librarian in charge to make it come to life. Since it was one of the first things people saw when they walked in, there was a lot of pressure. That and there was a slightly heated competition to have the most popular display. The metric for gauging popularity wasn't the most scientific; social media engagement and people stopping to take pictures were about the sum of it, but that made the competition even fiercer. Subjective results meant you had to blow away the competition.

"Need help?" Walter looked over Thea's shoulder in a decidedly non-facilitative way.

"Absolutely not." Thea shooed him. "Take your nosy bones elsewhere. There has to be some work for you somewhere in this library."

"I'm on desk," Walter said. "You might remember, the lady in charge around here scheduled me there this afternoon. She knows I like the face-to-face after lunch. But as you can see, there's no one in need of my services at the moment. Except perhaps you."

Thea didn't know how she'd forgotten she'd scheduled Walter on desk. If she'd remembered she never would have worked on the display today. Other librarians might watch her struggle and want to heckle her, but only Walter, and maybe Carrie, actually would.

The desk was fifteen feet from where Thea was working. Walter didn't really need to sit behind it to cover it, technically.

"With you standing here talking to me, how would anyone know you were available?"

Walter seemed amused, which was even more annoying. He could at least have had the decency to be properly offended by her petulance.

Thea turned back to her display. She swapped a couple of books and stepped back to reevaluate. As she did, she felt someone approach.

"I told you, I don't need your help."

Whoever it was hesitated briefly.

"Are you talking in general? Or with the work you're doing? 'Cause that looks great."

Thea didn't turn around right away. She let herself savor the brief, enjoyable anticipation of seeing Kit before she actually did.

When she turned around she wasn't disappointed. Her stomach leapt slightly at the sight of her, which was new and unexpected.

Kit was back in her construction attire, complete with slight coating of sawdust on her clothes and hair. Thea wouldn't have listed that among her top ten turn-ons, but she found it incredibly appealing when Kit was the one wrapped in the signs of a hard day's work.

"I've been battling it all afternoon. We're competitive about the displays so there's extra pressure to get it right. Walter's been heckling me." Thea waved at Walter.

"Will this help?" Kit offered one of two coffee cups she held. "I promise nothing weird. Just a plain, boring latte."

"You showing up and bearing gifts always helps." Thea took the coffee. Kit perched on a nearby chair.

"What do you get if you win?"

Thea was confused until Kit indicated the display. She wasn't used to sharing such mundane details about her work with anyone outside of her colleagues. Sylvia had never been interested in what she did all day.

"Ah. Bragging rights. Also, a hideous trophy. There's a cow wearing a clown hat on top and it says 'Udderly amazing. You don't suck.' Carrie found it at a yard sale."

"How do we make that trophy yours? It sounds incredible. Can I stuff ballot boxes? Rig a vote? Twitter bots?" Kit hopped off the chair, ready for action.

"I don't need to cheat. Whose office do you think the trophy lives in now?"

Kit threw her arms up in victory and let out a library appropriate, quiet whoop of approval. Thea couldn't help but notice how damn good her stomach looked when her shirt pulled up during her celebration. It was hard not to stare.

"You here for a meeting? Or just a coffee delivery?" Thea might have been caught staring.

"Can't it be both? The meeting doesn't start for a while, but I'm done for the day. I'd rather be here than go home for ten minutes. You do have to put up with my dusty ass, though. But I thought I remembered you saying you didn't mind that."

"You have a good memory." Thea hoped she wasn't blushing. Or drooling. "If you're going to stick around, I'm going to put you to work. I need your opinion."

"Yes, ma'am. We have an udderly amazing trophy to win."

Thea continued to tweak the display with feedback from Kit. She saw Walter watching at one point, but he didn't come over. She couldn't tell what he was thinking.

They were finally satisfied a few minutes before Kit's meeting. Thea had enjoyed having Kit's company and wasn't all that eager to give her up. Kit seemed to be thinking the same thing. She didn't seem in a rush to get to her meeting.

"Are you busy Saturday night?" Kit's question came out in one rapid-fire string of syllables. "And how do you feel about baseball?"

"I'm free Saturday. And I've always felt like I'd be great at baseball. Right up until I had to throw, catch, or hit. Otherwise, I love it."

"And how do you feel about watching baseball? With me? On Saturday?"

"I can't think of anything better." She meant it. Going on a date with Kit sounded fantastic, all her reservations aside.

*Wait, was it a date? Are we reading the same tea leaves? Are we both drinking tea?*

"I'm over the moon you're agreeing to be seen in public with me surrounded by thousands of people, but there will be at least two things better than me at the game. We need to expand your definition of 'nothing better.' Not that I'm complaining of course. And you can't back out now, you said yes. I'm taking you out Saturday."

"I'm sticking with my assessment. But for argument's sake, what are these other things that are supposedly better than a night out with you? I need convincing."

Kit shot her a roguish grin. She seemed to be enjoying the game they were playing as much as Thea.

"Well, it doesn't count as one of the things, but you'll be there with thirty thousand people, so for all I know, you'll join a group of bachelorettes out for a night of fun and have the time of your life. If that happens though, there will be massive amounts of sulking."

"I no-showed to my own bachelorette party." Thea patted Kit's cheek. "I think you're safe."

"I would like to hear more of that story, but to answer your original question, number one is the moment you first see the field. It's close to a religious experience. No one's on the field yet, but the grass is beautiful and waiting. The stadium is quiet and ready. The second is you can buy ice cream in tiny replica baseball hat bowls. There can't possibly be anything better than that, right?"

Thea couldn't help it, she laughed. Kit was so serious, so earnest, describing the wonders of ice cream in souvenir helmet cups. "You're serious about helmet cups."

"It's one of the few good memories I have from a time I'd rather forget," Kit said.

"When you were using?"

"No." She looked far away and sad. "Before then. Bad parents come in all different flavors, formulations, and doses. Mine were pretty mild, all things considered, especially compared to yours, but

I have no desire to spend time with them, then, now, or in the future. But they did give me baseball."

Thea put her hand on Kit's shoulder. She wanted to wrap her in a hug, but she was at work and she didn't know how Kit would feel about it. She never felt like it much mattered where on the spectrum of having shitty parents you fell. It wasn't a competition.

"Well, I guess my work here is done." Kit dusted her hands together. "I stopped by, delivered coffee, asked you out, and totally killed the good mood. I'd grade my performance a solid D-plus. Unbiased opinion, but you have yourself a catch right here."

Thea held her finger up to Kit's lips and swallowed hard at the flare of desire clear in Kit's eyes. She moved her finger away slowly and took a step backward before she did something professionally, and possibly personally, out of character.

"Get out of here or you'll be late for your meeting. And I'd give you a B-plus, for what it's worth. I'm grading on a curve because I'm pretty damn happy you asked me out."

Thea couldn't believe she actually had the balls to name their date as such. Not to mention telling Kit she was so damn excited about it. Thea was rewarded with an enormous smile and a wink.

*Score one for wild abandon.*

After Kit left for her meeting, Thea cleaned up the detritus from her work on the display and mentally went over what was left to do today and what could be pushed until tomorrow. Walter was off desk and the library was quiet.

Thea wandered through each row of books, looking for any out of place, forgotten coffee cups, or other unsavory items. What she found was Frankie, curled in a large leather chair adjacent to the biographies. She looked like she was crying.

She wanted to rush to Frankie and take her in her arms, but she had no idea if that would be something Frankie would appreciate. Instead, she kneeled beside her and gently touched her knee.

"Hey, kiddo, what can I do?"

Thea was completely unprepared for Frankie to launch into her arms. Thea landed on her backside with Frankie in her arms, sobbing on her shoulder. Sixteen-year-olds weren't exactly lap sized, but

Thea didn't try to reposition or move. She wrapped Frankie in a hug and held her as her body shook with the ferocity of her sorrow.

"My mom," Frankie said, finally able to get some words out. "They took my mom."

"Who did, sweetie?" If she needed to get the police involved, she wanted to get as many details as possible while it was still fresh in Frankie's mind.

"The cops. They arrested her. They found drugs and took her away. I know she's not coming back anytime soon."

Thea didn't know what to say. She squeezed Frankie tighter. She knew this pain. She fought her own childhood memories. This was about Frankie.

"Do you have a place to stay?"

"My aunt. She's moving in with me so I can stay at the same school until I graduate. She's nice but I don't know her that well. She didn't really want anything to do with my parents. I don't blame her."

"What about your dad?" Thea shifted so she could see Frankie.

"If you see him, let me know." Frankie swiped angrily at her tears. "He's been gone about three weeks. My parents suck sometimes, but they're still mine. Especially my mom. She tries. She tries hard. It's just the drugs got a hold of her and she fights, but there's no one else around that's clean. No one. How's she supposed to get straight in an environment like that? But she just started methadone. She was trying again. I don't know if it would have stuck, but she was trying." She put her head back on Thea's shoulder and sobbed.

"I imagine it's almost impossible without support," Thea said. "It sounds like you believe in her, though. Are your parents the reason you told Kit you didn't know anyone who was clean?"

"I never even thought it was possible. I still think Kit might be a unicorn. I mean, I know there are people out there. But they don't look like the people in my neighborhood."

Thea pulled out her phone and texted Kit. She hoped she would check her messages during the meeting.

"What are you doing?" Frankie sniffled and looked at Thea.

"Trying to pull the horn off a unicorn." Thea's phone buzzed and she saw Kit's message. "There's an NA meeting happening right now. It's an open meeting. Kit is there and she's invited you to join her. Would it be helpful right now to see some other folks who have struggled and gotten clean, or do you want to sit out here and keep talking? I'm happy to sit here all night if that's what you need."

Frankie didn't answer for a long moment. Thea worried she had missed the mark and Frankie was clamming up. Teens were fickle creatures.

"I'd really like to go to the meeting. Thanks for always knowing what to say, or what I need to hear. I'm hoping my mom can finally get clean in jail. Maybe there's some people in Kit's meeting that did that too."

Thea walked Frankie to the NA meeting. She wanted to take Frankie home tonight and keep her safe from the ugliness of the world, but she knew she couldn't. Frankie's reality would come calling no matter how hard Thea tried to shield her, and she had someone willing to step in and care for her. As a child Thea had been confused, lonely, and hurt. Now, as an adult, watching Frankie, knowing what she was likely feeling, her pain for Frankie felt overwhelming.

"My mom's not a bad person," Frankie said, and it wasn't clear if she was trying to convince Thea or herself. "She's not violent. Drug addiction is a disease, right? I've read all about it. I've read everything I can find about it. They'll see that, right? And maybe let her out? I can send them what I've read."

Thea wasn't sure and didn't want to offer Frankie anything that could be interpreted as a promise of any outcome. "Do you need me to call your aunt and let her know where you are?"

"She knows," Frankie said. "I told her I'd be home later."

Thea had texted Kit to let her know they were on their way down and Kit met them at the door. Thea hadn't been able to fill her in on why Frankie needed to sit in on the meeting, but Kit knew enough, and seemed to get a bit more from Frankie's red eyes and stricken expression.

Kit put her arm around Frankie's shoulder and said something to her that Thea couldn't hear. Whatever it was made Frankie smile. That was progress.

"Frankie, I'm going to be up at the desk. I'll wait for you to finish up and then we'll get you home, okay?"

Frankie nodded. "Thank you. Sorry I cried and snotted all over your shirt."

"If you've got more, let me have it. It should mix well with my sawdust," Kit said. "We'll be out in a bit, Thea. Thanks for getting in touch."

Thea watched Kit lead Frankie back into the community room. She still had her arm around Frankie's shoulder. As soon as they were inside, Thea ran upstairs, emotions hard at her heels. She didn't have a destination in mind, and halfway across the main floor she realized she should have gone to her office.

She turned to go back down and ran into Walter. She thought he'd left for the day. She wasn't sure she'd ever been happier to see him. His arms were full as he was on his way out, but she still wrapped him in a hug. He awkwardly tried to hug her back around his lunch bag and other items for home. By the sheer strength of an iron will she didn't know she possessed, Thea didn't cry.

"Should I put these things down, then?" Walter asked.

"No, no," Thea said. "I just really needed a hug."

"I'm always happy to oblige, but I suspect you're leaving out a detail or two. You aren't the most demonstrative with your affection."

"It's just Frankie's having a pretty terrible day. It reminds me of my own baggage. You don't remind me of those things and in fact, chase those things away. So, a hug."

"Is Frankie okay? I do have a soft spot for that girl. Where is she now?" Walter shifted his things to one hand and put his free arm around Thea's shoulders.

"She's downstairs with Kit at the NA meeting." Thea leaned into Walter's embrace.

Walter looked like he'd smelled something ghastly. "Are you sure that's a good idea?"

"Not at all. But I think it's what Frankie needs right now. And I fear there's nothing she'll hear in that meeting that she hasn't lived already."

"Poor child. I hope Kit is as careful with Frankie's trust and vulnerable soul as you are, my dear. Are you okay?"

"I really am okay, Walter. Thank you for the hug. Sorry to attack you."

Once she convinced Walter he could go and she settled at the desk, the NA meeting was almost over. It was just as well since Thea didn't want or need a lot of time to dwell on Frankie's situation or the overlaps with her own past. Her heart ached for Frankie. She wished she could whisk it all away, or at least provide some magic solution that would make it hurt less for her. Since there wasn't one, she would do what she'd always done—keep the library a safe, welcoming place for those who needed it. Just as it was for her.

## CHAPTER FOURTEEN

"You live on my couch, and all your clothes fit in a duffel bag. How have you been figuring out what to wear for an hour?" Josh asked.

"I pulled all your nicest jeans and shirts out of your closet." Kit buttoned up the latest shirt option and tugged on the sleeves.

"Hey. I thought that shirt looked familiar. Damn it. Looks better on you."

"Will Thea think so?"

Kit was nervous about her date. She'd been nervous before when the rules of the ballgame had been ambiguous, but then Thea made it official. Now the stakes were higher and Kit was feeling the pressure.

"Well, Thea's never seen my sexy ass in it, so she doesn't know what she's missing. But she'll be pretty excited to get you out of it, if that's what you're asking."

"Dude." Kit shook her head. "What the fuck?"

"What? Please tell me you remember how. I went through all the basics when you were a teenager. I'm not doing it again if that part of your brain was sizzled into oblivion during your break from reality."

For some reason, the flippant comment hit a nerve. "Is that what we're calling it now? You can call it what it was, Josh. I wasn't on vacation."

"Well aware, Kit. Wasn't a vacation for those of us on this side of it either," Josh said gently.

"I know. Sorry." There were so many things Kit wished she could take back, change, repair, erase about the past. If only it were that simple.

"Nope, none of that now. I know I started it, but I'm ending it." Josh made sure Kit was looking at him before he continued. "I wasn't trying to make you feel guilty. I know you do that enough on your own. Tonight, you've got a lady to charm. It's going to take more than my shirt to do that, so you better concentrate."

"Is that supposed to be a pep talk?" Kit looked at her outfit critically. "'Cause it sucked."

"Kit." Josh grabbed her by both shoulders and got uncomfortably close, looking her in the eyes. "You're going to be fine. I've loved you my whole life and I know all the worst things about you. Every one of them is outweighed by a million best things about you. Let her see those and don't worry so much about the other stuff. It'll work itself out. And you look fine, so stop pulling all my clothes out of my closet. I know you're not going to put them all back."

"You're a pain in my ass most of the time." Kit pulled Josh into a tight hug. "But sometimes you know just what to say, and I love you."

Josh waved her off. He grumbled about having recipes to try and not to wake him if she bothered to come home.

Kit flipped him off on her way out the door. If Josh was recipe testing it was a good night to be out of the house anyway. He was a master in the kitchen but, like many chefs, he was temperamental while cooking.

On her way, Kit texted Ethel to see if she had any advice since this was her first foray back into the world of dating. Ethel's reply, "don't blow it, sport," wasn't all that helpful. Ethel had been less insightful and available than usual the past couple of weeks, but Kit took it as a sign Ethel trusted the work Kit had done. Maybe she didn't need quite as much hand-holding as she had at first. Progress always felt good.

Thea had asked Kit to meet her at her house, which made the evening feel more like the date it was. Kit was eager to move their relationship outside the confines of the library. They had prescribed roles inside that building, but out here, there were no rules. Could anything be more exhilarating? Or more nerve-wracking?

The early evening was beautiful and Thea's neighborhood was quiet and tranquil. On any other night, Kit would have been content to stroll by herself, aimlessly, enjoying the peaceful bits of the closing daylight. But tonight she barely noticed any of the sights and sounds that usually gave her such pleasure. She was in a rush to get to the one thing that outshone them all.

When she turned the corner onto Thea's street, Kit slowed to take in Thea sitting on her stoop watching a couple of squirrels quarreling nearby. She was wearing a white sundress that flowed down to her ankles and a big floppy sun hat. Kit wasn't sure she could get her feet moving again. To say Thea was beautiful was like saying a waterfall was wet. Although accurate, it failed to capture just how exquisite Thea was.

"Are you coming over, or are you going to stand in front of my neighbor's house all night?" Thea leaned her head on her hand and looked Kit's way.

"Be right there," Kit said. "Need a minute to recover."

"From what? Are you okay?" Thea sounded worried.

"From you. Lost my breath for a second. It'll be back before the first pitch, I'm sure."

Thea left the stoop and headed Kit's way. Was it healthy for a heart to beat as fast as hers? Short of a tranquilizer there wasn't any slowing it.

"You promised me a baseball game," Thea said when she got near. "I already cleared off a spot on my desk for my helmet cup. So no passing out."

Kit had no idea why, but the idea of a souvenir helmet cup on Thea's desk was enough to thaw her limbs. A helmet from their date.

"I refuse to stand between a woman and a tiny souvenir helmet," Kit said.

"It better not be that tiny." Thea shot Kit a look. "I don't want to be cheated out of my ice cream."

Kit offered her arm, but Thea laced her fingers through Kit's instead. It took an inordinate amount of willpower for Kit to not leap off the ground and whoop with delight. She was afraid if she did, she would pull her hand free from Thea's. No celebratory exultation was worth that.

They walked in silence for a few blocks. It wasn't an uncomfortable silence, though. Kit was intensely aware of the feel of Thea's hand in hers. She had always felt a restlessness deep in the most out of reach recesses of her soul, but as soon as Thea's hand slid into hers, some of that churning quieted. Perhaps it was the newness of the feeling or her excitement at having Thea willing to hold her hand at all. Or maybe it was something else entirely.

"Penny for your thoughts," Thea said.

*Tell her you usually feel like a firecracker ready to explode, but when she holds your hand it feels like she extinguishes the fuse. I dare you.*

"If you're willing to spend two pennies, then I can tell you the two things I was thinking. The first is, thank you for taking a chance on me and coming out tonight. I don't imagine it's easy."

Thea nodded. "Kit, if being around you was hard, I wouldn't be here. I wanted it to be hard, but you're so damn likeable. What's my second penny get me?"

"I was thinking how beautiful you are, always, but I was thinking specifically tonight. I don't think I've ever seen you in non-work mode. I like it. I'd like to see more of it."

"You don't want to see how the rest of the evening goes? Play it by ear before you say you want more?"

"Are you planning on spilling nachos on me and heckling the home team?"

"That wasn't on my list of things to do tonight, no." Thea laughed and squeezed her hand.

Once they got to the ballpark and made their way to their seats, the game was just beginning. Kit loved baseball. She pulled a scorebook from the bag she'd brought and leaned forward to get a better look at the scoreboard. She was filling in the lineups when she felt Thea's hand on her cheek.

"I didn't get a chance to tell you earlier how incredible you look." Thea stroked her cheek, then pulled her hand away. "This shirt is now tied as my favorite Kit look."

"What's it tied with?"

"You in your work shirt, covered in sawdust." She looked a little embarrassed admitting it.

Kit wanted to kiss her but didn't. It didn't seem like the kind of thing Thea would appreciate so early on a first date. Kit wasn't usually so over eager, but Thea was making her react in all kinds of new and different ways.

"I'm sorry we were a little late to the ballpark and you missed your empty field magical moment," Thea said.

Kit was thrilled Thea remembered her joking comment and somehow understood that it really was something she thought was magical.

"I got something better when I saw you sitting on your stoop." Kit stole a look at Thea over her scorebook.

"What am I going to do with you, Kit Marsden?"

"Anything you want."

Thea's cheeks turned an adorable shade of red. Kit let her off the hook.

"Do you ever score games while you watch?"

"I admit I've never scored and don't know how," Thea said. "Which seems weird since it is completely in my wheelhouse of attention to details and predictability."

Kit didn't understand. "There's no predictability to baseball. You have no idea what the batter's going to do. Well, that's not exactly true, but you don't know how an inning is going to go or who is going to win. That doesn't drive you nuts?"

"Not at all. Because it's all in the framework of rules and structure. I can deal with the chaos of the game since it's contained within the rules that are predictable. I understand what will eventually happen. For example, the inning will end and the new one will start, so let chaos reign."

"I've never thought of it that way." Kit tapped her pencil on her chin. "Would you like to score with me?"

Kit was worried her offer was a little lame. She tried to view it from Thea's perspective. Who went through the motions of scoring the game anymore? Stadiums were multisensory distraction factories seemingly designed to get you to look at anything and everything but the actual game, and it wasn't like they didn't keep score anyway. There were much better and more exciting things to do than sitting and debating whether a slightly bobbled ball was an error by the shortstop or a clean single.

"Kit, relax. I already told you, I can't think of anything better than spending tonight watching baseball with you. And now I know you can teach me to score the game, and I'm assuming it's different from what we see on the score board over there. So, get to it. We've already missed half an inning. We'll miss another half when you buy me my ice cream."

Kit wasn't completely convinced, but Thea pointed at the scorebook and told Kit to get on with it. Kit started her quick and dirty explanation of how to score. While she did, Thea moved as close as she could in her seat and rested her head on Kit's shoulder. Kit didn't want to move for fear of ruining the moment. She also forgot all about scoring, but Thea kept asking questions and filling in the score sheet as the game progressed. Kit was happy to turn over control. As far as Kit was concerned, Thea resting her head on her shoulder was the only thing on earth that mattered.

❖

Thea breathed in the warm evening air and sighed with contentment. Kit squeezed her hand and looked at her, a question in her eyes. Thea had never particularly enjoyed holding hands with anyone, until she slipped her hand in Kit's.

"Nothing's wrong, if that's what you're worried about," Thea said. "I had a great time at the game. It's a beautiful night. I'm happy."

"There's nothing this night has to offer that holds a candle to you." Something fell out of a tree and thunked off Kit's shoulder. "Which is why the squirrels are throwing things at me."

Right on cue, a squirrel on a low branch started chattering at them as they walked past.

"I see you Nutsy von Squirrel," Kit said. "Catcalling a lady on the sidewalk is no way to behave."

"Are you defending my honor from a squirrel?"

"Only if you think it's charming. Otherwise, nope. I was performing a public service announcement on this very quiet street."

"You're a charmer. And you seem to know how to make me laugh. Two points in your favor."

"Ah, a points system. I can work with that." Kit's hair was a little windswept from being outside for hours and the expression on her face bordered on cocky. She looked roguishly handsome. Thea had a rash urge to grab fistfuls of her sexy shirt, shove her back against the nearest wall, and kiss her until she'd had her fill.

*Jesus Christ. Get a hold of yourself.* Thea involuntarily pulled her hand from Kit's and immediately felt the withdrawal acutely. It felt like switching off the lights the moment their hands disconnected, like the electricity was shut off.

"Hey, is everything okay?" Kit moved around so she was facing Thea. She looked concerned. "Did I say something wrong?"

"God, no." Thea put her hands over her face. Kit didn't deserve the whiplash. *Tell her the truth.* "I freaked myself out. I'm sorry."

"Freaked out about what?" Kit gently pulled Thea's hands away from her face.

*Don't tell her the truth. Don't tell her you want to pin her against a wall and kiss her until you both need oxygen.*

"Is it me? My past?" She looked incredibly sad and resigned.

Thea grabbed her hand and intertwined their fingers. It felt like the power was restored to the entire block. She put her other hand on Kit's cheek.

"No. No, Kit. Not about you. It's true you're dissimilar to anyone I've ever dated or thought I could ever date. This might sound familiar, but before, people were unsurprising and felt safe. You aren't predictable and I think I like that. But it's making me react in ways I'm not used to. And that's what scared me."

"The old 'it's not you, it's me' speech?" Kit said. Thea dropped her hands to her sides.

*This can't be happening.* Thea wasn't sure what else to say to make Kit understand. She was gearing up to try again when she felt Kit's hands on her face, then in her hair. Thea looked up. Kit moved closer so they were only inches apart. Thea thought she might combust.

"I told you I'll be reliable for you," Kit said. "If you need me to change something, tell me."

Thea put her hands over Kit's. "I don't need you to change. It feels incongruous to everything I need in my life, but I like being a little off balance with you. You still make me feel like I'm safe."

Thea was rewarded with a lopsided grin. "Next time you start to lose your balance, keep holding my hand." Kit tilted her head and leaned in…

Kit kissed Thea on the cheek, slipped her hand back into Thea's, and kissed the top of Thea's hand.

*Damn it.* Thea sighed internally, disappointed in the lost moment.

They walked in silence for a few minutes before Kit broke it.

"Tell me about these others you felt safe with but who didn't excite you."

"How do you know they didn't excite me?" Thea took a deep breath. She didn't want the comment to be true. "And is this really what you want to talk about at the end of our first date?"

"Because you said you never left your comfort zone." Kit kicked an acorn. "Falling in love isn't in the comfort zone, but it is full of excitement. And yes, because I want to know about you. They're not here now, so what do I have to worry about?"

"If you cheat on me, the wrath of everyone I know. Otherwise, nothing at all." Thea balled her free hand into a fist, then forced herself to relax.

"Hold up. Someone cheated? On you?" Kit stopped walking and looked horrified. "What kind of moron does something like that?"

"The ex-wife kind of idiot." Thea looked at the ground and bit the inside of her cheek to keep from crying.

Kit wasn't quite fast enough at hiding her surprise when Thea mentioned Sylvia.

"Does it really surprise you that much that someone would marry me?" Thea always felt vulnerable when she talked about the clusterfuck that was the end of her marriage. Or any part of her marriage, for that matter. She didn't know how she ever got herself into that situation.

"You mentioned your bachelorette party before. I'm generally familiar with what comes next." Kit tilted her head and gave her a small smile. "What I don't know is how someone who was lucky enough to marry you would be stupid enough to throw it all away. What was the marriage like for you?"

Thea thought about Kit's question, so plain and clear. Usually people asked questions about Sylvia. Thea'd asked herself over and over what she'd gotten from the marriage, or why she thought it was a good idea, since she'd walked in on Sylvia making a mockery of their wedding vows. The answer had always been elusive. Tonight, it was clear as a cloudless night.

"In the beginning Sylvia said all the right things, did all the right things. I believed all of them. Maybe she did too. Things were safe. Beige. Right in my comfort zone. Sylvia began to need more color in her life and figuratively started coloring in bolder, wilder colors. Outside the lines too, but I didn't know about that right away. It was paralyzing for me. Honestly, it was almost a relief to find her in bed with someone else." It felt strange to admit it out loud for the first time.

"No one should ever feel unsafe in their relationships." Kit put her hands on Thea's hips. "Physically or emotionally."

"To be fair, it wasn't all Sylvia's fault," Thea said.

"I'm going to be rude and interrupt you," Kit said. "I forbid you from taking any blame for someone cheating on you. We're moving on to other topics if you're going to blame yourself for being cheated on."

Kit's protectiveness made her smile. "Is that right? And what exactly would you like us to talk about?"

The look on Kit's face nearly made Thea faint. She didn't need Kit to answer to know exactly what she was thinking. Kit pulled herself together a lot faster than Thea did. Thea didn't mind. She wasn't ready to begin thinking of taking a peek under all Kit's sexy outer layers.

But even if she wasn't ready to do anything about it, it did feel awfully good to see desire in Kit's eyes and know she was the cause. To keep everyone safe, she moved Kit's hands from her hips. They resumed their walk, hand in hand.

When they reached Thea's house, she wasn't ready for the evening to end, but she wasn't ready to invite Kit in, either. Kit didn't look like she was in a hurry to get home, but she was clearly leaving the next step up to Thea. Thea appreciated that. She took thirty seconds more to make up her mind.

"Do you have to be home?" Thea asked.

"No curfew tonight," Kit said.

Thea wasn't sure if Kit was joking or if she usually had one. Maybe it was part of her recovery, or she had some legal entanglements?

"Do you usually?"

"Not unless Josh is feeling ornery and decides I need to be at work before the new day dawns. I guess that's not really a curfew. Just a self-imposed deadline so I'm functional in the morning. It means I make sure I'm tucked in tight in time for a good night's sleep."

Thea felt her emotion roil into something altogether unfamiliar. She couldn't quite pin down the feeling. She needed more time to sort it out.

"Have a seat, I'll be right back with something to drink."

"A porch picnic? Sounds lovely."

On her way inside to get drinks and a small bite, Thea took a quick inventory. Her emotions were usually comfortably familiar and rarely strayed outside of those she knew like old friends. This one, on the other hand, was like an old book, long forgotten. She was pouring lemonade when she realized what it was. Jealousy. It had been years since she'd been jealous of anything or anyone.

It wasn't hard to figure out why she was jealous now. Kit had said she was out late at night, bumping up against her curfew. Thea was envious of whoever was lucky enough to be keeping Kit occupied well into the evening. She'd been foolish to think Kit's eyes were only focused on her, and there was no reason to be upset she was dating other people. Suddenly the idea of extending their evening didn't seem as appealing. But she'd promised a picnic, so she brought lemonade and snacks outside.

Kit was leaning causally against the porch railing. Thea wondered if Kit had any idea how hot she was. Did she frequently cause car accidents just walking down the street? Thea would have trouble concentrating if Kit walked by.

"I realized I may have given you the wrong impression just now," Kit said.

She helped with the lemonade and sat on the stoop, making a spot for Thea to settle into between her legs. Against her better judgment Thea sat down and leaned back into Kit. Her body felt incredible. Thea could feel the strong muscles and solid body of someone who had a physically demanding job. But Kit also had the softness and curves Thea could spend days exploring.

*That's for another day. Get a hold of yourself.*

"Like I was saying, I don't want you to think I'm out at all hours of the night with anyone else. The only date I've been on since I got clean is this one," Kit said.

"Then why do you need the curfew?"

"My sleep isn't always great. Sometimes I go walking to help with that. The curfew gets me back home at a reasonable time. It's just another way to stay focused."

Thea was glad she was facing away from Kit. She was sure the relief was written all over her face and she didn't want to seem possessive or insecure. It was crazy to feel like this after a few cups of coffee and a single night of baseball.

"You live with your cousin, right? Tell me about him." Thea wanted to know more about Kit outside of what she got from their interactions at the library.

"Josh? He's the greatest. Don't get me wrong, we argue ninety percent of the time, but I'd know I'd done something unforgivable if he ever stopped giving me a hard time. At my lowest moments, he was always my connection to a different path. Since we were kids he's always been my grounding wire."

"You grew up together?"

"We were inseparable. About as close as siblings and we saw each other almost as much. My parents were never all that interested in the kid they had even before the drugs. But after? It was too much for them. Josh was the one who came to every family therapy session in rehab and treatment. He was the one who picked me up and drove me home no matter how many times I flunked out of this treatment or that until one finally stuck. Every time he'd say to me, 'Kit, you're not building a piano here. It doesn't have to be perfect or look all that great. In the end it just has to get built.' He never gave up on me."

"It's clear how much you love him." Thea wanted to meet the man who meant so much to Kit.

"Oh, don't go putting him on a pedestal just yet. He won't share his gourmet ice cream with anyone. He'll deny it, but the man loves romantic comedies. Josh, a box of tissues, and a chick flick is his perfect Saturday night. He'll do actual harm if you so much as look sideways at his mother starter. And he has no sense of humor about there being a Kool-Aid packet in the shower head."

"That did really knock him off his pedestal. What color Kool-Aid? I have no idea what a mother starter is so that one's probably safe."

"Blue. He looked like a Smurf. An angry, naked Smurf. The mother starter's a bread thing. He bakes every weekend. It's some kind of sacred bread holy grail. I nod and smile when he really gets going. I'll listen and nod if I get to keep eating the bread he pulls out of the oven."

"Seems like a fair trade-off to me." She snuggled closer to Kit. The evening wasn't cold. She had no reasonable excuse except she wanted to be closer to her. She couldn't remember an evening when she'd enjoyed herself more, which was impressive because they'd spent some of it talking about Sylvia.

Kit wrapped her arms around Thea and held her close. She didn't seem in any hurry to leave the date after-party either. They stayed that way for a long while. Cuddled together on the stoop, talking about all manner of things, and looking up at the stars. Thea ran inside to get a candle, ostensibly to keep the bugs away, but also because it seemed like it matched the mood of the moment. She could have sat happily on the stoop until morning, but eventually, Kit had to go.

When they parted Thea wasn't sure if she wanted the first kiss, or if she wanted more time. Kit saved her the agonizing by sweetly kissing her on the cheek and running her hand through her hair softly.

"I'm going to do what I had planned when we first got back. I'll make sure you get inside safely." Kit didn't look like she wanted to let Thea go inside.

"Kit, I've been in and out a bunch already," Thea said.

"I know. But if you go in now, then I can skip and dance my way down the street like a fool and you won't see me." Kit grinned. "Only the envious squirrels will know how happy I am after going out with you tonight. And they're jerks anyway, so who cares what they think?"

"God, you're cute." Thea's stomach flipped and she felt her smile down to her bones.

"That's good, right?" Kit cocked her head to the side. "I mean, puppies are cute, but you just coo at them and encourage them not to poop on the rug."

"It's very good." Thea patted Kit on the cheek and tried to hide the enormous smile that was threatening to break free. "I'm going inside now. You may commence dancing. But don't forget, I have windows."

Kit blew Thea a kiss as she walked backward down the street. Thea went inside but stole a glance out the window. As promised, Kit was doing a celebratory jig down the street. Thea loved it. She especially loved that it was for, and the result of, her.

Maybe sticking a toe or a whole foot outside her comfort zone wasn't such a bad idea after all.

# CHAPTER FIFTEEN

Thea was looking forward to dinner with Carrie and to talking about all the things going on. It seemed like ages since they'd caught up.

She spotted Carrie at the bar. Two martinis were in front of her.

"Cheers. I ordered for you." Carrie handed her one of the drinks.

"Oh, it's going to be that kind of night?"

"Isn't it always when we go out? You should have known what to expect. No surprises. And methinks you have some interesting things to tell me. If I'm right, drinks seem in order."

"What do you think I have to tell you that requires drinking?" Thea smiled and thought of turmeric coffee.

"You tell me." Carrie indicated Thea's drink.

The only time Thea really drank, and never even all that much, was with Carrie. She didn't mind Carrie pushing her outside her comfort zone, which as it turned out, seemed to be the theme of the week. As Carrie said, when she was with her, she knew what to expect, even if it was outside her normal routine. And it was usually a lot of fun.

Thea picked up her martini. She was about to ask Carrie a question, but Carrie cut her off.

"I know that look. You will not ask me any questions about children, books, or children's books. I do not want to talk to my boss about work. I want to have dinner with my friend. Do you accept my terms?"

*Busted.* "Fine. Accepted." Thea took a sip.

"Thank God. You've been holding out all the juicy bits about your new coffee delivery wizard. What else is she delivering for you? Does she look as good out of those clothes as she does in them? She was wearing a construction T-shirt the other day. Does she have a tool belt? Do you make her wear only that? I would."

"Stop." Thea nearly choked on her drink and felt her face grow hot. She was sure she was bright red. Sure, she had momentarily wanted to rip Kit's clothes off on their date, but Thea saw her as more than a hot body to drool over. She was a bit embarrassed to consider Kit that way, and a little jealous at Carrie's effusiveness.

"Kit is a friend. That's all."

"Well then, you, my friend, are blind. You're also a liar if rumors are to be believed."

"I'm not blind." She was definitely not blind. "She has a complicated history."

"So what? So do you." Carrie waved away her comment. "You still haven't denied the lying part."

Didn't she know it. "Yeah. That's sort of the problem. They may not be all that compatible. Her complications and mine, I mean. And we're way ahead of ourselves here. We've only been on one date."

"I knew it." Carrie looked triumphant. "And if you of all people have decided to go on a date with her, then you're not really all that worried about the compatibility stuff. Or you are, but you're willing to give it a go. You don't like being surprised by which way the toilet paper unrolls in the bathroom, so if you're willing to give a woman a try, she's special."

"There's clearly only one right way to install a new roll."

Carrie slid Thea's martini closer to her. Thea took the hint and another sip.

"As your friend I'm officially sanctioning the allowance of a little friction in your life. Breaking some of your rules isn't the worst thing. You tried to follow them with Sylvia and…well, here we are."

"You started strong, but really faded at the end there." Thea patted Carrie's hand. "But I appreciate it."

They moved on to dinner and other topics, but Thea was distracted. Now that Carrie had mentioned it, Thea was having a hard time not picturing Kit wearing a tool belt and nothing else. Combined with the sawdust, it was really hitting the sweet spot. And now that she knew what Kit's body felt like, it was a wonder she heard anything Carrie was saying.

Thea looked up and found Carrie with an all too knowing grin on her face.

"Not one word," Thea said.

Carrie held up her hands in surrender and made a motion like she was zipping her lips.

"Kit doesn't think Walter likes her very much." Thea tried a Hail Mary subject change.

"I'm assuming I'm allowed to join this conversation?" Carrie raised an eyebrow. "Kit would be right. He's not a fan."

That news hit Thea hard. She loved Walter like family. If he didn't like someone, she took notice. She was also confused as to why he had gone out of his way to help Kit if he didn't like her.

"Do you know why?"

"I quote, 'That woman's sniffing around like she's got designs on Thea. Thea can do better.' He doesn't think Kit's good enough for you. No one will ever be good enough in his eyes. But his eyes are focused on different things than mine."

"Do I even want to know what your concerns are?"

"He's looking for happily ever after for you. I see a hot woman who might be able to help dust off some cobwebs in your below decks. I imagine they haven't gotten much attention since Sylvia abandoned ship?"

"Would you please, for the love of all things holy, never think about, or mention, my below decks again? Seriously, never."

"Fine. Parting words. Tool. Belt."

"I don't know why I spend time with you." Thea shook her head and finished her drink.

"Yes, you do," Carrie said.

"If Walter's so against Kit, why did he find me when she was injured and needed help, or tell her where I am when she comes in?

Or why did he tell me to get the stick out of my ass and take some risks?" Thea went to take another sip of her drink and put it down again when she realized it was empty.

"He really said that?" Carrie stopped mid sip.

"No, of course not. But it was implied." Walter's behavior was a little unnerving.

"Honey, he's doing all that for you. He doesn't have to like Kit to love you. And loving you means doing what makes you happy and is best for you, his own feelings be damned."

"I don't know what to do with that." Emotions were complicated, messy. This was why she'd been avoiding them since Sylvia.

"You don't have to do anything," Carrie said. "Except send me a picture of hottie pants wearing her tool belt. Otherwise, keep following your heart for once, instead of your head. See where that takes you this time."

Thea wasn't sure she knew how to do that. The moment she let her emotions overrule her brain she'd freaked out and almost ruined the whole thing. But Kit hadn't seemed overly concerned, so maybe she shouldn't be either. Maybe they could figure it out together.

# Chapter Sixteen

Kit felt like she was still buzzing from her date with Thea. The guys at work had been all over her, making kissy faces, batting their eyelashes, and constantly asking if she was okay to operate the power tools. She'd find a way to pay Josh back for letting it slip she'd gone out with Thea. The guys said they were worried her head was too far in the clouds and her eyeballs were covered in hearts. She didn't argue. There was no point. Her feet felt like they were floating a foot off the ground. She was a walking, talking, post-first date, euphoric stereotype.

The two days felt unreasonably long since she'd seen Thea. Before, she'd never hesitated to stop by the library for no particular reason, but now she worried about seeming too eager. She was usually busy early in the week and didn't always make it to the library anyway, and now she wanted to be especially respectful of Thea's desire for predictability. Luckily, she'd been even busier than usual and hadn't had the chance to twist herself in knots over it. Tonight, she didn't need an excuse. Ethel would tie her in knots of a different kind if she missed a meeting for anything short of death. Especially a meeting after Kit ventured back into the wild world of dating.

Kit charged up the library steps. Feeling like something a dog regurgitated the first time she'd been on these steps barely registered now. At one point she never thought she'd think of anything else.

When she entered, Walter was at the desk and Thea wasn't in sight. Kit didn't want to be rude, but she wanted to spring past Walter and find Thea. Just to say hi, or hug her, or stand there awkwardly. "Ms. Marsden," Walter said. "Good evening."

"You can call me Kit. It won't kill you. Oh, God, will it?"

"It might." Walter regarded her coolly. "I prefer to keep things professional."

Kit didn't know if Walter was messing with her. He was a tough read.

*I will win this man over if it kills me.* "In what professional capacity are we interacting?"

Walter looked perplexed.

"Thea takes care of my library related needs and I don't see you outside of this building. If I did, it wouldn't be professionally motivated. Unless you have something you'd like to share with the class, you old fox?"

"Nothing I can think of at this juncture," Walter said, his head tilted slightly as he studied her.

*Not even a smile.* Okay. Maybe the truth would work, then. "Look, you don't like me. I'm not blind. I'm not good enough for Thea? My past is a disqualifier? You can't unsee the first time we met? You have an aversion to sawdust? What is it? She loves you, so I don't want you to hate me."

Kit was a little more aggressive than she meant to be, but the truth of the words hurt. Walter certainly looked taken aback. Seeing Walter had killed her good mood.

"I do not hate you, Ms. Marsden." He looked sad. "And I would never hold your past against you. On the contrary, I greatly admire your efforts and achievements in securing your sobriety."

*Securing my sobriety? I didn't get the last loaf of bread before a winter storm.*

"But I'm not good enough for Thea? You don't approve?" Kit felt her frustration rising. It wasn't Walter's fault. She couldn't make him like her, but it felt important that he did. She knew how much he meant to Thea. It would be hard for her to dismiss Josh's impression of someone if he didn't like them.

"No one is good enough for Thea in my estimation." Walter shuffled a few books on the desk. "And no one ever will be."

"Well, I guess we agree on something." Kit's stomach churned and she shoved her hands in her pockets.

"And I do agree your history and hers appear to be incompatible on the surface. But I encouraged her not to let that dictate her actions when it comes to you."

Kit looked up from the floor and stared at him. "So you don't like me, but you told Thea she shouldn't run away from me. I'm confused, Walter."

"Ms. Marsden, I never said I don't like you. You've said it and the rumor is certainly out there. I don't trust you. And before you ask, it's not because I worry you'll relapse. Rather, you appear to me to be a woman running from herself. And if you don't know yourself, how can Thea?"

Kit's first reaction was defensive because his words stung. She wanted to tell him to go to hell. That he was wrong. Instead she took a deep breath and asked another question. "If you don't trust me, I still don't understand why you would encourage Thea to not run from me?"

"Ms. Marsden, you make her happy. She smiles more lately because of you," Walter said. "And if I may be uncharacteristically crass for a moment, I'm really rooting for you to get your shit together soon. For the good of both of you."

Walter swearing was probably as rare as a leprechaun twerking with a yeti and Kit was the only witness. She was working out a reply when she was derailed by the feel of a hand trailing across her shoulders and down her right arm. She didn't wait for the full descent before she pulled Thea's hand into her own. The tension she'd felt from talking with Walter receded and was replaced with a jolt of excitement.

"That, Ms. Marsden. That's the reason. Right there. Mind what I said, for both of you."

"I feel like I missed something important," Thea said, her bright smile fading a little. She looked from Walter to Kit.

"Nope," Kit and Walter said in unison.

"Well, now I know I did. One of you will tell me later."

Walter waved his hand dismissively and walked away.

"He doesn't seem afraid of your serious voice." Kit watched Walter retreat.

"And what about you?" Thea moved in front of Kit but kept some distance.

Kit would prefer her closer, but Thea was still at work. "Oh, you scare me plenty," Kit said.

Thea looked pleased with that information.

"I'm glad tonight was a meeting night." Thea reached out and caught Kit's hand quickly before letting go. "I knew I'd get to see you and it saved me having to come up with an excuse to get you here without resorting to begging."

"You wouldn't have had to beg." Kit took a small step forward. "Although I wouldn't have minded if you did. But I wanted to respect what you've asked for. I'm not usually free the couple of days before my meeting, anyway, but I didn't want to change things up just because we had a date over the weekend, either."

Kit couldn't tell, but she thought Thea appreciated her being mindful of her need for a schedule.

"I really appreciate your thinking of that, Kit. But if we're going to give this a try, and you better not back out now, then I don't want you to overthink. If you want to come visit, please come visit. I like seeing your face. Don't wait two days because you think that's what I want. You're probably wrong."

Kit wondered how much of a goober she'd look like if she danced around a little bit. She played it a little cooler instead.

"I don't mind being wrong. But if you only want to see my face, I can give you a picture."

"You know that's not all I want." Thea's eyes glinted and her lips quirked in a sexy half smile.

"Tell me more about what else you want."

"I will not do that in the middle of the library, ten minutes before your meeting." Thea gave Kit a playful shove a few feet back.

"Can't blame a girl for trying." Kit grinned and hoped her desire showed in her eyes. "Can I take you out again?"

"You better." Thea smiled at someone walking past and took a small step backward. "I need to find out if we do second dates as well as we do firsts. Research is very important to librarians."

Thea walked Kit to her meeting and although they were no longer holding hands, Kit could still feel Thea's hand in hers. It felt like it had always belonged there. She missed Thea's touch. Was it possible to feel so close to someone you'd hardly spent any time with? Apparently, it was.

Frankie was walking out of the community room as they approached. She had a bag of trash.

"Hey, Kit. Hey, Thea. Just finished setting up. No one took the trash out, so I emptied it. The meeting's going to be a little aromatic. At least it's not dead fish. I'm going to stick around for a while, so if you need anything, I can take care of it."

Kit thanked Frankie and stole a couple of additional minutes with Thea before the meeting began. She wanted to be respectful of the fact that Thea was still in her place of work, but she couldn't stop herself from some form of physical contact. She touched Thea's cheek, rested her hand on Thea's waist, and briefly linked their hands. She felt a little like a high schooler again sneaking off behind the bleachers. It made everything more exciting, although the way Thea looked at her was all the excitement she needed.

She was daydreaming when Ethel slid into the seat next to her. She looked frazzled.

"Hey, kiddo. Haven't seen you much lately."

"You saw me last week." Kit looked Ethel over. She seemed different today.

"But no coffee dates. No breakfast. You don't call, you don't write. Tell me about your lady troubles. Or work problems? Which was it again?"

"Neither. Things are great." She was a little worried about Ethel. She seemed awfully stressed lately and a little distractible. She didn't know what the protocol was for checking in on how Ethel was doing. Was turning the tables okay? Ethel had her own sponsor and support system in place, but Kit was a friend and NA was peer support. They were all there for each other. Truth was, it felt like Ethel saved her life, so if there was something wrong, Kit would do just about anything to help, but she needed to know what it was first.

"You okay, old lady?"

"Don't you 'old lady' me, skip. I'm sorry I've been a little off my game, Kit. I've got something brewing in my personal life that's adding quite a bit of stress. I didn't think it was spilling over, but it clearly is."

"You know I'm always here for you, like you've been for me, right?"

"I know, ace, I know. But we need to keep your eyes focused on the prize right now. Feel like participating today?"

Kit thought about it. She had no idea what she would say. Ethel would probably tell her to talk about what she was feeling or share her story. But what was the point? She was sitting in this room, so everyone could deduce her story, or enough of it. Outside this room she wanted to be defined as someone else. She didn't know why, but actually standing up and talking here made it feel like that would be impossible. Like it would make it permanent in a way it wasn't yet. She was happy to admit it was weird, but she wasn't ready to share.

Once the meeting started, Kit was reminded, as always, why she continued to come. Despite her conflicted feelings about her identity, she was committed to her sobriety, and these meetings were integral to that pursuit. That was especially true today with insightful readings and powerful shares from the group.

Kit was lost in the flow of the meeting when the door opened suddenly, causing everyone to stop and turn to look. It was Thea at the door and she looked upset. Kit jumped up and went to her.

"I'm really sorry to interrupt," Thea said. "I need to speak to Kit."

In the hall, Thea took a shaky breath. "It's Frankie. She was doing some last-minute clean up and stumbled across a drug deal near the philosophy books. It's not usually well traveled, and she freaked out."

"Is she okay?" Kit reached for Thea and she willingly accepted Kit's embrace.

"No, she's really upset." Thea sounded upset too.

"Physically. Is she hurt?" Kit's pulse raced at the thought of anything happening to that sweet kid.

Thea shook her head. "One of the guys shoved her into a shelf when he ran off, but she says she's okay physically. She asked for you."

Kit knew this had to be eating her up. She'd been working so hard to keep her library safe and this had to feel like a slap in the face. Drug use was one thing. It was one person, struggling with their demons. Kit imagined drug dealing felt quite different, although both were often about survival, if different flavors.

"I'm okay for now." Thea extricated herself from Kit's arms. "Let's get to Frankie."

Thea led Kit to her office where Walter was showing Frankie how to fold an intricate origami frog.

"You will never stop amazing me, Walter." Kit leaned down to examine the frog. "Never change."

"Ms. Marsden." Walter nodded at Kit as he exited.

"That's not my name," Kit called after him. "I changed it to Sparkle Pants."

"You should definitely change it back," Frankie said. "And if she doesn't, break up with her." Frankie was looking at Thea.

"One date and I can no longer let my sparkle pants fly?"

"I think I'm going to stay out of this." Thea held up her hands.

"Good idea." Frankie looked at Kit and Kit saw tears in her eyes. "Did Thea tell you what happened?"

"Yes, sweetie, she did. She also said you asked for me. What can I do?"

That seemed to be all the invitation Frankie needed. She flung herself into Kit's arms. Kit could feel Frankie's tears hitting her shoulder. She wasn't sure what to do or what Frankie needed from her, but Josh always said she was a good hugger. She could do that.

After a while, Frankie seemed angry at the tears and pulled out of Kit's arms. She sat down in a huff in one of Thea's guest chairs.

"They shouldn't be allowed to do that in here," Frankie said. "Not in here."

"They aren't allowed." Kit got her a new tissue since she'd smashed the first one up into an unusable ball. "It's one of the sacred library rules. No talking loudly, no porn on the computers, no playing badminton with the books, and no drug deals in the stacks. Thea's serious about rules, you know that."

"This was just the one place. After my mom. This was the one place." Frankie's shoulders slumped and she put her head in her hands. "They can do it in the park. In the street. In my building. In my house. But not here. Just not here."

"You know how much I love this place." Thea squatted down in front of Frankie and put her hands on her knees. "And I will do everything in my power to keep it the safe place you need it to be. We'll figure out a way to increase security and have more monitoring, especially in these quiet hours. And I don't want you to wander by yourself. I'm not sure there's anything else we can do."

Kit mulled over options. She didn't like the idea of drug deals happening in the library. Violence could accompany drug deals when they didn't go well and she didn't want Thea or Frankie, or anyone else in the library, near that kind of stuff. She also didn't want kids like Frankie exposed to things they shouldn't have to be aware of. They would grow up soon enough without getting that seediness smeared on their Dr. Seuss.

"There might be something else we can do." Kit expelled a deep breath and ran her hand through her hair. She couldn't believe she was about to do this. "Is the library okay if you come with me on a field trip, Thea?"

"I'm coming too," Frankie said.

"Nope." Kit's chest tightened at the thought of Frankie and Thea out with her. "You don't even know where we're going. You wait here."

Frankie looked at Kit like she thought she was an adorable little chinchilla who'd given a good attempt at a new trick. Kit didn't like being looked at like that.

"What are you going to do to stop me? Call my parents?"

Kit knew her bluff had been called. She had no authority over Frankie. "Fine. For the record, I could threaten you with something that would matter enough to keep your ass here. But I'm not going to be that person today. It should be okay, but if anything goes sideways, you stick close to me and do what I say. Both of you. Understand?"

"Does this count as a second date?" Thea leaned close and whispered in Kit's ear. "Because I'm more into the flavor of the first one."

"You don't know where we're going either. This could be awesome. Although it's really not."

Once they were out of the library Kit headed into the park. There were plenty of people out enjoying the evening, but she was looking for someone specific. After a quick, fruitless search, Kit changed tactics. She walked over a small footbridge in the middle of the park, hopped the rail at the lowest point, and peered underneath.

Two men scrambled up from the embankment and tried to scuttle away.

"I'm not interested in what you're doing under here." Kit held her hands up and far out to the side. "And I'm not the cops. I want to know where Parrot Master is. Can you tell me?"

Both men shook their heads.

"You don't know, or you won't say?"

One of the men indicated he didn't know where he was, but he could get in touch.

"Tell him to meet me on the bench between the statue and the giant oak in fifteen minutes. Tell him Kilo's waiting." The words tasted foul coming out of her mouth.

*How deep a damn hole do I have to dig to keep Kilo buried?*

Kit wasn't ready for the feelings stirred up by waiting for her former drug dealer on a bench in the park. It felt too familiar. Too comfortable. The only thing keeping her from bolting or having a panic attack was the fact that Thea and Frankie were there. She didn't want to panic in front of Frankie, and this meeting was important for the library and Thea. Thea seemed to sense her discomfort and had kept some form of physical contact since they arrived at the bench.

*How does she know I need that? What does she think of me that I do?*

"Kilo, I knew you'd be calling," Parrot Master said as he flew, arms outstretched and zigzagging, toward the bench. The Zookeeper wasn't far behind. Her approach was more measured. She was sizing up Kit and her group. "What can I do for you?"

"I need a favor, Parrot." Kit managed to get the words out despite the bitterness of them.

"Like I told you before, Kilo, friends and family discount is yours. I harbor no ill will against those who fall out of the nest."

"This isn't Kilo, Parrot," the Zookeeper said, her eyes narrowed slightly as she studied Kit.

"My Queen, I didn't pack my eyeballs with the good glasses today, but this tall drink of water looks like our Kilo. How did my zesty tail feathers lead me astray?"

"Does she look like she's using again?" The Zookeeper rested her arm on Parrot Master's shoulder and pointed at Kit.

Parrot Master moved in uncomfortably close to Kit's personal space. He examined her face intently. He circled her, inspecting various body parts carefully. Kit allowed the examination. She needed their help, and despite their quirkiness, they had always been good to her.

"Kilo, you aren't using." It wasn't a question. "Why come to a drug dealer if you do not seek drugs? Why have you summoned me?" His arms were spread wide and his head was thrown back. Kit had always appreciated his flair for the dramatic.

"Like I said, I need a favor. This is Thea," Kit said, holding up Thea's hand.

"You're the librarian from across the park," the Zookeeper said.

Thea looked at Kit. Now it looked like Thea was the one who needed comfort. Kit guessed she didn't find being easily identifiable by these two to be particularly great news.

"I am," Thea said, her chin lifted as she turned back to the odd pair.

"There was a drug deal in there today. Some of your boys?" Kit looked from one to the other.

"So what if it was?" Parrot Master shrugged. "I'm engaged in a free market economy. I have pop-up shops all over town."

"If it was, then kids are watching and getting hurt. One of your boys shoved my friend here to the ground and you know that's the best-case scenario when someone interrupts a deal. That library is full of kids and people who aren't looking for any part of this life.

Thea's providing a safe place for everyone who walks through the door."

"Even you, Kilo?" The Zookeeper looked at her intently.

"My name's Kit now."

"I'm not asking about her." The Zookeeper crossed her arms and looked at Thea. "Is Kilo welcome in that library?"

"Everyone's welcome. I just want it to be a safe space," Thea said. "And there's only one Kit."

"Does she know that?"

Kit didn't like Zookeeper's scrutiny. The Zookeeper had asked her something similar the last time they met. She still didn't have an answer. Was Kilo a separate person? Was she trying to make her be something fully apart? Would she be easier to get rid of if she were?

Before Kit could fall further down the rabbit hole of self-reflection, the Zookeeper caught sight of Frankie, who had been hanging back behind Kit and Thea.

"Frankie, whatcha doing lurking behind these two? You the kid that got roughed up?"

Frankie nodded and moved forward. Kit was shocked when Frankie embraced the Zookeeper. It wasn't a tentative hug either. There was genuine affection and caring between the two.

"Don't look so surprised." The Zookeeper smiled. "Frankie and I go way back."

Frankie looked hesitant to let go but finally returned to Kit's side.

"I'm sorry about your mom, kid. Far as I know, she was clean. She was on our no-fly list. Those drugs didn't come from us and I don't think they were hers."

Frankie nodded. She looked relieved.

"What's the favor you want?" Parrot Master looked serious, a rarity for him.

"No drug dealing in the library." Kit stood a little taller. "And if you can arrange it, no drug use either. I know you don't control that, but you have some influence and people listen to you. There needs to be a safe place for the community where they know the outside world won't seep in."

The Zookeeper and Parrot Master stepped away and conferred. It felt like ages before they returned.

"This bird refuses to be caged by your terms and conditions," Parrot Master said when he returned. "But I offer a feather of peace in the form of a counteroffer."

"Let's hear it." She was encouraged that they were opening negotiations instead of rejecting her outright.

"No drug dealing inside the walls of the library. Grounds and surrounding areas are fair game." Parrot Master ticked off conditions on his fingers. "I still have a business to run. If I give that much ground someone else will move in. They won't be so accommodating."

Kit knew he was right. But she still pushed for more. "Nothing inside or within eyesight of any exit," Kit countered. "Is that okay?" she asked Thea quietly.

Thea nodded. "The windows are high enough you can't really see much directly below them, only into the park which is fair game now anyway."

"Acceptable," Parrot Master said, bellowing out the agreement loudly. "Zoo, I cede the floor."

The Zookeeper stepped forward and kissed him on the head as he stepped back with an elaborate bow.

"What you do on your own doesn't involve me. The library is too important for my own business dealings."

"And what is that? I won't have my library used for criminal activity." Thea stepped forward. Kit could see fire in her eyes.

"I like her, Kilo. She's got balls to tell us how to run our enterprise. Try not to screw things up." She turned back to Thea. "The business I'm referring to is not illegal and I believe is compatible with your stated goals of community safety. There are times I need a place, a safe harbor, to get certain individuals off the streets for their own protection. I have a list of locations for such purposes. I utilize the library when needed. I cannot guarantee, nor am I inclined to try to guarantee, sobriety when I drop off these individuals. That is not my purpose or concern."

"What is your purpose?" Kit put her arm around Thea's waist. "What danger do they bring?"

"What danger did you bring when I paid you to sit in a Laundromat all day babysitting my unmentionables?"

Kit thought back to her years of drug use and the times that the Zookeeper had asked her to do her laundry or other seemingly weird tasks. At the time she was happy for the extra money or promise of a safe place to enjoy her high. Now she wasn't sure of the motive.

"I fell out of my chair a couple of times." Kit dropped her arm from around Thea and looked at the Zookeeper. "Why *did* you pay me to watch the washer spin that day?"

The Zookeeper ignored Kit. Instead she kept speaking to Thea.

"There are women and young kids under my protection, whether they know it or not. Using drugs shouldn't sentence you to a life of prostitution, being sold into the sex trade, or being beaten or abused by some asshole out here. When the mood is rough or I know the traffickers are out I move my charges around to keep them safe. If I required sobriety, I wouldn't be able to protect them. I know that adds a burden on you. It's one I'm asking you to bear."

Kit was impressed with Thea, who seemed to take the information in stride and simply looked thoughtful. This had to be a difficult meeting given her history with individuals like Parrot Master and the Zookeeper. Although Kit wasn't sure there was anyone quite like these two. Kit didn't know why she was surprised though. Thea always put the needs of the library and the community she served first. It was one of the most impressive things about her.

Kit, though, was having a hard time squaring what the Zookeeper was saying with how she viewed herself and her time using drugs. She never thought of herself as needing the protection or the help of someone else, but clearly that wasn't true. Someone had been looking out for her after all.

"Why not get these women into treatment?" Thea asked. "Instead of hiding them?"

"Treatment has to be self-initiated, or at least the individual has to be on board. We've never stood in the way of anyone who wants to get clean. I've dropped people off myself. But I've also come to accept that I can't change reality. If someone doesn't want to change, they won't. Until they do, all I can do is keep them safe. It seems like we have that goal in common."

"And you supply them with drugs." Thea wrinkled her nose.

"If we don't, someone else will." The Zookeeper shrugged. "And at least we make an effort to make sure our shit's not laced with stuff that could kill them. We all just do what we can, lady."

The score that likely would have killed Kit hadn't come from these two. Their logic was sound, even though the subject was difficult.

Everyone waited while Thea thought over what the Zookeeper said. Kit was still chewing on all the times Parrot Master or the Zookeeper had shown up and dragged her to some strange location and insisted she stay put for a few hours or a few days. They had implied her access to drugs was at stake so she did as she was told. How would things have turned out differently if they hadn't been looking out for her?

"I want the library to be accessible and a safe place for everyone." Thea's words were measured, and she looked conflicted. "Keep the drug dealing out of the library. I won't stand in your way with the rest."

"Frankie, can I trust her?"

Kit wanted to punch the Zookeeper for questioning Thea's trustworthiness, but this was a negotiation, not a cage match. How did the Zookeeper view her?

"Thea's the best," Frankie said. "She's not lying."

"Then I guess our business is done." Parrot Master flew back to the proceedings in time to finalize the deal. "Welcome to the flock."

"I'm not part of the flock," Thea called after Parrot Master and the Zookeeper as they retreated back into the park.

Thea looked at Kit and Frankie. "That was a good thing. What just happened there, right?"

Kit nodded. "It means no more drug dealing in the library, at least to the extent they can make that happen. I think that's a good thing." It felt like the net gain from the meeting was positive, but the personal revelations were throwing her for a loop. Maybe it would be a good idea to get in touch with Ethel.

"Why is she called the Zookeeper? And why does she talk like she belongs in a Wall Street boardroom?" Thea tucked a stray strand of hair behind her ear.

Kit saw her hand was shaking. She looked closer. Thea's jaw was also clenched. Perhaps Kit wasn't the only one who found the meeting unsettling.

"Because of all the women she keeps under her protection," Frankie said. "She gives them animal names. Keeps them anonymous when she talks about them so everyone's protected. She's the zookeeper watching out for everyone in this crazy zoo of life. I'm Baby Giraffe."

"Do you know what she called me?"

Frankie shook her head. Kit thought it was probably better not to know. It could be something horrible like Guppy.

"She went to law school. That's why she talks like a lawyer." Frankie laughed when Kit and Thea looked at her like she had said the sky was pink and unicorns were real. "I don't know what led her to her current profession, if you're going to ask, but she's one of the smartest people I know. Aside from you, Thea. No offense, Kit."

Thea looked like she wanted to say something, but she opened her mouth and shut it again. Kit knew the feeling.

"You're wondering how I can be friends with drug dealers?" Frankie poked at something on the ground with her shoe.

"Yes," Thea said. "I was under the impression that was a life you wanted to get away from. And seeing the drug deal in the library upset you so much."

"I do." Frankie nodded vigorously. "More than anything. But I'm not away from it now. You do what you have to do to survive. And whatever their flaws, my parents made a deal with Parrot Master and the Zookeeper that they'd never sell anything to me and they'd never recruit me. But seeing the drug deal in the library was different from the rest of the world. That's the only place I really feel...felt, completely safe. I don't know why I didn't think to talk to them myself."

"Because you're not supposed to have to think of that kind of thing." Kit hated the idea of parents who had to make that kind of a deal for their kid, but it said something about them, too.

"Does what happened here help make the library feel safe again?" Thea asked.

Frankie nodded, but it was clear she was still deep in thought. She probably understood the ways of the streets better than any of them. If she felt the deal they made meant the library was safer, then it was.

"I'm probably naive, but why would Parrot Master and the Zookeeper agree to never recruit or sell to you?" Thea started back to the library. "Don't they want as many clients as possible?"

"Unfortunately, demand isn't an issue," Kit answered for Frankie, who still looked a little distant. "Look around the park. They have plenty without having to go after a client's kid."

"Am I supposed to like them?" Thea turned to talk to Kit as she walked. She looked like she was forced to eat something a few days past its sell by date. "Because they have a moral code of some kind?"

"I never said they were great people," Kit said. "But they helped us today, and maybe it will make things better in some way."

Kit's feelings about Parrot Master and especially the Zookeeper were as convoluted as always, but there was an extra layer of confusion now. And to make matters worse, it felt like the time she'd been using, which she'd been trying to bury and forget, had been shoved back in her face. She didn't want to think that she'd needed so much help and looking after. She also didn't want to think there were other vulnerable people out there now who didn't have the protections she did. She'd done what she could today, and for the moment, it needed to be enough.

# CHAPTER SEVENTEEN

On the walk back to the library, Frankie split off to head home. As Kit and Thea walked the rest of the way to the library, Kit slipped her hand in Thea's.

"I'm sorry I dragged you out of work to meet with drug dealers. In hindsight, I probably should have prepped you a little or given you a chance to wrap your head around the idea." Kit pulled their joined hands to her lips and kissed the back of Thea's hand. She quickly dropped their hands back down when she seemed to realize what she'd done.

Thea smiled and squeezed her hand. "When you just lay it all out there like that, it sounds insane. But you were doing something to help the library and me. I could see in your expression that it wasn't easy for you either. It wasn't a perfect situation, but I really appreciate what you did. Thank you."

"I'd do it again for you. And again, and again if you need it."

"And that is just one of many reasons you're so wonderful." Thea really enjoyed the embarrassed stammering that followed her statement.

The day hadn't been easy, but she knew it wasn't easy for Kit either. The fact that Kit hadn't hesitated to dive back into a world that she was trying to put behind her was quite a gesture.

"I still don't understand how we just trust that they will keep their word, but you and Frankie know more about this than I do." Thea stopped to pick up a stray paper and toss it in the trash.

"We don't have to trust," Kit said. "At least not fully. If we see more drug deals, we know they're full of crap. Then we call in the big guns."

"Tell me more about these big guns." Thea ran her free hand suggestively up Kit's arm. She was happy to flirt a little after the stress of the last few hours.

Kit didn't look sure if they were still talking about drug deals and the library.

"If we're talking about the library, I have no clue, so hopefully Parrot Master keeps his word. If you happened to mean anything else, you're welcome to explore anytime."

Kit moved in front of Thea and walked backward, facing her. Thea reached out and took Kit's other hand. She didn't think she'd ever get enough of the jolt she felt tingle up her arm when she took Kit's hand. She had no idea if it felt that way to everyone when they held hands with someone they cared about. She knew it never felt like that on the rare occasions she and Sylvia had held hands. She never wanted to stop holding Kit's hand.

"Oh, there are many things I intend to explore." Thea tried to pull Kit closer, but she stayed an arm's length away, teasing her. "But tonight, would you be willing to hold my hand and walk me home?"

Thea wanted more time with Kit. Just the two of them, no entourage of dotty drug dealers.

They stopped by the library quickly so Thea could grab her things. Kit carried Thea's workbag. It made Thea feel like her sweetheart was carrying her book bag home from school. She teased Kit about it, but that just made her puff out her chest and lean into the role. Thea thought she was goofy and incredibly hot.

They walked in silence for while, each lost in their own thoughts, connected by their joined hands and their weird earlier experience. Thea could honestly say she'd never met anyone quite like Parrot Master and the Zookeeper. That was probably for the best. The world could only handle so many like those two. Parrot Master seemed like his own kind of special bird, but she could see the intelligence and calculation in the Zookeeper's eyes that Frankie had mentioned. She didn't appear to have ill will behind her gaze, but she wasn't someone to be underestimated either.

Kit pulled her out of her musings.

"Can I cook dinner for you for our next date?"

Thea was surprised at the offer. She didn't take Kit for a cook.

"I'd love that," Thea said. Kit in the kitchen sounded pretty damn sexy. A vision of Kit cooking in nothing but her tool belt materialized. It was going to be a long walk home.

Kit looked thrilled. "Great. I'll tell Josh to get lost so he isn't bothering us all night. He's nosy as hell and the apartment isn't that big. He'd probably walk out in his underwear right when I was serving dessert."

Thea tried hard not to let her mind go to inappropriate places involving Kit, dessert, and underwear, but she wasn't all that successful. She had no idea this side of herself even existed.

"Why don't you come to my place and cook there? Then poor Josh can wander the house in his underwear in peace?"

Kit looked like a kid caught telling a wild tale.

"Well, damn, there goes all the hot chef points I was totally counting on. I can't come to your place to cook because Josh doesn't live there. I need him to pregame dinner with me, step by step, and then we'll all say a prayer I don't screw it up."

Thea laughed. "Why don't we just go out to dinner? Or I can cook for you?"

"No. I want to cook for you. You make me want to learn how to do these things. For you. But I was hoping I was going to get away with using Josh's help for longer than twenty seconds."

"For hot chef points?" Thea raised an eyebrow.

"Exactly."

"Do you own a tool belt?"

"A what?" Kit stopped walking for a second while she looked at Thea in confusion.

"What? Never mind." Thea couldn't believe she'd actually asked out loud. "So what will you be cooking for me, hot chef?"

"I don't know. I'll see what Josh has on the menu." She winked.

"I thought you packed lunch every day for the two of you."

"The best peanut butter and jelly sandwiches you've ever tasted." Kit pretended to shine her knuckles on her chest.

Thea thought Kit might be selling herself a little short, but it didn't matter. Thea was already counting down to dinner.

Usually she took the bus home, but tonight they were both happy to walk the extra distance. The mood of the streets felt different to Thea with Kit by her side. She didn't always feel comfortable walking the few blocks near the library alone, especially after dark, but Kit didn't seem bothered at all. Her comfort put Thea at ease. Kit made her feel safe in a way she wasn't sure she'd ever experienced.

She was happy she listened to Walter and was following her heart's lead and not her head. That damn thing could lead her to some lonely places. Thinking of Walter triggered the memory of the strange conversation she'd walked in on between Kit and Walter earlier.

"What were you and Walter talking about earlier? And before you tell me it was nothing, remember you said I scare you. I'm not afraid to use that to my advantage."

"Why don't you think you can scare it out of Walter?" Kit looked like she wanted to bolt.

They were walking past a row of brick, single story, small businesses that were closed for the day. There was a small alley between two of the buildings. Thea pulled Kit into the narrow space and pushed her against the wall. She pinned Kit's hands above her head and pressed their bodies together. She leaned close but stopped with her lips inches from Kit's.

"I can't do this to Walter." She wasn't sure where this side of her was coming from. But now that she was out, she was going to let her play. This was quite a turn-on. From the look in Kit's eyes, it was working pretty well for her too.

"He'd be dead right now." Kit was breathing erratically and looked like she was having a hard time keeping her hands where Thea wanted them. "Most people are scared of that."

"And what about you?"

"My heart is beating really fast and I'm sweating." Kit glanced at Thea's lips. "That happens when you're scared, or having a heart attack, but I don't think that's what's happening right now."

"Who says this is the scary part?" Thea leaned close to Kit's ear and spoke softly. She felt Kit shiver. She released Kit and pushed off the wall. She headed back to the sidewalk and heard Kit's loud groan behind her. She ran to catch up with Thea.

"Okay, you're right. The fact that you can do that to me, what you just did, and then leave me high and not at all dry, is actually terrifying. But I don't think it was all one-sided. I saw it in your eyes."

Kit was right. Thea's brilliant plan had backfired rather spectacularly. She might have made her point to Kit, but now she was wet and turned on as well. At least they could both be uncomfortable for the rest of the walk to her house.

"What did Walter want with you?" Changing the subject seemed safest right now.

"I'm seriously considering being obstinate to see if you can keep your hands to yourself or if you shove me up against another wall," Kit said. "But I'm not sure either of us is ready to scandalize the neighborhood just yet. And you're too classy a lady to be groped behind a dumpster in a back alley."

Thea appreciated Kit pumping the brakes. Letting her wild side out for a spin had been fun, but she didn't know where to go after she had Kit pinned to the wall. Even though she wasn't ready for more intimacy than she'd already initiated, she wanted to get her hands on Kit. She settled for looping her arm around her waist. Kit responded by putting her arm around Thea's shoulder and pulling her close. Kit felt strong and solid. Maybe she wasn't ready tonight, but she was looking forward to exploring all of Kit soon.

"To answer your question…" Kit said.

Thea couldn't remember what question she'd asked.

"Walter doesn't think anyone, perhaps especially me, is good enough for you. We were discussing my worthiness, among other things."

All Thea's goodwill toward Walter evaporated and indignation filled in the gap. He had no right deciding who was and who wasn't good enough for her. And if he had an opinion on the matter, he sure as hell shouldn't be telling Kit about it.

*That's the kind of crap a father would pull.* Thea stopped short and Kit looked at her quizzically. She seemed to understand at least some of what was on her mind.

"He loves you. No one will ever be good enough in his eyes. I don't disagree. But I'm really freakin' happy you're thinking I'm at least worth a shot," Kit said.

"You already know that's true." Thea narrowed her eyes and stared at Kit with mock horror. "Are you fishing for a compliment?"

"I wasn't, but if you're offering…" Kit posed in the middle of the sidewalk. "Pick whatever you like best and compliment away."

Thea circled her slowly, just to enjoy the view. She wasn't going to turn down the excuse to ogle Kit without worrying about getting caught. When she was back in front of her she stopped and tapped her in the center of her chest.

"If I were to compliment you, I would praise this."

"My sternum?" Kit looked down at Thea's hand against her chest. She seemed to like what she saw. "A little weird, but okay."

Thea swatted her playfully.

"Not your sternum. I'm sure it's outstanding, but you know that's not what I'm talking about. You have a good heart."

"It pointed me to you, so it's earning its keep." Kit smiled almost shyly.

They walked the rest of the way to Thea's house talking about their respective days at work and other rather routine things. It felt so routine that Thea almost didn't notice how comfortable she felt with Kit and how unlike her that felt. For once she didn't want to analyze or examine. She just wanted to enjoy the walk with a woman she really liked. A woman who made her happy.

# CHAPTER EIGHTEEN

I saw my old drug dealers yesterday," Kit said.

Josh was helping Kit prep dinner for Thea. He'd dubbed it "Operation hot chef." The knife he was using to chop onions slipped and he sliced his finger.

"Ow. Shit. What the fuck, Kit. You do not just drop something like that on a man when he's chopping onions. My eyes are already blurry from the onion tears and then that? Now there's blood in your fancy dinner onions and you would deserve it if I dumped all of it in the pot and made you start over without my help."

"Jesus. You could just say you're worried about me. No need to drag the damn onions into it. They aren't part of this." Kit handed him a paper towel to press to the cut.

"Fine. Why did you meet your old drug dealers? You know if you're struggling you can talk to me. Have you talked to Ethel?"

"It wasn't like that." Kit paid a little more attention to the mushrooms Josh had put her in charge of slicing. "They were dealing drugs in the library. I needed them to stop. I tried to call Ethel about something else that came up, though. She couldn't talk. She's busy, I guess. Personal stuff."

"I know I'm not her, but I'm a good listener." Josh pulled the paper towel away from his finger and checked his wound. "And we've got at least an hour prepping stuff for your dinner here."

"Why do people cook?" Kit rolled her eyes and flicked a mushroom at him. "This takes forever."

"Because it's delicious. It's satisfying. You get to spend time with those you love and tell your favorite cousin what's troubling you. A million reasons. Pick your favorite."

"It's so hard to pick just one," Kit said.

Josh threw a towel at her. "I don't have to help you, you know. I can walk at any point."

"You wouldn't." Kit glared at him. Josh had picked a really complicated recipe. He'd said it would impress Thea. Now she wondered if it was so he could threaten to walk away and leverage her desperation.

"Keep chopping, Mr. Zesty." Kit pointed her knife toward the onions. "I'll talk."

She wasn't sure where to start. There were a number of things that rattled her about her encounter with the Zookeeper.

"I know that look," Josh said. "Get out of your head and don't filter. You don't have to be two people with me. I love all of you, so don't censor whatever it is you're embarrassed about, or wrestling with, or trying to hide; knock it off and tell me."

"Fine." Kit put her knife down and grabbed a soda from the fridge before returning to lean against the counter. She turned the can around and around between her hands. "The Zookeeper said I was under her protection when I was using. She'd dump me somewhere for a day or a few hours and get me out of the target range of some of the very bad people that prey on the vulnerable. I didn't know that at the time."

"And you what? Don't like that someone was looking out for you?"

"I don't know, Joshy. I guess I view that time as me, this little island, doing this thing, and now it's done. But now, someone else was involved."

Josh stopped his prep, leaned across the kitchen island, and looked at Kit. He'd done this up in her face eye contact thing when he had something important to say since they were kids. As always, she wanted to back away, but he'd just keep coming until she backed herself into a corner. She held her ground.

"Did you use by yourself back in the day?"

"Not usually." Kit shifted her weight and scratched the back of her neck. "Too risky if one of us overdosed."

Josh nodded like he expected that answer.

"One more question. Why did you, no matter what shape you were in and how many times your number changed, always make sure I had a way to get in touch with you?"

"Because if something happened, or if you needed to get in touch, I wanted you to know where I was. And I always wanted to be able to reach you." She had an idea where Josh was going with this.

"I know you feel like you were all alone, Kit. And maybe you were for the most part. I can't begin to understand what it was like for you. But maybe it's okay you weren't an island? If someone kept you safe, then I'm eternally grateful. What is the Zookeeper anyway? A person? A vending machine? A radio shock jock? A monster truck?"

"She's a person." Kit laughed, picturing the Zookeeper driving a monster truck through the park. "And for some reason, it feels harder to leave that part of myself dead and buried if I know she was involved in watching out for me."

"I know I've asked you this before, by why does that part of you have to be buried? It's part of who you are. Doesn't have to be the biggest part, or the only part, but it's not the worst part either. Despite what you might think."

"Oh really? What's my worst part?"

"The fact that you never clean the toilet and since you were five you've hogged the best slice of pumpkin pie whenever it's available." Josh didn't even hesitate.

Kit couldn't argue. Although she probably should clean the toilet now and again. Maybe they could trade and he could vacuum.

"The part I can't get over," Kit continued, "is if I felt that alone and vulnerable and I had someone looking out for me, what's it like for those that don't?"

"Do you know the answer to that?"

Kit nodded. She didn't need to explain to Josh some of the things she'd seen.

"I guess the question then is, are you going to try to bury those feelings along with everything else, or are you going to use them to do something good?"

Josh turned back to dinner prep and left Kit to her thoughts. He always seemed to know when to push her and when to back off and let her think. She let it be for now. She'd chew on it a while, but there were more pressing matters at hand. Like dinner. Josh put her back to work. They easily slipped into their familiar banter and soon the mood of the kitchen was light again. Kit couldn't wait for Thea's arrival, but she was glad she'd talked to Josh. He was right, he was a good listener.

❖

Thea didn't care that Kit kept insisting Josh was actually responsible for the meal she'd just eaten. The food was delicious, and she was giving all the hot chef points to Kit. As promised, Josh had scooted as soon as Thea got there, but not before giving Kit a kiss on the head and telling her to behave. Kit had said something to him that Thea couldn't hear, but she could guess at the content based on Josh's reaction. Kit had shoved him out the door before he could respond.

Thea didn't have siblings so she had no idea what a sibling relationship was like. She liked to think it was very much like the one between Josh and Kit. It was obvious how much they cared for each other even when Josh was giving Kit a hard time.

"Can I get you anything?" Kit interrupted Thea's musings. "We don't have alcohol in the house, but coffee's always available."

"I wondered about that." Thea trailed her fingers over Kit's stomach lightly as she walked past. She thrilled at the feel of Kit's muscles tightening beneath her touch. "Alcohol, I mean. I'm not much of a drinker and certainly don't miss it tonight. Coffee is always welcome."

Kit stammered a little. "Some people think alcohol's okay since that wasn't my drug of choice, others don't agree. I prefer to abstain. Anything that alters my state of mind is a risk I don't need. At least, that's how I see it."

Thea liked when Kit told her a little about her recovery. It helped her understand and let her in on that part of Kit's life. She wanted to know all of her and that was something that, at least for now, was a large part of Kit's day to day existence.

Kit and Thea took their coffee to the couch. Kit sat in the corner and opened her arms. Thea was happy to be back against Kit's strong, solid body. She leaned her head against Kit's chest. Even on a day without work, Kit smelled vaguely of sawdust.

*Likes: sawdust, tool belts, lumberjacks, hot construction workers...Kit.* She forced herself to focus. "Did you always want to work for Josh?"

Thea couldn't see much of Kit's face, but she could feel her tense. She didn't mean to hit a nerve.

"You don't have to answer if what I just asked upsets you. That's the last thing I want to do."

"It's okay," Kit said. "Things tend to work out and I love working with Josh. Now I can't imagine doing anything else. But I wanted to be a pediatrician. I got in my own way though."

There were deeper things to say on the subject, but somehow that didn't feel right. "It begs the question." Thea leaned against Kit's shoulder and looked up at her. "Did you want to be a pediatrician because you were born fluent in teenager, or did you study teenager in preparation?"

Kit's laughter shook Thea's whole body. It felt good to be so physically connected.

"Born fluent. If you'd known some of the interesting characters in my family, you'd know it was important to be able to speak multiple languages. Teenager was one of them."

"Do you still keep in touch with your family?"

It was less noticeable this time, but Kit tensed again. Thea kept stepping in it, apparently. A family you weren't all that keen on looking back on was something Thea could relate to. Her grandmother had died years ago, so there was no one left who warranted a Christmas card, let alone a relationship.

"Josh is the only one. We're both the black sheep of the family. I think he keeps in touch with some of them. Certainly, his parents. But we have each other and that's all I need."

"Black sheep, fish out of water, ugly duckling. There's been some great stories written about the ones who don't quite fit in," Thea said. "They're usually the heroes in the greatest tales."

"Are you saying I'm destined to be a superhero?" Kit winked.

"Funny, I don't think that was quite what I said."

"Yep, totally what I heard." Kit flexed her bicep. "I wonder what my superpower's going to be. You said I'm not Batman, so I'm definitely getting a superpower. He was just a rich guy who dressed up and played with toys."

Thea shot out of Kit's arms and turned to face her. She managed to set her coffee down without spilling it, which was its own superpower. She couldn't let such an offense stand. She was kneeling on the couch in front of Kit with fire in her belly. Kit looked surprised at Thea's sudden departure from their cozy seating.

"Batman is so much more than a 'guy who played dress up.' He's a symbol of right and wrong and an example of living life with guiding principles and a strong moral compass." She was just getting started.

Kit got up from her seat and mirrored Thea's position.

"Given how passionate you are about him, maybe I'm regretting not being a Batman."

"Don't." Thea held up her hand. "He's also brooding and dark. Not to mention, unwilling or uninterested in settling down and committing to someone."

Kit moved closer. "And that's a deal breaker for you."

"I have the divorce to prove it."

"Good thing I'm a one-woman kinda woman." Kit moved even closer. They were only inches apart.

*There's that sawdust scent again. Why is that such a turn-on?*

Thea wanted to grab Kit and pull her down on the couch. She'd wanted to get her hands on her since the second or third time they met. She felt confident Kit was leading up to kissing her. What she didn't understand was why each second felt like a week of Sundays.

"The question is—"

Thea got tired of waiting. She reached up with both hands, tangled her fingers in Kit's hair, and pulled her close. In the moment their lips met, Thea wondered why they had waited until now. Kit wrapped her arms around Thea's waist and with gentle pressure closed the small distance remaining between them. She pulled away from the kiss briefly and looked at Thea with a question in her eyes.

"You were taking too damned long," Thea said.

That seemed to be all Kit needed. She returned to her half seated, half reclined position and pulled Thea with her so that she ended up seated in Kit's lap.

She leaned in to resume the kiss that felt like it redefined the entire experience, but Kit stopped her.

"You are so beautiful," Kit murmured against Thea's lips. "I wanted you to hear that before I kissed you again."

Kit's lips were soft and welcoming. Thea felt Kit's tongue sliding along her top lip, gently seeking entry. Thea didn't allow it right away, making Kit wait. Kit turned the tables on her, letting her hands wander. She moved one hand up Thea's back and slowly ran the other up Thea's leg, working her way to her thigh. Thea deepened their kiss before Kit got close to the apex of her thigh. She felt like she might combust if Kit had moved higher.

Although Thea wasn't ready to move beyond kissing this evening, she was more than willing to get a sense of what she was missing. If Kit could tease her, she was happy to return the favor. Kit softly bit Thea's lower lip, then ran her tongue along the bite. Thea pulled Kit's shirt up enough to slide her hand under and then groaned into their kiss. Kit's body was even more than she had pictured and she'd done plenty of picturing.

She ran her nails up and down Kit's abs, enjoying the feel of Kit's muscles quivering under her touch. Kit broke their kiss and threw her head back against the couch cushions. Thea shifted so she was straddling Kit's lap. She kissed her way down Kit's jaw to her neck to the strong curve of her collarbone. Kit's breath was hitched, and Thea felt drunk on the power of making Kit shiver under her touch.

Thea slid her hands to Kit's sides and inched closer and closer to the underside of Kit's breasts. She wasn't trying to torture Kit, but having her so responsive under her hands was intoxicating. Kit's body was indescribable, and she wanted more.

Before she got to Kit's breasts, Kit put her hands over Thea's, stopping her progress.

"If you don't want this to go further than kissing tonight, please have mercy on me."

"I blame you," Thea said.

"Me?" Kit raised her eyebrow. "Why blame the victim? I'm just sitting here."

"Yes." Thea kissed her again, then again. "Completely innocent in this scenario."

"And if I'm not? What are you going to do about it?"

Thea knew exactly what she wanted to do about it. She couldn't believe she and Kit were in this situation together. They were the definition of opposites attracting, but she was so thankful they had. Their chemistry was undeniable. Even if she couldn't explore all of Kit's enticing landscape, she fully intended to kiss her quite a bit longer.

# CHAPTER NINETEEN

"So," Carrie said. "How's operation tool belt going?"

Thea was in her office working on the staff schedule for the upcoming month. Carrie had a habit of popping in to chat when she was in the middle of an aversive task. Thea had always joked that Carrie had bugged her office.

"What exactly is operation tool belt? Do I want to know?"

"Of course you do." Carrie looked incredulous. "Operation tool belt is getting your sexy woman out of her clothes and into only her tool belt. Obviously. What's your progress?"

Thea ran her hands across her face. This wasn't what she needed to be thinking about in the middle of her workday. Not when she was supposed to be working on staff scheduling.

"I know that look." Carrie wagged her finger at Thea. "Loosen up. It's not like you weren't already thinking about her. Probably thinking about her in her knickers, too. I know there's a dirty mind buried in there somewhere. Bring it out to play and let it chat with me."

"Don't you have work to do?" Thea crossed her legs tightly under her desk and looked back to her computer. She wasn't willing to concede the facts to Carrie just yet.

"It's the end of the day, which you know as well as I do. It's okay though, you can keep your secrets. I'll make up my own story."

Carrie cleared her throat and began reciting what sounded like an erotica story. Thea wasn't interested in hearing Carrie's erotica at any time, and certainly not in her office, or about herself and Kit. She didn't want Carrie even thinking of her, Kit, and erotica together, ever.

Thea flew from behind her desk and clapped her hand over Carrie's mouth to get her to stop, but Carrie just kept up her narration with the volume up. She licked Thea's hand, which was gross, but Thea should have seen it coming. Since Carrie upped the stakes and hadn't stopped her shout-talking, Thea poked her in all the spots she knew Carrie was ticklish, trying to find the mute button. Carrie retaliated and they both ended up in a twist of arms and headlocks an MMA fighter would have been proud of.

Thea was happy the workday was over. It was behavior unlike her, but she and Carrie were laughing and it was oddly freeing to act like a complete child with your best friend in your office at work.

They were trying to untangle when Thea heard laughter at her office door.

"Do you think they require our assistance?"

*Walter. And he's not alone. Please don't be—*

"It looks like they have it under control…ish."

*Kit.*

Carrie extracted herself from Thea's grasp. She never lost the crazy grin she'd had on her face since she walked into Thea's office. She propped herself on the edge of Thea's desk and started chatting with Walter and Kit like playing human pretzel in Thea's office was the most natural thing in the world.

When Thea finally turned around Kit was looking at her as if she'd been waiting all day, just to look at her in this moment. She looked amused, but Thea didn't get the feeling she was laughing at her. The feeling of embarrassment she'd been feeling was gone as soon as she and Kit locked eyes.

"Well, shoot, there goes my dinner date." Carrie threw up her hands. "Walter old man, you free tonight? Or do you have to run home to a hot toddy and a saucy romance novel?"

"I'm not ditching you for dinner." Thea moved closer to Kit so she could touch her but looked to Carrie. "You promised me we're going to…that place. What's it called again?"

"Tool Belts." Carrie examined her nails and refused to look at her as she said it.

Thea glared at Carrie. All she got in return was a not at all innocent smile.

"It is new?" It was cute how much of the unspoken Kit was missing. "I haven't heard of it. Josh loves food. If it's good, let me know. I'll take him and listen to him drone on and on about some tiny detail I didn't even notice."

"Don't encourage her to give you any more details," Thea said. "Were you stopping by to say hi, or was there something else?"

"Yes, was there something else?" Carrie was suddenly right over Thea's shoulder batting her eyelashes at Kit dramatically.

"Go away." Thea shooed Carrie away and out the door. She was a handful at times, but she did love her.

"I'll meet you upstairs for our dinner date. Always wonderful to see you, Kit." Carrie blew Kit a kiss on the way out. Walter went with her.

"Hi." Kit reached out and took Thea's hand.

Thea was happy for the connection. She'd missed Kit's touch even though it hadn't been long since they'd last seen each other. "Hi. Sorry about Carrie. She thinks we're living a romance novel and she's written herself in."

"That's okay with me," Kit said. "The romance novel part. I'm okay with Carrie too as long as she's not a villain or interested in a thruple."

Thea rolled her eyes dramatically. "I'd say the most you'll get with her is some light voyeurism."

"You have good friends. I like them."

"They like you too. Well, Carrie does." Thea's shoulders sagged and she examined a scuff mark she'd never noticed on her shoe.

"I'm working on Walter. He'll like me too in the end, you wait and see." Kit lifted Thea's chin. "Sorry for coming by without letting you know. I clearly caught you at a bad time. I just wanted to say hi. And do this."

Kit leaned in and kissed Thea. It felt as electrifying as the first time. If Thea had known kissing could feel like this, she would have ditched Sylvia a long time ago and kissed everyone she could find until she came across this feeling. Although, maybe it was only if she kissed Kit, in which case, timing was everything.

"You're always welcome." Thea wrapped her arms around Kit's neck and kissed her again. "Especially if you stop by to kiss me."

"I left something for you at the desk upstairs. I know you have dinner plans, so I won't keep you." Kit took first one of Thea's arms from around her neck, then the other and kissed each of her hands.

Before she could cancel her plans for the evening and drag Kit back to her place, or out somewhere, or deep into the stacks for more kissing, Kit was off. Thea sighed. It was probably better she not lose her head anyway. Not that Carrie would be much help with that. She seemed to be well and truly in love with Kit already.

Thea made her way to the front desk, eager to see what Kit had left for her. Carrie and Walter were waiting. Walter was holding a single red rose. Carrie was trying to snatch it from him, unsuccessfully.

"Your Ms. Marsden does have an old-fashioned romantic flair, which I applaud," Walter said. "She came round to leave the rose for you before taking her leave, but I escorted her to you. Little did I know you were engaged in a game of Twister with Carrie. Next time, should I call first?"

"Can it, old man." Carrie swatted Walter on the shoulder. "Enough speechifying. Give her the rose already."

Walter handed over the rose. Carrie teased Thea about looking dreamy eyed as she clutched the rose when they headed to dinner. No one had ever gotten her flowers before, so Carrie could tease all she wanted. She was going to enjoy all the feelings such a sweet gesture elicited.

It didn't take long for dinner to settle into their normal routine. Carrie refused to talk about work, but then usually had a question that she needed Thea to answer. Thea tried not to give in to Carrie's grilling about her personal life, but she always caved. It was harder now that there was Kit and everyone at the library knew her.

Although, surprisingly, she would have been happy to talk about Kit all night, there was something else she was hoping Carrie would share an opinion on.

"I met Kit's former drug dealer the other day in the park," Thea said.

"Whoa." Carrie paused, fork halfway to her mouth. "Things are moving awfully fast, don't you think? Why didn't you tell me? Are we going to need to go wedding dress shopping soon?"

Thea's jaw unclenched and her shoulders relaxed. Why had she been nervous to tell Carrie? "Her name's the Zookeeper. I think you'd love her."

"I am a sucker for a good nom de illicit activity." Carrie put her fork down and leaned forward. It was her "ready for a good story" pose.

"I know you are. She's also apparently a lawyer, but I don't have the full story there. But she alerted me to something happening in the library that I was unaware of. It's been bugging me. Not that it's happening, but that maybe we could be doing more to help."

"And that's where I come in? Problem solver extraordinaire?"

Thea wasn't sure where to begin. She'd been giving her conversation with the Zookeeper a lot of thought. It was admirable that she was getting the women she saw as under her protection out of harm's way when they needed to be off the streets. But as Thea had been reminded of recently, her library wasn't a true community library unless it served everyone in the community.

"You don't need to have all the answers, or the problem laid out fifteen steps ahead." Carrie reached out and took Thea's hand. "Just talk to me."

Carrie was right as usual. Thea didn't know where to begin so Carrie had told her.

"The Zookeeper and Parrot Master agreed to stop selling drugs in the library."

"Wait," Carrie said, interrupting. "The Zookeeper and Parrot Master. We're going to have a serious conversation about two people with those names featuring prominently?"

"We are," Thea said.

Carrie looked bemused but waved her hands to indicate Thea should continue.

"Kit arranged a meeting so we could get their agreement on the drug selling issue. You heard how Frankie stumbled on a deal that could have turned out far worse than it did?"

Carrie nodded. All the staff knew and liked Frankie and Thea had let everyone know about the drug deal. She wanted folks to be extra cautious if they were alone in less populated areas or if they saw anything suspicious. Then Thea explained the Zookeeper's refusal to encourage or insist anyone in their sphere abstain from drug use in the library.

"She has a network she uses to get mostly women and kids off the street if it's unsafe. The library's part of the network. If the women and kids had to be clean before she could help them, she'd never help anyone. So she stashes active drug users in our library occasionally, just to make sure they're safe from whatever threat she perceives could affect them at the time."

"So what?" Carrie took a bite of salad and waved her fork for emphasis. "We've set up the sharps containers in the bathrooms. You have naloxone just in case. We're a community library. All are welcome."

"But is that enough?" Thea leaned back in her chair. Her foot was tapping rhythmically. "Cleaning up the mess, literally and figuratively, if something goes wrong? Asking people who can't walk or stay awake to leave? I do more than that for Mrs. Zalenski when she calls every afternoon at twelve fifteen."

"And we all thank you for continuing to take her calls." Carrie tipped her imaginary cap to Thea with her fork.

Thea knew the irascible Mrs. Zalenski wasn't the most popular library patron, but she didn't mind the daily phone call.

"That's my point," Thea said. "If I can read the weather report and box score to Mrs. Zalenski every day, why can't we do more than provide a sharps container and a kinda, sorta, maybe promise we might be able to not let you die if you overdose, to others who come into the library?"

"Well, if you hang Mrs. Z over my head, of course I'm going to agree with you," Carrie said. "But you do have a point. I've done all kinds of stuff over the years to help the kids upstairs with what they bring into the library. Parents' divorce, illness, bullying at school, autism and developmental delays. Feels like we've seen it all. And we've updated and changed programs, ordered new, different, and diverse books, made the space more adaptive and sensory integrative, had social workers come in to offer groups for the little guys."

"You've done an amazing job up there." Thea ran her hand through her hair. "It's been one of our greatest successes at molding our offerings."

"Shouldn't be any different for the Zookeeper's contingent when you break it down," Carrie said. "Just takes a little rethinking on my part to see that her group and my kids are the same in terms of needing what the library has to offer. Probably happens a lot, now that I think about it. Not being seen as worthy of help or services."

"I want to be better than that." Thea balled her napkin. "I need to be better than that."

"Hey, what's going on?" Carrie reached out and took Thea's hand.

Thea felt her face heat and she looked down. She couldn't look her best friend in the eye. "Since I talked to the Zookeeper I've looked at every woman who walks in differently. I've been trying to figure out if they're one of hers and if they're a threat to the library. That's not fair to them. I'm ashamed of myself. But I need that library to be safe for kids like Frankie, so I'm caught in some judgmental twilight zone."

Carrie scooted her chair around so she was sitting next to Thea. She put her arm around her. "For kids like you too, right? Little Thea probably wouldn't have felt all that great having the Zookeeper's women prowling your library as a kid."

Thea pushed the food around on her plate so she had something to do. "Little me doesn't get to make decisions for adult me."

"Maybe not, but I'm sure she isn't afraid to share her opinion. Frankie's not the only kid in there that has seen what she's seen. Or has parents like yours. Your instincts to protect them aren't wrong."

Thea thought about Frankie and the women who were probably a lot like Frankie's mom within the walls of her library. She thought about how much Frankie loved her mom and how devastated she was when her mom was arrested. What if some program, service, or connection through the library was able to help Frankie's mom, or a woman like her? What if there'd been someone to help Thea's mom? There were a lot of layers at which to serve a community.

"No, but you're not wrong either. We're a community library. Everyone should be welcome. My personal history is not the fault of anyone who walks through the doors." Thea sat up a little straighter and looked Carrie in the eye. "So what do we do to improve things?"

"No idea," Carrie said. "But I'm confident we can figure it out. And I think you should ask Kit. I bet she'll have some ideas too."

Thea and Carrie eventually moved on to other topics while they finished dinner. On her way home, Thea revisited the conversation. She was happy Carrie had validated her feelings, and had also helped her come to the obvious conclusion that they should do more to support everyone who walked through the door.

There was nothing she could do to change the nature of the neighborhood surrounding her library. The only thing she could do was live up to her values and make sure the library served the neighborhood where it resided. Part of that meant putting her own fraught personal history aside and welcoming everyone through the doors. Tonight felt like a step in that direction. She didn't realize how good that would feel.

Once home, she kicked off her shoes and leaned against the closed front door. She smelled the rose Kit had left for her. She closed her eyes and pictured Kit's face. That was something else that felt good. Maybe too good. She and Kit were so different. Kit still came with so much baggage. Could it possibly work?

She looked at the rose in her hand and smelled it again. She ignored her overly analytical brain and listened to her heart. The future was just that. Today she was happy.

## Chapter Twenty

"Where are you taking me?" Thea swatted at a determined fly.

"Just a little bit farther. It'll be worth it." Kit hoped that was true and it wouldn't be an uncomfortable forty-five-minute drive back to the city. She hadn't been here in years. It used to be her favorite spot to laze away an afternoon. She didn't think it had probably changed much since she had last been there. Wide-open spaces didn't tend to. It was people who did.

Kit helped Thea climb over a crumbly old rock wall. Thea was wearing another stunning sundress as the late fall day was unseasonably warm. She looked like she was painted into the beautiful scenery surrounding them. Kit could see their destination in the distance.

"Are you sure we should be trespassing on someone's private property?" Thea asked.

"The owners won't mind." That was bullshit, but there was almost no chance the owners would find them way out here. Kit was willing to risk it. She wanted Thea to see this place. She didn't understand why it felt so important, but this was something she needed to share.

"We're going to that oak tree." Kit pointed to a majestic oak standing alone atop a hill.

"There are oak trees all over the park near home." Thea shaded her eyes and looked where Kit was pointing.

"Not like this one." The view was just as Kit remembered. She spread the blanket she'd brought next to the massive trunk and began unpacking the picnic.

Thea wandered down the hill a little and stopped and stared across the expansive view stretching out seemingly forever. Kit was happy to let her take it in. She'd been awed by this view for as long as she could remember. Now she understood. Letting Thea experience it was why she'd brought her here. She hadn't been sure what had driven her to return here, but watching Thea react to everything around them gave her the answer. This place still held so many positive memories and she wanted to make new ones with Thea.

"This is incredible." Thea joined Kit on the blanket. "How do you know about this place?"

"I grew up here. Well, in that house." Kit pointed to a house just visible in the distance.

Thea jumped up and craned to get a better look. "You grew up here?" She motioned all around her. "In that…castle?"

"My mother insisted on calling it a chateau." Kit rolled her eyes and shook her head. "Which tells you just about all you need to know about her."

"I have so many questions." Thea knelt in front of Kit, invading her personal space. "Are you a princess?"

"What? No. Do I look like a princess to you? How horrifying." Kit didn't like the mischievous look on Thea's face. "Absolutely not. I don't care what you promise, I'm not wearing a tiara."

"I haven't even presented my offer yet," Thea said. "It's okay, we can circle back."

Kit could see more questions forming. Thea's expression changed subtly as they occurred to her. Kit had wanted to share this spot with Thea because of what it had meant to her as a child, but she should have realized Thea would want to know more.

"I'll answer what I can," Kit said. "But if your first question is 'can we go visit' then I'm afraid I'm going to disappoint you. I already told you I don't keep in touch with anyone in my family. There's a good reason."

"But you said they wouldn't mind that we're out here." Thea put her hand out and stopped Kit.

"That's true." Kit continued opening containers from the picnic basket. "Because they'll never know." She filled a plate with food and offered it to Thea. She accepted and sat down on the blanket once more. Kit made herself a plate and stretched out, resting her head on her hand with her elbow propped.

"Tell me why you brought me here." Thea reached out and stroked Kit's arm.

Kit didn't think Thea meant the gesture as anything but a point of connection and support. The result, however, was quite distracting. Kit felt like Thea's touch was the match lighting a cascade of fireworks going off all over her body. It was pleasantly electric but made formulating thoughts a challenge.

"Why did I bring you here? Right. I told you Josh and I are the black sheep of the family. His parents have a house over that hill." Kit waved in the general direction. "This was a meeting place for the two of us more days than not. But even if he wasn't around, I'd come out here myself. No one bothered me here, or expected anything of me. I could lie in the grass and stare at that breathtaking view and be anything I wanted to be. It still feels that way when I look at it. I guess I wanted to share it with you. You told me about your library when you were a kid. This was my version of that."

"Thank you for bringing me here." Thea leaned forward and kissed her. Kit wanted to deepen it, but Thea pulled back.

"How did young Kit imagine herself when she dreamed out here under the big oak tree?"

"There were the usual kid things." Kit smiled. "I wanted to be Wonder Woman, or Captain Marvel. Either would have been fine. Or a ninja. There was a brief, but intense time where Josh and I were obsessed with becoming garbage men."

"An honorable and underappreciated career if ever there was one," Thea said.

"When I was here by myself, as I got older, I really just wanted to be seen. For who I was. Not who my family needed or required me to be. I wasn't ever going to live up to their ideals of the perfect daughter. Everyone was miserable trying to make it happen."

Thea looked confused. She scooted closer to Kit on the blanket. "But you're wonderful. Why wasn't that enough?"

"I don't know. My parents had an image of 'a daughter' they wanted to present to the world. Unluckily for them, they got me. You can't just hide away the parts of a person you don't like. A person comes with all the messy bits too."

Kit stopped and thought about what she'd just said. She groaned and flopped on her back on the blanket. "Damn it, Josh."

Thea leaned over her, looking concerned.

"I'm fine." Kit rubbed her temples. "Well, actually, I'm totally screwed because I have to tell Josh he was right about something. He's never going to let me hear the end of it. Maybe I'll just tell Ethel instead and not mention it to Josh. But she's been so weird lately. I should probably figure out what's going on with her."

Thea kissed her. It wasn't a soft tentative kiss, but a take charge, possessive kiss. She pulled away a few inches but kept her hand in Kit's hair.

"I think you were short-circuiting. Better?"

Kit pulled Thea on top of her. She tried to kiss her again. A day like this. A view like this. Lying under a tree in the middle of a field. This day was made for kissing. Not worrying about something she couldn't do anything about right now. If only she hadn't opened her big mouth.

"Oh no, you don't." Thea put her finger against Kit's lips and pushed her back down flat on the blanket.

She kept Kit from kissing her but stayed on top of her. She couldn't tell if Thea was pressing her leg into Kit purposefully or if she had the best accidental aim on the planet, but the impact was the same. She was on fire and having trouble concentrating. If Thea wanted to have a serious conversation, any conversation, Kit needed some relief.

She gently repositioned them so Thea was snuggled along the length of her body with her head on Kit's chest. Kit held Thea close with one arm and used her other arm as a pillow. Now at least she'd be able to listen without all nerve signals heading south.

"Sorry." Thea propped herself on her elbow so she was looking down at Kit. "Were you uncomfortable before?"

One look was all it took. *She knew exactly what she was doing to me. I like that.* "Was there something you wanted to know?" Kit huffed. "Or can we go back to kissing?"

"Are you pouting?"

Kit thought she might be laughing at her, just a little bit. "Absolutely. An amazingly sexy woman is lying in my arms, but she wants to talk about my cousin. And heroin."

"I do see your point," Thea said. "I'll make it quick. And I'll make it up to you."

That got Kit's attention. "What would you like to know?"

"What was he right about?" Thea slipped her hand under Kit's shirt and rested it on her stomach. Thankfully, she didn't increase the torture by stroking her or digging in her nails.

"He's been telling me I don't have to run away from my past. It can be a part of my future. He's very Yoda Zen master."

"He's also not wrong. Look at the impact you've had on Frankie's life. I'm not sure she would trust you as much as she does if she didn't know you understood where she comes from."

Kit thought about what Josh had told her. How he'd loved her, all of her, even the ugly bits, her whole life. Ethel was always trying to get her in touch with her addict side and the Zookeeper wouldn't let Kilo die. Even Walter seemed to think Kit needed to figure this out.

At the moment, the only person who mattered to her was sprawled on top of her looking windswept and more beautiful than Kit thought her heart could handle.

*Is this what falling in love feels like?*

"And what do you think?" Kit was sure Thea could probably feel the butterflies doing an Irish step dance in her belly. "What happens when we walk into a fancy library jamboree and everyone knows you're on the arm of an addict?"

"Two things," Thea said. "First, who cares? Second, are you imagining you'll be wearing a custom sign or announcing yourself every time you enter a room? If you get a sign, I'm designing it. Something green will really set off your eyes."

Kit couldn't help it. She laughed. Thea had a knack for cutting right through her anxiety and her bullshit.

"Thank you for very nicely pointing out I'm full of crap," Kit said.

"You're not full of crap. I know this is hard for you. But you're more worried about people knowing about your past than I am. Why wouldn't I be proud to be on your arm? You're sexy as hell, you make me laugh, you make me think about the world differently than I'm used to, and I'm happy when I'm with you. Everyone should be so lucky."

Kit marveled, as she had many times before, at the difference in how she was perceived by those around her and how she expected to be perceived. At least by those who knew her and cared about her. "That part of my life was so awful and consumed everything in its path. I think there's part of me that's afraid if I let any of it out, even if there's something decent that could come from it, it will engulf me, you, everything, again."

Thea looked thoughtful. "Will you tell me about it?" Thea brushed some hair off Kit's forehead and kissed her. "I don't want you to feel like you have to hide that part of yourself from me."

"I try to hide it from everyone, but for some reason, it's not that easy with you." Kit pulled Thea closer but remained on her back. It was easier to talk if she was staring up at the tree.

"When did you start using?" Thea stroked Kit's stomach lightly.

"My story isn't that different from millions of others around the country. I was in college. I was playing soccer and studying pre-med." Kit's chest felt tight. She could do this; she could get through this story.

"You wanted to be a pediatrician, right?"

"I did, but knowing what I know now, my being around a prescription pad would have been a very dangerous combo." She shifted. The ground felt uncomfortable under her. She felt uncomfortable in her skin.

"Or maybe you'd have been the best pediatrician in the state."

"I guess we'll never know." There was no point focusing on maybes. "Anyway, I was playing soccer and I got injured. When the pain stopped, my desire for the pain meds didn't. It happens to people every day."

"When did you switch to heroin? I know it's not uncommon to go from one to the other. But it feels like that must have been, I don't know, a big moment?"

If only Thea knew how little she cared the day she switched from pills to heroin. All that mattered was the rush. Today there was no craving stalking her while she talked. What a welcome relief. Maybe she had Thea to thank for that.

"I switched as soon as I ran out of an easy supply of pills and I started to run out of money. Heroin's cheaper and a dealer hit me up in my dorm room, promising it was way better than the pills he knew I'd been on. I dove deeper and deeper into my drug habit, and eventually school just wasn't on my daily priority list. I never finished my junior year."

"And eventually you found your way out. You are amazing, Kit Marsden."

Kit felt Thea's grip tighten on her side. She felt grounded again. Her chest loosened and she took a deep breath.

"I had a lot of help. Buprenorphine helps physically. But Ethel and Josh are the ones I owe the most. Especially Josh. I was never so deep that I let go of Josh. He tried everything early on to get me to stop. He yelled, rationalized, pleaded, bargained, anything and everything. Finally, he just stayed close and waited. No matter how many times I changed my phone number or drifted from place to place, I always made sure he could reach me. He was my anchor to another world."

"How many people know that story?" Thea propped herself so she and Kit were eye to eye.

"Not too many." Kit usually retreated long before this point, but there was nowhere to go and she didn't want to run from Thea. She needed to know why Thea wasn't running from her. "Why aren't you worried my past won't flare up and engulf both of us?"

"Who says I'm not worried?" Thea moved so she was draped across Kit's chest and they were face-to-face. The weight of her felt good.

"Worried isn't the right word. Aware is probably better. I'm aware of what could happen. I can only empathize with your experience, but I grew up in and amongst the chaos of active drug use. I have no desire to stumble upon someone overdosing again. But I refuse to run away from you because of something that could possibly one day happen. You make me too happy to be scared away by nightmare scenario eventualities."

"Were you the one who found your dad?"

Thea nodded, her eyes glassy. It was Kit's turn to offer comfort.

"Why do you carry naloxone after what you've dealt with?" Kit held Thea tight.

"When my father OD'd I had no way of helping. I don't think it would have mattered, but I'll never know. Now, there is something I can do to help. And if I let my personal stuff get in the way of saving someone in my library, I don't think I could live with that." A few tears ran down Thea's cheek.

"You really are Captain Naloxone the Super Librarian. And I think I…like you very much."

"Excuse me? Captain what?" Thea sat up and Kit could see she was full of questions.

"It's a compliment." Kit held up her hand defensively. "My sponsor and I called you that before I knew your name. I wanted to go with Captain Sexy Pants. Or Beautiful Book Lady."

"I would like to hear more about how sexy you find my pants and how beautiful you think my books are. Quick question though. What is that?"

Thea pointed at the branch above them. A decaying slab of wood was mounted on the tree limb. It wasn't recognizable as the two foot by two-foot-piece of plywood Kit knew it once was. Just visible were three metal poles coming together in a point. Near the plywood and poles was the remains of a chair seat and back sitting on the branch as if perched there by a giant. The chair didn't look fit for sitting any longer, but the elements hadn't done so much harm that it wasn't recognizable.

"That was one of my viewing stations." Kit looked away from them. "There are three more up there in higher branches."

Thea got up to get a better look. She walked around the tree and Kit assumed she was looking for the other stations.

*Why did she have to look up?* She sighed and played with a blade of grass.

"What was a viewing station? And how did you get up there?"

"I climbed. Then I sat in the chair and, it's hard to see from down here, but those metal poles are a tripod base I made. I'd bring my telescope, or binoculars, or a gun scope I stole from my dad, and just look at things. There's so much to see from up in a tree."

"I'll have to take your word for it." Thea looked melancholy. "I've never climbed a tree."

Kit was shocked. She couldn't imagine any kid not climbing trees. For as long as she could remember, if it had bark, she climbed. It felt like her way of escape.

"Do you trust me?"

"Yes." Thea drew out the word and looked less than fully trusting.

"Fantastic. We're going up."

"Up where?" Thea looked around as if the answer was written on the grass nearby.

"The tree." Kit pointed up. "The most important rule about tree climbing is the rule of three. You have four limbs and three of them should be in contact with the tree at all times. Two feet and a hand, two hands and a foot. You get the idea. Stay close to the trunk and move slowly. We go down the same way we go up. Sound good?"

"Not at all." Thea shook her head and took a step back. "Remember me, planful, not at all spontaneous? I don't climb trees. And I'm wearing a dress."

"If dresses were problems, girls would never have learned how to climb trees. If you don't go up, you'll miss the view." Kit held out her hand and waited for Thea to take it. "I won't let you fall."

They looked at each other for a long moment. The air felt like it crackled between them with something unspoken.

"I know you won't," Thea said softly, taking Kit's hand.

*Jesus. I won't let her fall, but it might be too late for me.* She took a deep breath and turned toward the tree, breaking the connection.

Kit had climbed this tree hundreds of times as a kid. Even after all these years she felt like she could do it in her sleep. The branches, footholds, and grips were exactly where she expected. Thea asked that she go first so she could watch. Kit explained her hand and foot choices as she went. Luckily, this oak had a low branch on the opposite side of their blanket, so it was easy to hoist into the tree. Once up, it was a matter of climbing from limb to limb.

Thea was cautious, as Kit expected, but once she was up she didn't cling to the tree or refuse to stand and look around. Thea was careful and methodical, but Kit knew she wasn't afraid of new experiences. That being said, she knew what a big deal it was that Thea was spontaneously climbing a tree. And that she trusted Kit enough to let her lead.

"Okay, fearless leader, I'm up. Now what?" Thea's cheeks were flushed and she looked like a conquering hero.

"What do you want to do?" She felt a rush just being up here again and with Thea.

"You promised me a tour of your viewing station."

"So I did. Follow me, please."

A leaf stuck in Thea's hair and Kit thought about not saying anything. It made Thea look wild and like someone who should be traversing branches in a great oak. But she didn't think Thea would want leaves in her hair all afternoon.

They moved around the tree until they were on the branch with the viewing station. The picnic was laid out on the ground below them. Although Kit was tempted to take her seat in the chair she'd dragged up here and screwed to the branch years ago, she wasn't sure it was solid enough to hold her. The last thing she wanted was to end the date by needing rescue from her parents. She moved to an adjacent branch so Thea could move closer.

"I see why you set up in this direction." Thea stood tall and stared at the horizon. "And you were right about the view. It's incredible. It feels like you can see to the edge of the world."

"That's exactly how I used to feel. Like what I wanted was out there somewhere if I just looked hard enough, or far enough."

"And how do you feel now?" Thea looked back at Kit, her eyes ablaze with something Kit couldn't identify.

Right there, standing in a tree with Thea, Kit's world felt like it flipped on its head. Her whole life it felt like she'd been running away from or toward some unseen...*something*. Suddenly, it felt like she just stopped. It felt wonderful and a little scary.

"I feel like maybe I don't need to look as far away as I used to in order to find what I want." Kit heard the words as they came out of her mouth, but wasn't sure when she grew the balls to voice them.

"I was hoping you'd say that." Thea smiled shyly and looked back over the picturesque expanse in front of them.

Kit wanted to hop over to Thea's branch and take her in her arms, but she'd be breaking every tree climbing rule she'd just told Thea. And she really did want Thea to enjoy the view. Maybe it was the overwhelming beauty that had them speaking with a bit more openness and honesty than they both had been willing to up to this point.

They stayed in the tree a while longer and Kit pointed out the landmarks she remembered. It was harder without binoculars, but it also allowed them to narrate a story where they both contributed. Thea had a much better sense of direction than Kit, so she oriented them to places that were meaningful to both of them. They found the ballpark where they had their first date, were reasonably sure they found Thea's neighborhood, and Kit pointed out a few construction sites she'd worked on recently. Although they couldn't see it with the naked eye, they stared in the direction of the library and pretended it was right there, just within sight on the horizon.

The descent clearly made Thea nervous. Kit moved quickly down and stood on the ground to help Thea find her footing. As Thea was placing her foot for the last step to solid ground, her foot slipped and she tumbled into Kit's arms.

Kit was worried the small stumble might negatively impact Thea's rating of the climb. However, when Thea regained her footing and looked at Kit, fear, disappointment, or regret weren't the emotions Kit saw dancing in her eyes.

Thea pulled Kit close, wrapped her arms around Kit's neck, and her touch was purposeful and passionate.

"Thank you for helping me climb a tree." Thea looked jubilant.

Kit's answer was muted by Thea covering her lips with her own. As with her touch, her kiss was fierce and hot. She nipped Kit's lower lip then soothed it with her tongue. Kit's mind hadn't caught up with the attention when Thea's tongue teased her again, seeking entry.

Thea's tongue was in Kit's mouth, her hands were on Kit's ass, and all the blood in Kit's body felt like it was rushing south or following Thea's touch. It meant she felt like a teenage boy already revved and ready, but her brain had short-circuited with no blood supply to reboot.

"If you're okay being done with the tree, get on the blanket." Thea tugged at the hem of her shirt.

"Fuck me," Kit said, out of breath and a little dizzy.

"That is exactly what I had in mind," Thea said. "And hopefully you'll return the favor."

They stumbled to the blanket, not breaking the kiss or their frantic caresses. They landed in a tangled mess, Thea on top. Kit sat up and Thea straddled her.

Kit broke their kiss and began exploring Thea's neck and shoulders. Her skin was smooth and pebbled with every touch of Kit's lips. She dipped lower and followed the line of the V-neck of Thea's dress. Kit felt Thea shudder and dig her fingers into the back of Kit's hair.

She pulled the fabric lower and trailed her tongue along the top of Thea's breast. Thea moaned. She tried to direct the fabric of her dress lower to give Kit better access. Kit gently moved Thea's hand away. For this part, she wanted to take her time.

Thea wasn't satisfied and yanked Kit's shirt free from her jeans.

"Is this okay? I want to see at least some of you," Thea said.

Kit stopped her own explorations and let Thea remove her button-down and undershirt. Her skin felt like it danced everywhere Thea looked. She'd give anything to keep her looking at her that way.

Thea kissed her again, hard. Her hands were all over her newly exposed skin. She caressed her back, her abs, her sides, and across her nipples which were puckered beneath her sports bra. Thea's exploration fueled Kit's fire. She was wet and ready, but she wasn't done building up Thea.

Kit pulled Thea's dress down farther, exposing her breast. She traced her teeth along the soft skin. She teased the area around Thea's nipple, enjoying the gasps and whimpers from Thea the closer she came. Finally, Kit sucked her nipple into her mouth, caressing Thea's other breast with her hand.

Thea was holding Kit close, encouraging her to suck harder. She was rocking her hips on Kit's lap, clearly looking for some relief. Kit understood, since she was wet and throbbing too.

Kit eased back to a semi-reclined position with her back against the tree trunk. Thea followed her as she reclined, rekindling their fiery kissing. While they kissed, Kit moved Thea farther up her lap. She danced circles up Thea's legs until she dipped under her dress and reached the apex of her thighs.

Thea stopped kissing her and rested her head on Kit's shoulder as Kit started teasing Thea's center. Thea was soaked and knowing Kit had caused it was a heady experience. She applied more pressure to Thea's clit.

"Fuck, Kit, you feel so good." Thea gasped softly against Kit's shoulder.

Kit liked that Thea was a sex curser.

"Is this how you want to come?" She knew Thea was close.

"Inside," Thea said.

Kit teased Thea's opening with two fingers. Thea rose slightly allowing Kit better access. Kit slipped in and then back out. She let Thea set the pace and rhythm. Once she knew Thea was comfortable, she slipped all the way in. Thea threw her head back and held Kit's shoulders. Kit thrust gently as Thea rode her hand.

Thea's orgasm built quickly and crashed intensely. She kissed Kit with a fiery passion while she rode out the last aftershocks. Kit slowly pulled out and lowered Thea onto the blanket, covering Thea's body with her own.

"Okay, hot stuff. Climbing trees and fucking in fields. This has been quite a date. I can't wait to see what you have planned for the next one." Thea lay with her eyes closed and her face turned toward the sun, a small smile on her swollen lips.

"I try to anticipate all of your needs and come prepared. How'd I do?" Nothing about this date had gone as she'd planned, but she had no complaints.

"I think you know exactly how well you're doing." Thea opened one eye and looked at Kit. "But there's one more thing I need you to do for me to make this date perfect."

"Anything."

"Get your sexy ass up and walk around to the other side of the tree. I'll be right there."

Kit was a little surprised by the request, but she did as she was asked. She would have rather stayed on the blanket and had Thea take care of the throbbing between her own thighs, but if needed she could take care of that on her own later.

"Are you where you're supposed to be?"

Kit leaned against the tree trunk, one foot propped against it. "Yep. You going to come join me? It's lonely over here."

Thea joined her. Kit thought she might come just from the sight of her. Thea had ditched her dress and was wearing the button-down shirt she'd pulled off of Kit. Kit was quite a bit taller than Thea so the shirt fit like a very short, very sexy dress. It was the best piece of clothing she'd ever seen.

"You said no one would bother us here, right?" Thea trailed her finger down Kit's chest.

Kit could only nod.

"Good." Thea reached for Kit's belt and unbuckled it. While she worked open the button and fly, she kissed Kit's face and neck. Once she had Kit's pants open she pushed them down, along with her boxer briefs, then kissed a trail down Kit's chest, abdomen and finally knelt in front of her.

She looked up at Kit.

"Do you know how long I've wanted to do this?"

"Strip me naked in a field and fuck me against a tree?" Kit was more turned on than she could ever remember being. Almost all of it had to do with Thea, but a small part was also knowing they technically could get caught since they were out in the open. It felt very unlike something Thea would do and that was thrilling too.

"I would have been happy doing this anywhere," Thea said.

Kit was going to come up with some snappy comeback, but Thea ran her tongue along the entire length of her clit and Kit lost all coherent thought. Thea gripped her hips and dipped her tongue in again, circling Kit's clit. She teased and toyed with her until Kit didn't think she could take any more. When she thought she might have to resort to begging, Thea sucked all of Kit into her mouth.

Kit bucked her hips and was vaguely aware the cries she heard were her own. What Thea was doing was magic and she was so close to coming. She felt like she was about to tumble over the edge when Thea stopped. She kissed Kit's inner thigh and stroked her abs.

"I was so close." She sounded pathetic.

"I know," Thea said. "I wanted it to last just a little longer. It'll be worth it, I promise. This time, come for me."

Kit thought she could come if Thea simply kept talking to her about sex for another few minutes, but she really wanted Thea's mouth on her again. She nodded. Thea teased her again with the feather light touch of her tongue. Kit tried to seek more but Thea wasn't giving in.

Thea moved her hand to Kit's leg and lightly scratched her way from her calf to her ass. Kit's muscles jumped at the sensation. Thea continued her ministration around the front of Kit's thigh until she turned her hand and slipped two fingers inside her. Pleasure exploded, and before she had a chance to fully comprehend the new wave of pleasure, Thea sucked Kit's clit back into her mouth.

Kit dropped her head back against the tree trunk and hoped her legs would hold her long enough to let her orgasm crest. It wouldn't take long. Thea thrust into her while she sucked her and she held Thea's head in place, urging her to suck harder. She bucked her hips faster as her orgasm built.

She felt her muscles clench around Thea's fingers as she came. She thought she cried out in pleasure, but sound was rushing in her ears, so she wasn't sure.

Thea stood up and pulled Kit's pants up for her.

"Now that was a date."

Kit nodded, assuming she'd never be able to walk or form sentences again.

Thea refused to give Kit her shirt back. She let Kit have her undershirt, but she kept the button-down and wore it over her dress. As they climbed over the fence and back the way they came, hand in hand, Kit couldn't remember ever being happier. Thea made her happy. She surprised her. She challenged her. She made her laugh. And apparently, she was creatively amazing in bed, or under a tree, too.

# CHAPTER TWENTY-ONE

"Oh shit, Kit, look. Guess someone forgot to give you some important news about fifteen years ago. You got some child support back pay due," Felix said.

"Damn," one of the other guys said. "I didn't take you for the type that would piss off a girl so bad she wouldn't even tell you she had your baby."

"What the fuck are you guys talking about?" The day was already taking too long without the guys riding her. Since getting out of bed this morning, she'd been counting down the minutes until she got to see Thea later.

"The kid over there waving at you like she finally found the one person in the world she wants to meet. Do you know her? Or should I get my phone so I can record the moment you become a daddy?"

Kit turned. Frankie was on the other side of the construction fence trying to get her attention. She looked at her watch. For a day that was dragging, somehow she'd managed to let time get away from her. She shoved her gloves in her back pocket.

"That's Frankie. Not mine, although I'd be lucky to have a kid that great. Act like you're potty trained when she's around." Kit shot a warning glare in the direction of all the guys.

A couple of the guys barked as Kit made her way over to Frankie. Outside the library, Frankie looked a little less confident and a little bit more like the teenage kid she actually was.

"Were those guys saying something about me?" Frankie glanced nervously in the direction Kit had come from.

"Yes. No. It wasn't about you. They were busting my balls." Kit pointed back at the guys. "They saw you waving and said you were here to hand me paternity papers and a life changing surprise."

"That's a dumb joke, since you're a woman, and we're friends."

"Of course it is." Kit smiled. "Every joke here is a dumb joke. Even the ones we think are actually funny would never pass teenage inspection. Come on, let's go find Josh." She clapped her hand on Frankie's shoulder hoping to relieve some of the tension radiating off her.

Kit led Frankie through the work site in search of Josh. Frankie had asked Thea for help with a project at school, which required interviewing and profiling a local business owner. Thea had suggested Josh. Now Kit was playing tour guide so Josh and Frankie could connect for the first of three scheduled interviews.

Josh was ass up with two other guys looking at the foundation of the building they were working on. He straightened when he heard them approach.

"Problem?" Kit asked.

"Usual stuff." Josh shrugged. He wiped his hand on his pants before holding it out to Frankie. "You must be Frankie."

They shook hands and Josh showed Frankie to his high end office on the tailgate of his truck. Kit stuck around so Frankie had a familiar face close by. Kit knew all the guys here and that they were all big teddy bears, but Frankie didn't. She didn't want her to be uncomfortable. And she said she'd walk her home.

While she waited, Kit put out a few fires with the crew that didn't need to escalate to Josh, tried to collect her tools, and she texted Thea. They'd texted and talked on the phone since their date to the oak tree, but they hadn't seen each other. It was driving Kit nuts. It seemed like they reached a new level of intimacy, not just physically, and Kit was sure Thea felt it too. But the longer they went without seeing each other, the harder it was to hold on to that feeling and solidify it so they could build on it.

"Hey, lover boy, you mind moving over so those of us who are working today can do our job?"

Kit jumped. She had no idea how long she'd been standing still, holding a hammer in one hand and daydreaming. She flipped off her hecklers and resumed collecting her tools. When Frankie was done with her interview, Kit was finally packed and ready to head out. She tossed her tools and gear in Josh's truck and she and Frankie headed toward the library. The closer they got the more Kit's stomach began to flip and flutter.

"You don't have to walk me, you know," Frankie said.

"I know you don't need a chaperone," Kit said. "Humor me."

"It's not that. I don't mind the company, but if you want to run to the library to see Thea, I understand. Because she's super smart, and some kind of librarian rock star, and nice on top of it all, and really hot." She flinched. "NOT. Really *not*, I meant to say not. Really not. Like, I mean, really not an asshole like she could be because she's so amazing."

Kit knew Frankie wouldn't appreciate it, but she found it really endearing how much of a hero crush she had on Thea.

"I'll stick with you." Kit glanced at Frankie and caught her smiling. "Someone said patience is a virtue, although I think that someone was full of crap, or had to wait for something and wanted to feel self-righteous about it. I think Thea will forgive me if I take a few minutes longer so I can walk you home. I'm going to a meeting anyway, so I might not get to see her at all."

"I'm actually going to the library too. It's easier for me to get my homework done there. My place is too chaotic. Do you need a college degree for your job with Josh?"

"No. I don't have a degree. Josh does. If you want to be an architect or engineer, you need bachelor's, usually graduate degrees. But the tradesmen usually follow a different path. Why do you ask?"

"Can you start right out of high school?"

Kit was startled by the quick subject change from Thea and homework to post-high school employment. She started to think now she was being interviewed. She replayed what Frankie had said about completing her homework at the library. Thea said Frankie had asked for as many hours at the library as possible and now she wanted a job as soon as she graduated.

"In theory, yes. You'd need to get an apprenticeship usually. When you dream of your future, are you working in construction?"

Frankie kicked at a can and looked down at her toes as they walked. She wouldn't look Kit in the eye.

"Let me tell you a story." Kit searched for the right words. "When I was younger, I couldn't stand living at my parents' house any longer. I had to get out. I didn't care where I went or what I did, as long as it was out of where I was. So I made a rash decision because I was young and stupid. But I'm older now and only a little less stupid. I can look back and see that I should have taken a little more time to think about what was best for me, not just the fastest way out of the situation I was in at the time. It might have saved me a lot of trouble if I'd figured out the best thing first, not just the first thing I could do."

"Are you saying I shouldn't try to get a job as soon as I graduate just to get away from where I'm living now?"

"You said that, not me." Kit put her hands in her pockets and purposefully avoided looking at Frankie. "I just asked you what you see when you dream of your future. And because we're becoming friends, I told you a story from my past. Isn't that what friends do? Oh no, did the rules of friendship change while I was making drug use my full-time job?"

Frankie assured Kit she was quite old and that wasn't really what friends did at all. Apparently, friends liked, tagged, and shared memes and other social media content with each other. Frankie listed what felt like a thousand social media platforms Kit had never heard of. Even though the age difference was only a decade, Kit began to wonder if she and Frankie were even the same species.

They walked in silence for a while. Kit didn't push Frankie to answer further questions. She'd never been good with being prodded into doing or saying something she wasn't ready for, so she certainly wasn't going to pressure Frankie.

Frankie, though, wasn't quite done with the conversation.

"It's stupid." She kicked at the can again. "What I see when I dream is a lawyer. I want to be a lawyer. To help people like my mom who had no one on her side." She glanced at Kit as though expecting to see ridicule.

"You'll be a great lawyer, kid. Do not let go of that dream. Sometimes college comes with dorm rooms, and if you want to go to college, then focus on that. Keep talking to Thea. Keep talking to me. Talk to your aunt or your dad, whoever you trust. It feels weird to say this, but ask the Zookeeper what law school was like. We'll help you make a plan. How is your mom?"

"She's okay, I guess," Frankie kicked the can hard enough this time that it shot into the street. "I mean, that's what she tells me at least. There's a real nice guard there, her name's Reggie. She lets me give my mom a quick hug if no one else is around. I think she looks out for her too, if she can."

"Don't give up on her." Kit wasn't sure if it was wise advice, but it felt right.

"Nah," Frankie said. "Haven't yet."

They walked up the steps to the library together. Kit reached for the door to hold it for Frankie, but she grabbed Kit's arm to stop her.

"Do you want me to go in first and you can come in a few minutes later singing and dancing in your underwear or something? You know, some fancy entrance to get her attention?"

Kit opened the door. "Get inside. Singing and dancing in my underwear would definitely get attention. And get me arrested. Not quite how I'd like to spend the evening."

As soon as they walked through the doors, Kit could tell something was wrong. The usually quiet library was buzzing. There wasn't anyone at the desk. Quite a few patrons were standing and looking toward the back of the library, speaking to each other in non-library voices.

Kit's heart started to race. All she could think about was Thea. What if the Zookeeper and Parrot Master had gone back on their word and a drug deal had gone wrong in the library? What if something else had happened and Thea was injured? Kit was about to charge off in the direction everyone was looking, ready for whatever Thea needed, when Thea herself sprinted by. Thea didn't glance their way as she ran past. Kit thought she looked scared. It took her a second of processing and then she realized why. Thea was sprinting at full speed through the library carrying her naloxone supply.

❖

Thea couldn't remember a time when she'd felt as scared as she did now. She raced after Walter toward the bathroom near the community room. Her worst fear was finally materializing. Someone was overdosing in her library.

*Where's Kit? Please don't be Kit.*

"Do you know who it is, Walter?" Thea was hyper aware of her surroundings and every sensation. Every footfall felt like it ricocheted around her head.

"It's not Kit."

She shouldn't be happy. Someone was barely clinging to life in the bathroom of her library. She couldn't help it, she was overcome with relief. She didn't know what she would do if it was Kit she was rushing to save.

Although she knew how to administer naloxone and thought she was prepared, the closer she got, the less sure she became. What if it was a man who looked like her father? What if she couldn't save them? What if it was already too late?

She gripped the box holding the naloxone doses tightly as they rounded the corner. Her palms were hot and sticky with sweat. She pushed through the small crowd outside the bathroom. A woman was lying on the floor of the bathroom. Her skin had an unnatural blueish tint and although her eyes were open, when Thea leaned over she could tell she was unconscious. Thea could hear a gurgling sound coming from the woman's throat. Fear marched along her spine at the sound of the "death rattle" It was time to get moving.

Thea quickly unwrapped the first dose of naloxone and handed the box to Walter. She put her hand under the woman's neck and put the applicator in her nose. She depressed the plunger, gave the dose, rolled the woman onto her side, and waited.

"How long?" Walter looked as ill as Thea felt.

"Sometimes right away, sometimes a couple minutes." Why was her voice so even? It scared her she was so calm and it terrified her that that might change. "If nothing happens and the paramedics aren't here by then, we give another. Naloxone works by—"

"I don't need to know how it works."

"But I need to tell you. It boots the responsible drug off the opioid receptors. Fentanyl and a few other opioids aren't especially interested in giving up their seats on the receptors and are harder to reverse. This is taking too long."

Thea prayed to every God she could think of that this woman wasn't going to die right here in front of her, under her care. How could she live with herself if she did? She studied every detail of the woman's face looking for a sign of improvement, losing the battle to hold the anxiety at bay. Hours passed in each second they waited.

Ten seconds passed. Fifteen seconds. Thirty seconds. Suddenly, the woman gasped and sat bolt upright. There was fury in her eyes.

"What the fuck did you do to me?"

She got to her feet on wobbly legs and stood over Thea. Thea was intimidated by her anger. She was unprepared for the rage and aggression some experienced coming out of overdose she'd read about. There wasn't much room in the bathroom. She felt trapped. Where was the door? How could she get away?

"I was fine. Now not only did you ruin my high, but now I'm in fucking withdrawal." The woman's fists were clenched, and she began to lift one.

Thea tried to scramble backward away from the impending hit, when she was pushed back down by someone stepping in front of her quickly. She looked up in time to see the woman punch Kit in the face.

Kit raised her hands in self-defense, clearly trying to placate the woman. "She saved your life, Ethel. Don't you ever raise your hand to her again."

"You here to fight me, ace?"

"No, Ethel. I'd like to help, if you'll let me." Kit dropped her hands to her sides. "A lot of us here would."

Thea was finally able to stand. She moved to the bathroom doorway as she watched Kit talk to Ethel. Kit had mentioned that name before, but Thea wasn't sure how they knew one another.

Now that Ethel was revived and the immediate danger had passed, Thea wanted to slide down the wall and cry. But she couldn't because she was still at work and there were people all around. People who had witnessed her reversing an overdose and needed her. Before she could focus on that she had to gather her scattered thoughts. Thea couldn't believe Kit had just taken a punch for her.

She had no idea how to mitigate what had happened or what was continuing to play out. She wasn't sure she could even if she knew what to do. Ethel took another swing at Kit, which brought Thea back to the moment. Kit dodged but kept her hands at her sides. She clearly wasn't going to defend herself.

"Fuck you," Ethel said. "You think you can help me? You, the one who's constantly running? The one who's so embarrassed by all of us you can't bear to say anything in a meeting. Why do you keep coming, Kit? You clearly think you're better than all of us. It can't be for the coffee."

Thea heard the paramedics arrive and Walter directed them in.

"Take care of yourself, Ethel," Kit said, and she turned to leave. Ethel took one last swing and connected again with the side of Kit's face but she never stopped walking. Blood dripped down Kit's cheek from a cut above her eye and it was already starting to swell.

Thea reached for her as she passed. Kit looked at her, but Thea wasn't sure she saw her. She looked haunted and far away.

Thea needed Kit. She needed Kit to take her home, to hold her and tell her she wouldn't always feel like she did right now. Thea had hoped reviving someone from an overdose would make her feel good. Instead, she felt drained, tearful, and a little traumatized. Kids had seen this. Kids like she once was. She was thrown back to the day she walked in her front door as a child and heard the death rattle for the first time. It didn't bring her much comfort that these kids had seen a happier outcome. Images of her father's body growing still made her feel sick. Just as she hadn't been protected then, she hadn't protected the kids here. Kit looked like she needed comfort too. Thea wanted them to find shelter in each other.

"Kit." Thea reached for her again. "Wait."

"I have to go." Kit pushed through the medical personnel and the lingering crowd and was gone. Thea could no longer contain the tears she'd been holding in. She considered it a victory that she managed to only let a few streaks run down her cheeks and she didn't dissolve into full ugly cry.

*Where'd she go? She's bleeding.*

"Come on." Walter gently guided her toward the door. "Let's get you out of here. You don't need to be here any longer. I think you've served the community admirably this evening. Library's just about shuttered for the evening anyway. I'm taking you home."

"Kit just left, Walter. She just walked out."

Thea was getting angry. She'd asked Kit never to walk out on her again and she just did. Thea needed her and Kit was nowhere to be seen.

So much for dependable and reliable.

# CHAPTER TWENTY-TWO

Thea would have preferred to be alone since the one person she wished to have around wasn't, but it didn't seem that was an option. Walter had insisted on staying, and as soon as the library closed Carrie came over too. Now Thea was making dinner for houseguests she didn't want, trying to make sense of an afternoon that felt beyond logic.

She hadn't expected to have such a reaction to reviving someone from an overdose. In hindsight it was laughable to think she wouldn't struggle given her childhood experience, but she felt sure it would have been worse had she watched helplessly on the sidelines, just as she'd had to do as a child. That would have been even closer to home. At least she'd been able to take action, something she never felt capable of as a child. Knowing that wasn't making the aftermath easy even if she'd somehow thought she'd feel like a superhero saving someone's life. She figured she could add that to the pile of things throwing her for a loop about the whole situation. After all, she had chosen to carry naloxone. She'd chosen to be available and made it clear her staff should call her if ever she was needed. Hypotheticals were one thing. Being faced with a dying woman in her library had proven to be quite another.

It seemed she had also underestimated the impact of Kit. Being with Kit had personalized things in a way they hadn't been before, which was saying something. But she really cared about Kit and Kit knew this woman. Thea was having trouble shaking the fear she'd felt when she thought it might be Kit she'd find lying on the floor of the bathroom. What would she have done? It wasn't exactly out of the realm of possibility, and that made the bile rise in the back of her throat.

"I ordered us pizza and Walter's going to get wine." Carrie tentatively put her hand on Thea's back.

"I'm cooking dinner, Carrie," She didn't mean to snap at Carrie.

"Sweetie, if you eat that, we'll be trying to revive you. And frankly, I don't have the balls you do, so please don't make me try."

Thea looked at the stove. She couldn't remember what she'd been cooking, but it was a blackened mess now. It was a small miracle the smoke alarm wasn't blaring, and her stove wasn't on fire.

"No wine." Thea wiped away a rebellious tear. "If Kit comes here tonight, I don't want there to be alcohol."

When the pizza arrived, Thea forced everyone out to her front porch. She felt claustrophobic inside. It was too much like the tiny bathroom earlier, but being out on the porch made her miss Kit.

"Why did Kit walk away?" Thea asked as she picked at her pizza.

"She's probably the only one who could satisfactorily answer that query," Walter said.

"I feel like she probably had a reason," Carrie said. "I heard she got punched in the face. Maybe she had to deal with that?"

"Well, she's not answering my texts, so I guess I'm stuck here with you two making up wild guesses." Thea knew it wasn't fair to take out her fear on her friends, but they were here and she couldn't chase away the terror by shouting.

Thea could clearly see Ethel's fist connecting with Kit's face and the blood dripping down Kit's cheek. Kit hadn't tried to defend herself and Thea hadn't pursued her to make sure she got medical help. *The only one she protected was me.* Still, she'd left without a word, and Thea couldn't help but wonder if she was okay, if she needed to talk. If this could push her over the edge to using again. She let the tears fall and accepted the napkin Carrie passed over without a word.

After they finished eating, they sat in silence for a long while. Although Thea had been annoyed at their presence before, she was glad for her friends' company now. They seemed to know what she needed, even if she didn't.

"Well, thank all that's holy tomorrow is Friday," Carrie said. "I don't think I could take a Monday staring me in the face. I don't know about you two."

"I would not relish a meeting with Monday, no," Walter said. "Will you be in tomorrow, Thea?"

Thea thought about the question. It seemed ridiculous, but it was reasonable for him to ask. "Where else would I be?"

"My vote would be Tahiti." Carrie didn't hesitate. "But that's just me."

Thea had to admit a vacation did sound pretty amazing. But Tahiti only worked for her if Kit was there, strutting around in her birthday suit. And right now, that didn't seem like it was in the cards. Thea would settle for knowing where Kit was and that she was safe.

"Maybe I'll spend the day in world history. Or ordering new travel books." Thea reviewed the schedule. Even for a Friday, it was light. She'd need to fill her time or spend the day struggling.

"And what if there's another occurrence like this afternoon?" Walter asked. "Will you wish to be summoned?"

"Of course, Walter. The alternative is someone dies. I could never live with that. What I'd always thought was my worst-case scenario happened today. But someone dying in the library would be unimaginably worse." She shuddered.

"As I thought. It looked like your Ms. Marsden knew the woman you revived today."

"Oh shit," Carrie said. "That must have been hard for her. Did she watch the whole thing?"

"She stepped in front of me and took a punch meant for me. And she does know her," Thea said. "I've seen them together. I'd ask her about it, if she were here. I tried to talk to her after, but she said she had to go. I want to respect her space, if she needs it, but I really need her to get in touch and tell me she's okay."

"If she knows this woman, she may be hurting too," Walter said gently.

Thea knew Kit was hurting. She'd been seeing Kit's haunted look over and over all night. What she didn't know was why Kit walked away from her and why she hadn't heard from her. When she thought of herself coupled happily, she'd seen two people who bonded together when things were tough, not each of them running in opposite directions.

"I can't force her to want my support or comfort." Thea looked up at the stars, hoping if she kept her face up, the tears wouldn't be able to fall. "But it hurts like hell that she doesn't. Especially since hers is what I want. I asked her once to promise she wouldn't walk out without talking to me about what she was thinking. But here we are. And I really need her right now. After it was over earlier, all I could see were the kids who saw the whole thing. I was that kid. I know they walked out of the library different children than they were when they walked in. I'm really struggling with that right now. There's an entire rabbit hole of my childhood I'm trying not to fall down."

"It's only been a couple hours." Carrie took her hand. "You don't know how either of you will feel once you see each other again."

"I know." Thea pulled her knees up and wrapped her free hand around herself. "I'm not making any grand proclamations. But I told her how much I need someone I can depend on. I've never had that before. No one except you two. But never someone who was just mine."

Walter looked thoughtful. That usually led to wisdom Thea wasn't often dumb enough to dismiss out of hand.

"Ms. Marsden and I have our differences." Walter smiled wryly. "But I greatly respect her sobriety and what it has taken to achieve it. My strong suspicion is that today may have tilted her axis on that front."

*How could it have not? Please, Kit, just let me know you're okay.* She got up and got her cell phone, just in case Kit tried to call. She set it on the pizza box and sat back down on the porch with her back to the sidewalk. "When you came to get me and I was running to the bathroom, I didn't know who I was running toward. I was scared I would be too late, scared I would freeze, but the thing I was scared of more than anything was that I was going to find Kit overdosing. And I've struggled with that feeling ever since. Will that fear always be with me? I feel guilty that I even thought it. Kit and I talked about it, but today was the first time it felt like it wasn't some hypothetical from an alternate reality. God, what would I have done if it were her? I can't walk in on someone I love on the floor, dying, again."

The words were barely out when she saw Carrie glance over her shoulder, close her eyes, and shake her head.

"So you're okay with everyone else knowing I spent years shooting heroin, but you're not really okay with it when it comes to yourself?"

Thea's heart felt like it lodged in her throat. Her stomach knotted. She stood. Kit was halfway up her porch stairs. She looked terrible but was still the most gorgeous woman Thea had ever seen. Walter and Carrie got up and went into the house.

"You know your past doesn't bother me." Thea reached out, but Kit backed away.

"Kinda sounds like it does." Kit's shoulders were hunched like she was waiting for another blow. "And with good reason, Thea."

It looked like Kit had tried to clean the blood from her face, but she hadn't gotten all of it. Her hair looked like she'd been running her fingers through it for the past ten years, and her shirt was covered in something unidentifiable. When Thea got close she realized Kit smelled of alcohol.

"Where have you been? I've been really worried about you. Have you been drinking?" Thea tried hard to keep any accusatory tone from her voice. She was worried about Kit, not mad at her.

"A moron spilled a beer on my shirt." Kit crossed her arms and took another step back. "I didn't show up on your doorstep drunk, if that's what you're worried about."

"No, Kit." Thea followed her down the steps. "I'm worried about you. I've been worried about you since you walked away earlier. I've been worried, and scared, and sad. I know how much drug use can hurt everyone in its orbit and I know it's hard to be there for someone, but today was really hard for me. I was scared your friend was going to die and it would have been my fault somehow. Now all I can hear is the death rattle the day my dad died. I never thought I'd hear that sound again. And I really wanted you to help me feel safe. Because you're the one person who seems to be able to do that. And I was hoping you'd want me to be there for you, too. Except you weren't here and I don't know why."

"I couldn't be here." Pain swept across Kit's face. "I had some places to go and you couldn't come with me."

"Why not?"

Thea wasn't sure she wanted the answer. All the crap from earlier faded away and was replaced by a new set of worst-case scenarios.

"Because I couldn't look you in the eye if you were there. Leave it at that, Thea. Please."

"No." Thea stepped closer to Kit. She wanted to pull her into a crushing hug, but she hesitated. "I'm not willing to leave it there. I care about you, Kit. You took me to your tree, so I know you care about me too. Who was she? The woman today?"

Kit didn't answer. She didn't even look at Thea for a long time. When she did, she had the same haunted look she'd had after Ethel came up swinging.

"Stay here tonight. Stay with me," Thea said. "I need you. It looks like you need someone too. Let me be that someone, please? I want to be that someone for you."

Thea tentatively reach out and touched Kit's cheek. Kit leaned into the touch and kissed Thea's palm.

"You're scared one day you'll find me with a needle in my arm. You should be afraid of that. I don't come with any guarantees. You deserve someone who does. I told you sometimes I'm scared my past will consume everything in its path. I won't let you be consumed. You mean too much to me. I can't stay. And from what I overheard, you're not really sure you want me here either."

"Please don't do this, Kit. Don't make the decisions for both of us and don't tell me what I want."

The problem was, Kit was right. Thea wasn't sure what she wanted. She didn't want Kit walking off to wherever she seemed determined to go, but it wasn't easy to ignore the potential for instability Kit represented.

"I'm sorry." Kit leaned in for a kiss.

Thea stopped her.

"Are you kissing and then leaving?"

Kit looked confused and nodded.

"Oh hell no." Thea's hands were trembling and her legs felt a little wobbly. "You do not get to kiss me good-bye after I've been begging you to stay. You don't get to kiss me good-bye and walk away so that I can worry about you all night. If you're going to make unilateral decisions about what's good for me after I told you not to do that again and leave me freaking out about whether or not you've relapsed, you walk your ass out of here without any kiss from me. I'm not sanctioning any of this with a good-bye kiss."

"You tell her, girl," Carrie said quietly from the doorway.

Kit clearly wasn't expecting Thea to argue with her. She looked surprised and maybe a little embarrassed. Thea was done asking her to stay. The day had brought up a lot of memories she would have preferred not to revisit, she was hurting, and feeling a little lost. She could admit Kit's past, for the first time, was giving her a moment's pause, but she wanted to spend tonight soothing each other's hurts. Tomorrow they could problem solve, together. She'd laid her cards on the table. Kit had to make up her own mind. Either Thea was where she wanted to be or not.

"I've had a fantastically crappy day," Thea said. "The thing I worried about the most happened in the library and the kids I so badly want to protect saw the whole thing. I need someone to lean on. Are you staying or not?"

"No." Kit almost whispered it. It looked like the word was painful coming out of her mouth.

"Damn it, Kit. Don't you dare do anything stupid. Do you understand me?"

Kit nodded. Thea couldn't stand on the porch looking at her any longer. It hurt too much knowing Kit was going to leave and there was nothing she could do about it. If she was going to spend the rest of the evening worrying about what Kit was up to, she might as well get on with it.

Thea turned and walked back inside. She didn't look back. She knew what was behind her. It felt like her heart was breaking. They hadn't said this was the end of what they had, but how were they supposed to move on when Kit kept pushing her away when things got tough? Thea couldn't live like that. She wanted to be with someone who ran toward her, not shoved her aside. She thought about where Kit might be going. What if she used and ended up like Ethel? Like Thea's dad? What if no one was around to find her? Thea picked up the pace and headed for the bathroom. She thought she might be sick.

# CHAPTER TWENTY-THREE

Kit flopped into a chair at a grimy table in a dive bar she used to frequent. Shock made her numb. She hadn't meant to leave things the way she had with Thea. She hadn't really meant to do anything in particular when she went there. She just wanted to see her.

Thea was well within her rights to be mad at her, but not because Kit didn't want her comfort. Kit craved it. But seeing Ethel overdosing had cracked the foundation she'd built her sobriety on and for a few hours it felt like it might all crumble down. She wasn't proud of the fact that she'd run, but that was what she'd always done. Old habits were hard to break, and this time she'd just needed to get away from the situation. And in the moment when it felt like she was losing control, Thea was the only one she'd wanted to see.

But when she got to Thea's house, Thea was worrying about the possibility that Kit would be the next victim she'd need to revive on the bathroom floor of her library, and Kit couldn't offer Thea any promises. That didn't feel fair because there was no way to know if she could keep them. Walter and Carrie were better choices to help her navigate the trauma of the day, both past and present. Thea needed someone whose life hadn't recently resembled the horror Thea was forced to relive earlier.

At least, that's what she told herself.

Kit knew Thea would be mad at her. Thea had asked her not to make impulsive, unilateral decisions before, but this time felt different. Today everything felt different.

Kit's scotch arrived. She rolled the glass between her hands. She was desperate for the numbness the amber liquid could provide.

*Still need a little work on your coping skills, Marsden.*

Kit placed her phone on the table and turned it on for the first time since she left the library. It nearly vibrated itself off the table with texts, missed calls, and voice mail notifications. The only one she returned was from Frankie. She didn't want Frankie doing anything stupid, like coming looking for her. She really hoped Frankie hadn't been behind her watching Ethel being revived. She couldn't remember if she was, her entire focus had been first on Ethel's chest, searching for signs of life, and then on getting Thea out of harm's way. She wasn't in a state right now to help Frankie anyway. She'd let her down too.

The last text was from Josh. Kit wasn't looking forward to the conversation with him when he arrived.

"Well, well. A Kilo in a bar isn't something I thought I'd see again."

Kit spun around in her chair. The Zookeeper was in the doorway.

"You look like shit, you know," she said and pulled up a chair at Kit's table.

"That seat's taken," Kit said.

"I can see that," the Zookeeper said and pointed at the other chairs. "This one is reserved for self-pity, despondence over here, and I sat on moodiness. Are you just torturing that scotch, or do I really need to worry?"

"Why would you worry about a former client returning to the fold?" She really wished the Zookeeper would leave her alone. She wasn't feeling chatty.

"I'm a human being, Kilo. I'm allowed to have complicated, messy, conflicting, contradictory feelings."

"Are there any other kind?" Kit stared into her drink.

A new text notification showed up on Kit's phone. It was from Thea. Kit's heart ached.

"Any of those fifteen unread texts the reason you're sitting in a bar looking worse than something I usually scape off my shoe?"

"It's complicated." Kit still didn't look at the Zookeeper.

"Of course it is." The Zookeeper nudged Kit's phone. "You planning on writing back?"

"Nope." Kit turned her phone over and shoved it away. "I don't know what I'd say."

"Oh, for fuck's sake. Start by telling her you're not dead. Cause when she called me that's what I sensed she was most worried about. Although if you keep up this shit, I just might throttle you, so you might want to warn her about that. Then tell her you're sorry. When you're done with all that, tell her I say hi."

"She called you? Why does she have your number?"

Kit didn't want company and she really didn't want the Zookeeper involved in her personal life. And yet, it was good to have someone there to distract her from the whirlwind of negativity buffeting her.

"After our chat it seemed wise to keep the lines of communication open. Thus, the exchanging of numbers one day when we crossed paths. And of course she called me. She's worried about you and you turned off your damn phone and disappeared. Piece of advice, that's not how to treat a lady."

"Look, I appreciate your checking on me." Kit rolled her glass a little too aggressively and sloshed scotch over the edge and onto her hand. "But Thea doesn't want to hear from me. She—"

"Kilo, was that bullshit tasty coming out of your mouth?" The Zookeeper had fire in her eyes. "If you can't figure out why she'd want to know you're safe then I'll tell her myself you aren't worth the effort. But both of us seem to think you are. Maybe it's time you did too."

"Zoo, I've had a shitty day." Kit's shoulders slumped. The weight of everything hit her hard. "Can you give me this pep talk another time? Or maybe not at all?"

Her eyes softened and she covered Kit's hand with her own.

"I know what kind of day you've had. I'm sorry about Ethel. But my pep talk's true any day, even the shitty ones. I told you once not to fuck it up with Thea. So unfuck it. It's obvious you two are crazy about each other. That's not easy to find. I'll let her know you're okay for now, but you have to do the rest. Ethel's problems aren't yours. Don't make them."

The Zookeeper got up and hooked her thumb over her shoulder. Kit looked where she was pointing. Josh was standing by the bar waiting for them to finish and made his way over as the Zookeeper walked gracefully out of the bar.

*Fuuuuuuck. This is going to be fun.* Josh sat down and neatly folded his hands. He looked at Kit and waited.

"How twisted are your panties?" Kit asked.

"My balls are *blue* there's so much torque." Josh leaned forward and did his uncomfortable, intense eye contact thing. "You want to tell me what's going on?"

"Why do you assume something's going on?" Kit wanted to face-palm, but the fuse was already lit. All she could do now was fasten her seat belt and wait for Josh to explode.

"Are you shitting me right now? You're pulling that sitting across from me in a bar? With your face covered in blood and a drink in your hands? After Thea called me in a panic because you were some combination of complete asshole and sad puppy before you stomped off into the night? And just to add a cherry on top of this fucking crap sundae, look me in the eye and tell me that wasn't your drug dealer you were talking to."

Kit wasn't quite sure what to say. She expected Josh to be worried, maybe even mad, but this level of anger caught her off guard. "She was, in the past. But that's not what we were talking about. She was yelling at me too, weirdly."

"I'm not trying to yell at you, Kit. I'm scared out of my mind here. Thea called me and told me what happened today and I couldn't find you. Even at your worst, I could always find you."

Kit felt the familiar wave of guilt settle over her. It was like an old friend she couldn't seem to let go of. "How did Thea get your number? How did you find me?"

"Thea got it from Frankie, I think. And I'm glad she did, or I'd have no clue what was going on. I found you when you turned your phone on." Josh picked up her phone and slid it across the table to her. It landed in her lap. "And then I could see you were in a bar by using that stalker app we put on last year."

"Gave you the warm fuzzies, right?"

Kit wanted to lighten the mood. She'd been so blinded by her pain earlier she hadn't given much thought to how her actions would impact anyone around her. She'd clearly made quite a mess of things. She was good at thinking about herself first. Not as good at thinking of others, it seemed. Thea was better off without her.

"What's going on? You don't have to shut out the people who love you."

Josh was still leaning forward forcing eye contact she didn't want. She felt like he could see into her soul.

"I've never shut you out." Kit took a long time to dig her phone out of her lap and reestablish eye contact.

"You don't have to shut Thea out either. No, I take that back. Don't shut Thea out."

"She deserves better than me, Josh." Kit threw up her hands. "Look what happened today when I got scared."

"I love you, Kit, but you are a fucking idiot."

Kit felt anger flare. It felt better than sadness or guilt. "Why does everyone keep telling me that?"

"If it's reached a quorum, maybe you should admit you're outvoted and listen to us," Josh said.

Kit resumed rolling her scotch glass between her hands. She thought about what the Zookeeper had said. At least everyone in her life seemed to be consistently on message. Maybe they sent around talking points.

"Ethel overdosed today, Josh. I knew she was struggling with something and I didn't push. I didn't ask what was going on. Maybe I could have done something to help her. I should have tried."

Josh looked as sad as Kit felt. She felt tears welling. She'd held the emotions at bay all day, but now, with Josh, they were starting to leak out. She'd felt like this, raw and exposed, when she'd arrived at Thea's too, but then it all went to hell.

"I'm really sorry, Kit. She gonna be okay?"

Kit nodded. She thought about Ethel's reaction to being revived and wondered where she was now. Kit didn't stick around to see if she went with the paramedics or not. Ethel could have gone right back out and gotten more drugs. Jesus. Why hadn't she stayed to check? Some friend.

"Hey, wherever you just went, it's not your responsibility to solve Ethel's problems."

"She saved my life, Josh. Don't I owe her something for that?"

"No, because you saved your own life. She helped you find the way and you can be grateful, but you did the work. If you want to reach out to her now, fine, but you did the work. I was there, I saw it. She's got to reach out to her support system now if she needs it. This is not on you."

Kit looked at the scotch and the bar. Suddenly, she wanted to be anywhere but where they were. She threw some money on the table, got up, and headed for the door. Josh followed. Kit didn't have a destination in mind, she just needed to walk.

"You could have warned me we were going for a jog," Josh said. "I would've peed."

"There's a tree right there." Kit picked up the pace. "But no one's making you follow me."

"Keep talking." Josh jogged next to her. "I believe we'd just gotten to the part about all the good work you did in your recovery."

Kit stopped short and turned on Josh. "Ethel did that work too, Josh. She did all the work I did. She goes to all the meetings I go to. She taught me everything I know. Everything. And she knows a hell of a lot more than I do. She's been sober for years. And this morning I watched Thea shoot naloxone up her nose and prayed the death rattle wasn't prophetic. She started using again. What hope is there for me?"

"Is that what this's about? No one can predict the future, Kit."

"Exactly, but I can face reality. You said it yourself, I should accept my past. I wasn't before, but now I am. I'm a heroin addict. I am now, I always will be. Doesn't matter if I'm clean or not. That's who I am. And Thea deserves better than that. She shouldn't have my drug use hanging over her head constantly. She shouldn't have to wonder if that's what she's going to have to face one day. And I know she worries about it because I heard her talking to her friends when I went over there tonight. Her dad OD'd when she was a kid. She shouldn't have to worry her partner will too."

"So what, you're just going to get it over with? You believe you're going to use again, so there's no use in getting close to someone? Screw the people who care about you? Screw the work you've done and the life you've built for yourself? And screw letting a woman who cares about you use her own damn free will to make her own decisions?" Josh jabbed her in the chest.

Kit was confused. Why wasn't Josh understanding her?

"That's not what I'm saying. I'm not going to use again. Not today, at least. But I am who I am."

"Jesus, you certainly are. You're a stubborn, black-and-white thinker who drives me crazy sometimes. You don't have to be one thing or the other, Kit. You don't have to choose one at the expense of the other. You can be both and they can live together, peacefully. That's what I've been trying to get through that thick skull of yours. You've swung your pendulum too far the other way. How about a little middle ground, for all our sakes?"

Kit flopped down on a bench. She scrubbed at her face hoping she could keep the tears at bay. When she reached her swollen cheek she was reminded of Ethel's physical reaction at being revived. She gently probed the area.

"What happened to your face?" Josh tried to get a better look. Kit shooed him away.

"Ethel wasn't all that grateful Thea saved her life. The naloxone threw her into an aggressive withdrawal." Kit resumed gently probing her cheek. "It's not a very pleasant experience."

"Ever happen to you?"

Josh asked it quietly and Kit knew it probably hurt for him to voice the question. She shook her head. But she'd seen it work enough to know. And a few times when it didn't.

"How do I do that?" Kit turned to Josh and didn't shy away from eye contact this time. "How do I be both? How do I not let the fear of what could happen overwhelm me?"

Josh shrugged. "No idea. But I'm here to help. I'm willing to bet there are a lot of people in your meetings who have had the same struggle. And Thea's a pretty damn smart woman who, for some reason, seems to put up with you. Stop pushing her way. I'd argue you should have had this conversation with her, instead of doing whatever it was you did that had her calling me scared out of her mind."

Kit didn't even need to close her eyes to see Thea's face as she'd realized Kit was leaving after she begged her to stay.

*What did I do?*

"I screwed that up pretty bad, Josh. I did the thing she asked me to never do to her again. I really wanted to protect her. I'm still not convinced it was wrong, even though my heart really fucking hurts."

"Usually people don't need protection from those they love, Kit. She doesn't need protection from you. She needs you to be there for her like anyone else in a relationship. Everyone comes with baggage, babe. Yours is different from mine, but we all have it. You just have to be willing to set it down every once in a while."

Kit started to protest.

"Nope. I know the concept of one day at a time is important. Apply that liberally. Give her the benefit of the doubt. And for God's sake, let the woman make her own decisions."

The tears fell freely now. Josh wrapped his arms around Kit's shoulders and let her cry. She appreciated his solid strength and comfort. If only she'd realized earlier she wanted a different shoulder to cry on.

# CHAPTER TWENTY-FOUR

Thea didn't feel like going to work for the first time in her life. She truly couldn't remember a time when she considered calling in sick just because she didn't feel like going. Today she thought about it but wasn't sure she would go the next day either if she let herself off the hook today. Not only did her library not feel as much like the sanctuary it once had since she'd had to revive Ethel, the joy of seeing Kit was also gone. What remained were reminders of her tucked into the stacks, waiting to be found like an unwelcome jab to the heart.

Then there was the matter of the letter. Kit had slipped it into her mail slot the day before, but she'd not yet worked up the courage to read it.

She paced the living room, letter in hand, staring at the blank, neat, structured space. Previously, Thea would have described this room as a perfect example of what she needed in life—calm, predictable, orderly. Now when she looked around her home looked sterile and gloomy. She acutely felt the lack of color. It was alarming and invigorating. She knew what, or more accurately, who, sparked the change.

She flopped onto the couch and ripped open Kit's letter.

*Thea,*

*First, if you don't read any further, please know I wasn't running from you the night Ethel overdosed. I was running from myself. You were all I wanted. You're all I ever want. But I owe you more than someone who runs blindly through the world. I should have been there for you and I wasn't, and for that I'm sorry.*

*What I want right now is to figure out how to be the person you deserve and believe I can be. I think the other night proved I'm still a work in progress. You should get the best of me. I'm not giving up on us. Please don't give up on me. I need a little time to, as Walter said, "get my shit together" so I can be the stable, reliable person you need.*

*I'm sorry.*

*Kit*

Thea read the letter again. And again. She wanted to forgive her, tell her there was nothing to keep them apart, and fall back into her arms, but she couldn't, not yet. She'd asked Kit not to walk out on her again, and she had. She'd needed Kit and she wasn't there. And now her entire prior, beautifully ordered, predictable life looked bland and boring and Kit was the reason. But her childhood had been anything but bland and she knew her experiences left a deep, lasting mark. It was impossible to repair something that was shattered so thoroughly that key pieces were still missing.

The ironic part was Kit felt like some of those missing pieces, if Thea could trust Kit wouldn't bring everything else crashing down around her, again. How could Thea trust something neither of them could guarantee? The reality of what it would mean if Kit relapsed was more vivid today than it had been a week ago and that was hard to set aside as inconsequential to their relationship. If she was going to be all in, she needed time too, because it wasn't fair to Kit if she bailed after six months. Knowing that and actually moving through her life without Kit were at odds, however, and her chest ached knowing she didn't need to rush through her days because her evenings wouldn't include Kit.

When she arrived at the library Walter greeted her. He didn't give her a pitying look like some of the other staff did.

"You ready for today?" Walter looked like he wanted to hug her, but he didn't.

Thea nodded. After she'd administered the naloxone there were discussions of whether other staff should be trained to administer it as well. She'd also raised the issue of the women under the Zookeeper's care and how best to serve them. The staff had been energized, brainstorming ideas and coming up with plans to serve this segment of the community. Thea was proud of them and motivated by their enthusiasm.

"Let's get the gang together," Thea said.

She and Walter opened the community room, which was the best space for a full staff meeting. It was a day the library didn't open until the afternoon, but everyone had agreed to come in early.

"How are your spirits?" Walter turned his full attention her way. It felt like an invitation.

Thea busied herself moving chairs and tidying. "I don't even know where to begin answering that."

"Why don't you begin by telling me about what is causing you to move through the day like it pains you?"

Thea sighed and paused her busy work. "I miss her, Walter. I wasn't prepared to miss her this much. She wrote me a letter saying she needs time. I think I do too, but why does it hurt so much if it's what we both need?"

"I am confident that your story with Ms. Marsden has not yet seen its final chapter," Walter said.

Thea wanted to believe that. Desperately. But right now, it was hard to see happily ever after through all the hurt. "How are you so confident?"

"Because I still firmly believe that your Ms. Marsden will get her shit together."

Thea was stunned into silence for a few beats.

"Excuse my salty language." Walter's face was a delightful shade of pink.

"No apology needed. That gave me more joy than anything lately, by far. Kit said you used that language in her letter to me, but I thought she was employing creative license to make a point. How are you so confident she'll get her shit together?"

"Because I believe she wants to. And she's trying. And mostly, I believe she'll do whatever it takes to get back to you." Walter examined her closely. "Is that what you are desirous of? Her return to you?"

*If she wants me so badly, why does she keep waltzing out the door?* "Yes. But it was easier to ignore the implications of her past drug use before her friend was dying in that bathroom." Thea gestured over her shoulder. "She'll never be able to prove to me she won't use again. It's not possible. I guess I have to make sure I'm okay with the uncertainty. That's not something I'm good with, especially not uncertainty that hits so close to home. I want my life so predictable and ordered precisely because of the hurricane drug use created for me as a kid. But my biggest problem is her impulsively running and making decisions for me every time something unpleasant happens."

Walter looked pensive and Thea waited him out. He couldn't be rushed even if a train was coming and he was thinking deep thoughts on the tracks.

"I imagine it's easy to swing wildly when you haven't yet found your anchor point," Walter said.

"And if she never does?"

"I guess you have to decide if you love her enough to accept her as she is or you have to live without her. I will support you no matter your decision in this matter. It is okay to take a leap of faith, or to step back and protect a heart which has seen too much trauma in a life so young."

Thea didn't give Walter a choice about embracing her this time. She needed the comfort of a good friend. The respite was short-lived. The rest of the staff bustled in, full of energy she didn't feel and happiness she wanted to forbid. Walter started the meeting, but it quickly dissolved into barely controlled chaos as almost all staff meetings did. Thea hated the frenetic energy, but today she was willing to embrace it for a good cause.

Before Thea had to stand on a table or set off the fire alarm, Carrie stood up and whistled loudly. Everyone quieted.

"All right, folks, contents of your pockets on the table in front of you." Carrie slapped her hand on the desk. "Don't be shy."

Everyone complied. Thea never knew how Carrie was able to get people to do the weird things she asked of them without any explanation.

Carrie went around the room inspecting pocket treasure.

"Winner." She held up a Captain America action figure. "Only the good captain here is allowed to talk. We'll pass him like a hot potato, but raise your hand if you want a turn with his fine ass. Since I've got him now—Thea, we already voted, we want the naloxone training."

Thea looked around the room. To a person, there were nods of agreement. She felt a little choked up.

"Are you all sure? I don't want you to make this decision lightly. I also want to make it clear, just because you go through the training, you aren't required to carry naloxone, or administer it. It is completely voluntary. There will be no judgment from me or anyone else if you choose not to participate."

"We know, Thea. We're in."

"Okay. Thank you. Now let's talk about a few other things."

They spent the rest of the time hashing out some rough plans to better serve the larger community around the library. Thea was nervous that the new initiatives might not be well received. She should have trusted her staff. Not only were they on board, but eager for the new changes. Many of them expressed the desire to do more for the clients they served, be it kids, teens, or adults since addiction impacted so many in their community, either directly or secondarily.

After the meeting adjourned Carrie lingered.

"Have you also prepared a speech?" Thea wasn't sure she could take another pep talk.

"Speeches are more Walter's thing." Carrie hopped up on the conference table and crossed her legs dramatically. "I'm more of a gossip."

"Barking up the wrong tree then. I've got nothing interesting to share."

"Oh, my love, you *are* the intrigue. But don't worry, I collect, I don't share."

"I still don't have anything interesting." Thea turned to leave. She really wished people would stop poking her wounds.

"Fine. How about I ask you questions, and you can answer them?" Carrie jumped down and followed her.

"How about we talk about the meeting we just had, or we go to work?" Thea tried to pull open the door, but Carrie zipped in front of her and blocked her exit.

"Nah, that doesn't sound like fun at all. Have you heard from Kit?"

"No, not exactly. Sort of. What did you think of the proposal to limit time in the bathrooms?" Thea tried again to reach the door handle, but Carrie swatted her away.

"Bathroom plan made sense to me. How do you sort of hear from someone? Do you want to hear from her? Do you want her back?"

"I don't know. She wrote me a letter. Walter told her to get her shit together and so she's doing that. I get to decide if she's worth the wait. Do you think it's feasible to set up some of the other community services we talked about?"

"Sure, why not? If anyone can do it, it's you." Carrie pushed away from the door and lifted Thea's chin so they were eye to eye. "I'll circle back to Walter's role in all of this later. Do you want it to work with her?"

Thea didn't answer right away. She felt like the right answer was probably no. That seemed like the safe answer. The answer she would have given in the abstract before she met Kit. But things were different now, even if her rational brain had been putting up quite a fight since Ethel's overdose. She thought about what Walter said about living with Kit as is or living without her. The tug on her heart was her answer. "Yes. I do."

"What would it take? To win you back?"

"I'll have to give some of the services we talked about some thought. I think there's a way we can put them in place without disrupting normal operations. And they would benefit more than just the Zookeeper's women."

"You didn't answer my question," Carrie said. "Are we talking showing up naked in nothing but her tool belt or sonnets from the rooftops?"

"You are really hung up on that tool belt." Thea ducked around Carrie and held the door for her. Thinking of Kit naked wasn't what Thea needed right now. It was a lot harder to remember why they wouldn't work when she thought about how perfectly they fit together.

"Can you think of anything sexier?"

"Yes," Thea said quietly.

"Wait, you didn't?" Carrie stopped halfway out the door. "No? You did? And you didn't tell me? You know this means I have so many more questions."

"No, you don't. You're done." Thea pointed Carrie down the hall. "You've been extremely helpful. I'm going to work. And so are you."

"Sarcasm, I detect sarcasm. I'm immune, of course. It's my superpower, but I can still detect it."

Thea waved to Carrie and retreated to her office. She sat down heavily in her chair and pulled out her phone. Her lock screen was a picture Kit had taken of her in the giant oak.

Despite everything that had happened since, thinking about that day still made Thea's heart race and not just because of the sex. It had felt like she and Kit had created a world just for themselves and they were the only ones who would ever inhabit it. She wished they were still there.

Thea opened her phone and pulled up another picture from that day. This one was of Kit. She was leaning against the tree trunk looking at Thea. Her hair was rumpled and she had a half smile. At the time, Thea had been ecstatic to have captured Kit at her suave sexiest. When she looked at it now, it felt like her heart broke all over again.

She ran her finger over Kit's face in the picture and let the tears fall. She didn't answer Carrie's question because she didn't know what it would take to get her back. She didn't know how to answer that question. She didn't know how to build a solid foundation on something that felt like quicksand. Kit could provide some of the answers, but she needed to find the others herself. Or maybe she needed Kit to help her, to be the anchor Walter had mentioned Kit was also searching for.

*Damn you, Kit. Give me something I can grab on to. Get your ass back here with something we can both use to help rebuild my broken heart.*

## CHAPTER TWENTY-FIVE

Kit tried telling herself this was just like any other time she'd dropped by unannounced, but it sure as hell felt different.

*Everything is different this time, champ. Put on your big boy underwear and knock already.*

She knocked and waited. No one answered so she knocked again. She was about to pound on the door when it opened.

"What do you want, ace?" Ethel didn't look happy to see her.

"I don't want anything." Kit held her hands out to the side as a show of peace. "I'm here for you."

Ethel's jaw bunched and she held the door tightly. "I punched you in the face. What makes you think I want your help?"

"You punched me twice, but who's counting. And let's skip the grumpy teenager. I think we've both earned more than that from each other, don't you?"

"Tough love? You know that crap doesn't work." Ethel opened the door a bit wider.

"Ethel, you've given me more than I can repay. You helped me find my way to sobriety and gave me the tools to maintain it. I'm not playing games with you."

Ethel waved Kit in. They sat on the couch and Ethel pulled out an e-cigarette.

"I gave up cigarettes twenty years ago, but fuck if the cravings for every vice I've ever had aren't strong as shit now. Why are you here, Kit?"

"I told you." Kit shrugged. "I'm here for you."

"But why? I said some horrible things to you—unfortunately, I remember it—and I took a couple swings at you. So again, why are you here?"

"Ethel, no one should be judged on their worst mistakes. I've made plenty since Thea revived you. But I'm trying to be better. I used to think I had to shove my past away never to be seen again. Turns out that didn't work. Blew up rather spectacularly, actually. You kept trying to warn me, so no need to say you told me so. After you overdosed, I sort of swung the other way. I'm trying to find some middle ground."

"You look me in the eye right now, skip. Did you use again?" Ethel was rivaling Josh for uncomfortable eye contact.

"No, ma'am." Kit squirmed but she didn't look away.

"All right then. Let's talk about middle ground," Ethel said.

"That's not what's important right now." Kit shook her head. "I'm here for you, not for me."

Ethel put her hands over Kit's. "That's not your job, kiddo. You know about Star Recovery, right?"

Kit nodded. The time she'd spent working with them could have been life altering if she'd had the balls to stick around.

"Well, I reached out to them a couple of days ago. I'm going to start working with one of their peer recovery coaches. I'm going to get a handle on this again, Kit. My path isn't one you're guaranteed to walk. And if you do slip, you have as many supports as I do to find your way back."

"I know that now. I'm not a one trial learner." Kit ran her fingers through her hair and let out a deep breath. "And I know service and accepting my place in the recovery community is part of my sobriety, not a hindrance to it. I'm sorry it took me so long to realize that."

"There's no timeframe for any of this," Ethel said. "Can you do me a favor? Can you tell that lady you're keeping company with thank you for saving my life? I know I was a real asshole about the whole thing. I'm sorry I hit you, Kit. And I'm really sorry for the things I said to you. They were unforgivable."

"Thea and I aren't really keeping company right now. But I'll let her know if I see her."

"What did you do?" Ethel looked disappointed.

"Why does everyone assume it's me who screwed up?"

Ethel gave her an "oh, please" look.

"Okay, it was totally me." Kit looked up at the ceiling, hoping there were answers to be found on the blades of Ethel's ceiling fan.

"So win her back, tiger." Ethel patted Kit's knee.

*It sounds so easy when she says it.* "I have to get my shit together first," Kit said. "And then I have to convince her to trust me."

"Meet me tomorrow at Star Recovery." Ethel used Kit to hoist herself off the couch.

"Why?"

Kit wasn't sure she wanted to go back there after the way she'd run out the last time she was there.

"Because it seems like we both have some shit we need to get together. Maybe we can help each other."

Kit left Ethel's feeling better than she had since she dropped off the letter asking Thea not to give up on her, or them, while she worked out a few things. Kit had never had a broken heart, but some things you didn't need flashing neon signs to recognize. It was killing her to stay away from Thea even an hour more, but she couldn't go back to her until she knew she wouldn't do the same thing the next time something spooked her. She needed to prove that she had things figured out. That she wasn't scared of who she was. She had to try.

❖

Luanne's intense stare was discombobulating. Kit had been welcomed cordially, but Luanne hadn't been nearly as open and warm as she had been on Kit's last day of work. It probably had something to do with Kit's panicked sprint for the door. Funny how all you left in the dust when you ran was pissed off people. It's a wonder she had any friends left. "Luanne, I think I owe you an apology," Kit said. "Zeke, too."

"I'm listening." Luanne folded her hands on the table. "Knock my socks off."

Kit spoke honestly and plainly, knowing that was the only way. "I loved working here and I'm in awe of the work you do. But when I was working in the office I was scared of being identified as a recovering drug user. Setting foot in this building scared me, even though I was so drawn to the work that you do. So, when Zeke started talking to me about being a peer mentor, I freaked out. It would seem I have a bit of a bad habit of running like hell when I freak out. So, I'm sorry for running like hell."

Kit waited anxiously for Luanne's response. Running was much easier than waiting around to hear people out. And the stakes here were relatively low. The tough ones were still to come.

"You aren't the first one to get scared and scamper off, Kit," Luanne said. "I understand the running. You back because you're less scared?"

"Oh, fuck no." Kit laughed. "I'm still scared out of my mind. But I'm tired of running away from something. Maybe I'm ready to head toward something instead."

"That's sort of my wheelhouse." Luanne slapped her hand on the table. "I know you came in here to support a friend. Is there something else you had in mind when you walked back through my doors?"

She'd only come because Ethel had asked her to, but now that it was out there, something occurred to her. "Actually, yes," Kit swallowed and took the leap. "Do you think I could talk to Zeke?"

## Chapter Twenty-six

In theory, Thea was reviewing orders for new books for the children's library. In reality she was staring at her computer, not seeing a word on the screen. Her mind was flitting between the new plans for the library, some of which went into action this morning, and Kit. Always Kit.

Kit had still been coming to meetings, which gave Thea comfort. It seemed like Kit looked for her when she walked through on the way to her meeting, but Thea no longer sat at the front desk waiting for her. It was too painful. Carrie kept her updated on Kit's movements, as well as how hot she continued to look. Thea couldn't decide if it was helpful or not. At least she knew she was attending meetings. Ethel was back too, which was a great relief.

Thea thought about what Walter said. Would she be willing to accept Kit exactly as she was? Was it fair to Kit to say no? Was it fair to her to say yes? Wasn't that part of loving someone? Accepting them for who they are? Accepting the things you cannot change?

*Back up. Do I love her?*

"You are certainly looking contemplative," Walter said. "I feel like I should bring in some thinking spirits for you to tuck into your bottom drawer for after-hours chats. It would liven up the mood."

He took up residence in the chair in front of Thea's desk. He calmed the air in a way only Walter could.

"Are you implying I'm morose? I certainly am contemplative and it's all your fault," Thea said.

Walter cocked an eyebrow and rolled his hand, encouraging her to continue.

"I was mulling over our conversation about Kit. I miss her, Walter. And I don't just miss certain parts of her. I miss all of her, even the impulsive, wrong-headed bits, because that's part of who she is."

"I sense a but." Walter leaned forward, leaned his elbows on his knees, steepled his hands, and waited. He looked like Yoda.

"But I'm still me." Thea rocked side to side slightly in her chair. "Risk averse and careful with a whole messy history of my own to contend with. I feel like my heart is shattered and I want to blame it all on her for walking away, but it isn't all her fault. That feels so much scarier. Trusting us both enough to take that leap of faith…How do I do that?

"Thea, my dear, I do not believe I can provide the answers you need. I believe only you and Ms. Marsden have the answers you require."

Thea looked at Walter and stuck her tongue out. It felt childish and fun. She hadn't done anything fun in quite a while. "A lot of help you are."

Walter smiled. "I am always available with a shoulder to cry on. But advanced notice is always appreciated. I'll choose my outfit appropriately. It's more difficult to get tear stains and nasal secretions out of some of my sweaters than others."

"I'll keep that in mind." She knew Walter was full of it. He'd let her snot all over any sweater he owned.

"Did you come down here for something specific?"

Walter nodded and pointed to the box in the corner of Thea's office. There were shiny new naloxone kits ready for distribution. A member of the department of health had come by to train the entire staff earlier in the week.

"The lockboxes have been installed in the common areas and we're ready to disperse these," Walter said.

"What are we standing around here for?" Thea pushed away from her desk and stood.

She grabbed a box and handed the other to Walter. Ethel's overdose had one positive side effect. It had galvanized the staff into an overdose prevention super team. Thea was impressed at how eager her staff was to turn the library into a safe place for all. In their last staff meeting, one of the teen librarians had put it best. She said "we have to accept the community we have. There's no point fighting the tide. Now we just have to figure out how to serve those who walk through our doors."

Thea and Walter walked around the library with the naloxone kits. They'd decided against only having them at the desks, although they stocked quite a few kits there so any staff member could get to them easily. They also put a few kits in the bathrooms, in lockboxes. All staff members had keys to the boxes and could access the kits easily if required. Thea didn't want someone to have to run to a desk if they were already on the scene of an overdose.

They put one, unlocked, in each bathroom as well. It was under the sink, but someone could easily find it if they looked. The plan was to keep an eye on if and how quickly they disappeared. They didn't want to be a source of unlimited naloxone, but if someone needed it, it was better to get it where it was needed.

"This is going to save lives, Walter." Thea looked around the library, her library. For the first time in days it looked, once again, like the sanctuary it always had. "But I want everyone to know it's voluntary. No one has to use these kits."

"You've made that clear." Walter put his hand gently on her shoulder. "But having them throughout the library will make it easier for us to respond."

Thea thought about the first time she met Kit. She'd had naloxone in hand ready to revive her after Walter had shouted about a woman overdosing on the front steps. How many times had she asked people to inject a little farther away from the front door so kids wouldn't walk by them on their way in after school? How many times had she asked clearly intoxicated folks to please go back out into the park if they couldn't stay awake? The problem was larger than anything naloxone kits could solve. Thea sighed.

"What about our other plans?"

"In progress," Walter said. "I took care of securing permission from the library higher-ups. They were rather eager to agree after your heroics. I know you were reticent, but a security guard is overdue. They will not restrict access, only ensure safety. I've begun interviewing for two new bathroom monitor positions. The process has drawn a colorful cast of characters. Two of our volunteers requested their duties be expanded to include collecting used syringes on our property and a reasonable perimeter in the park."

Thea was impressed. They had only begun talking about these changes a few weeks prior. Walter moved quickly.

"Very good work, Walter. And what about the community outreach efforts we spoke about?"

"I can't take all the credit," Walter said. "Everyone around here's been quite motivated. You've provided an easy leadership to follow."

Thea felt the praise deeply. She coached herself not to cry. Now was not the place. But his support did, and had always, meant the world to her.

He patted her shoulder again. "Our community outreach champion is right over there, why don't you check in with her about our progress?"

Thea saw Frankie sitting behind the desk huddled with one of the adult librarians. She couldn't help but smile at Frankie's furrowed brow and look of deep concentration. Whatever they were talking about was something new to Frankie, who always looked that intense when she was taking something in.

Since the overdose, Frankie had asked to be involved in the new initiatives around the library. Thea was resistant at first. Frankie was still a kid, even if she was about to start her senior year of high school. But she'd quite clearly taken issue with that argument and pointed out that what had happened to Ethel was normal for the kids in the neighborhood. Seeing drug use and used syringes was common. She wanted to be part of helping her community and reminding everyone, especially the kids, that this wasn't normal and it didn't have to define their lives. It was hard for Thea to deny her.

"Hello, you two. What's causing so much consternation over here?"

"The schedule. I can't make it work." Frankie looked defeated and ready to throw the computer.

"Why don't you tell me what the trouble is and maybe I can help?" Thea moved around the desk and looked over Frankie's shoulder.

The other librarian looked grateful and happily gave up his seat.

Frankie pointed at the computer screen.

"See. The food pantry's not a problem. It doesn't need anyone monitoring it. The security guard is within sight and there's a camera in that part of the library anyway, just to make sure no one takes off with all the food at once. But we wanted to have community health outreach workers here one night a week and social services organizations here another night. The new security guard is only working late these two nights."

Frankie jabbed at the screen.

"And community health can only come this night. The government benefits group can only come this night. Women's social services can only come these two. And Star Recovery here. How do we make it all line up?"

Frankie flopped back in her chair with the dramatic flair only teenagers seemed able to manage.

"You reached out to all these groups to get them on board?" Thea glanced at Frankie who was still staring intently at the computer.

"A lot of them. I had help. Walter helped me with what to say and how to ask for what we were looking for. I had an in at Star Recovery, so that one was easy."

"I'm really impressed." Thea didn't follow up on Frankie's cryptic Star Recovery comment. Frankie could tell her if she wanted.

"But look, it's not going to mean anything if it doesn't work on the schedule." Frankie waved her hand wildly at the computer again.

Thea pondered the computer screen for a few minutes. She'd been putting together the staff schedules for years. There was a solution to this problem. She saw it quickly but kept staring a little longer to consider all her options.

"What if we moved everyone to Tuesday? They're all available then. We can just have one night of community health. They all fall under that umbrella more or less."

"But the security guard doesn't work late that night."

"They do now." Thea snapped her fingers. "It probably makes sense for them to work late every night, actually."

"You can just do that?"

"You can when you're the boss," Thea gave Frankie a wink.

Now Frankie looked impressed.

"Since everyone's coming on the same night, we have a free night on the schedule. Carrie told me you had an idea for something that didn't make it to the final round for implementation. Why don't you tell me about it now?"

Frankie turned bright red. Thea wasn't sure if Frankie was going to bolt or melt into the floor, but she sure didn't look like she wanted to share her idea.

"Frankie, it's me. I want to hear your idea. Carrie said it was a good one."

"She shouldn't have said anything." Frankie started shoving things in her backpack. "I thought…I mean, I was thinking maybe, it could be nice. Um. Family dinner."

Thea didn't follow. She waited for Frankie to elaborate, but Frankie was still packing haphazardly.

"What's family dinner?"

"Uh, you know. Where people get together and eat a meal together."

Thea was pretty sure she shoved the library stapler in her pack. "Frankie, I'm familiar with the definition," Thea said gently. "What does it mean to you in this situation?"

"I was thinking maybe the library could host family dinner," Frankie said. "You know, for the neighborhood. There are a couple of soup kitchens around, but they're really small and don't have a lot of room. There's more space here. If the weather's nice, people could eat outside."

Thea felt like the proudest mama bear in the forest, even if she had no claim to Frankie as her own. How this sweet child had such a giving heart after all she'd experienced was beyond her, but it reinforced everything Thea wanted to accomplish at the library. Frankie was the embodiment of all Thea wanted the library to stand for and be in the community. Strength, hope, compassion, and assistance.

"I'm going to make some calls. Frankie, family dinner is a wonderful idea."

Thea rounded the desk, and her first instinct was to find Kit, to share this with her. The fact that she couldn't hit her like a sledgehammer to the chest. How could they fix this?

# CHAPTER TWENTY-SEVEN

"You nervous?" Josh poked Kit.

"What gave it away?" Kit swatted at his hand. She could provide water for an entire town with the sweat her palms were producing.

"The pacing, the sweating, the food you threw away instead of eating, the talking really fast and then not talking at all…"

"Aren't you supposed to say 'everything's going to be fine, Kit, nothing to be nervous about'?"

"We promised a long time ago not to lie to each other." Josh shrugged. "And I have no fucking clue if this is going to be fine. You dug yourself a pretty deep hole. Time to find out how good your climbing skills are."

"You are probably the worst motivational speaker on the face of the planet. I should throw you down a deep hole." Kit scrubbed at her face with her hands.

"Promises, promises," Josh said. "Are we leaving or what? We're going to be late."

Kit panicked and looked at the clock. There was still plenty of time. She punched Josh hard on the shoulder as she walked by him and out the door. He should know better than to mess with her today of all days. She was nervous enough about talking to Thea without Josh adding extra stress. Hopefully, she'd left a bruise.

Josh didn't come in right away when they got to the library. He'd come in closer to the meeting time. Kit didn't want an audience when she talked to Thea.

She bounded up the library steps as always. When she walked in there was a security guard posted by the door. She looked like a brick wall that swallowed a bulldozer. But she smiled, and for all that solid mass of womanhood, she looked relaxed and friendly.

*Well, the library is safe from battering rams, tanks, antiaircraft missiles, and puny humans with her at the door. Hope that brick house isn't throwing me out on my ass in a few minutes.*

Kit walked to the desk. Walter was there, her own personal bouncer. "Hi, Walter. Is Thea here?"

"Ms. Marsden," Walter said. "I'm not overly inclined…"

"Walter, please."

Walter considered her for what felt like the entire life cycle of a star. "She's in her office."

"Thank you, you beautiful man."

Kit leaned over the desk and kissed the top of his head.

"Off you go then," Walter said, looking flustered.

Kit walked as quickly as was polite through the library and took the stairs two at a time down to Thea's office. Now that she had something to say, she couldn't wait to see her. Even if Thea threw her out, or had Tonya the Tank Engine upstairs do it, at least she would get to see her again.

It didn't matter that the exile was self-inflicted or necessary. It had been painful and lonely. And, Kit hoped, it was coming to an end.

Kit skidded to a halt outside Thea's door. She was sitting in front of the computer but didn't look to be concentrating on anything. She looked tired and sad. Kit felt an intense pang of guilt. *Don't be so arrogant. She might not be sad about you, you ass.* Kit took a deep breath for courage and knocked on the doorframe to announce her presence. Thea waved her in without looking up. Kit walked to Thea's desk and stopped in front. Thea still didn't look up immediately. She seemed not to register Kit had entered the room.

Kit was about to say something when Thea looked up and whispered, "Sawdust."

"Excuse me?" It wasn't exactly how she expected to be greeted.

"You smell like sawdust." Thea's smile was gentle and her eyes looked far away. It only lasted a moment before her expression shuttered closed. "What do you want, Kit?"

"You," Kit said. "All I've ever wanted is you."

Thea stood up and looked like she was going to protest.

"Before you say it, I know I've got a really fucked up way of showing it. You don't have to tell me. I'm well aware. I'm not proud of how I've treated you. I'd be a rich woman if everyone who told me I was an idiot threw me a little money along with their wisdom."

"You're not an idiot, Kit."

"Oh, but I am." Kit didn't know what to do with her hands, so she shoved them in her back pockets. "I ran away from the best thing in my life. *You* are the best thing in my life. And I may have ruined that for good because I was so scared of myself. You found all the parts of me that I was trying so hard to bury and never once did you turn away. Only I did that."

"Kit, I'm not innocent here," Thea said. "Maybe I didn't turn away, but I took a few steps back. You asked for time, but the truth is, I needed it too. I couldn't in good faith come back to you if I was too scared to be fully yours. But that meant I wasn't there for you and I'm sorry. I was hurting after Ethel overdosed and I wanted you to take care of me. I didn't realize how much you needed me. I begged you to stay, but maybe I should have run after you sooner."

Kit shook her head. "You'll have to trust me on this, running isn't a very good way to deal with problems."

Thea smiled and Kit's heart felt like it started beating again for the first time in weeks. That smile did things to her. The best kind of things.

"I've missed your smile."

"I've missed you." She said it almost too quietly for Kit to hear.

Kit reached for her, but Thea didn't reach back. The desk still stood between them.

"Where do we go from here?" Thea asked.

"Will you come to my meeting today?" Kit reached for Thea's hand, and this time she took it. "It's an open meeting and I'd really like you to be there. Josh is coming and I asked Frankie to be there too."

Thea looked surprised by the seeming change of subject. Kit figured she had been looking for a little less concrete answer.

"Please? I hope it will answer your question if you come. That's why I came down here. To ask you to the meeting. But you looked so beautiful, I got a little ahead of myself. You do that to me."

"I'm already going to say yes." Thea squeezed Kit's hand. "No need to lay it on so thick."

The sparkle in her eyes let Kit know she was teasing, and hope fluttered in her heart like a newly born butterfly.

*She wouldn't tease me like that if she didn't still care, right? Although cats tease mice before they kill them.* Kit led the way to the community room. There was a chipper looking young woman, probably just out of college, sitting on a stool outside the bathroom. She was wearing a library identification badge.

"Bathroom monitor," Thea said in Kit's ear.

Kit jumped. She liked Thea whispering in her ear as a general rule, but this time it caught her off guard.

"Since when?"

"Start of the week. There have been a few changes around here. You probably saw Daisy at the front door."

"That human armored vehicle is named *Daisy*?"

Thea didn't say anything, but Kit swore she thought it was funny too.

Inside the community room, Frankie was already seated. She waved them over. They took their seats and Josh joined them a few minutes later. Kit felt her heart rate ratchet up as the minutes ticked closer to the start of the meeting.

When she didn't think she could stand it any longer, something sharp poked her in the kidneys. Kit whipped around to confront her poker.

"Isn't this cute, ace. You brought the missus, junior, and your best man. Does that mean you're going to actually get off your ass and say something? If you want them to stick around, don't wait forever to tell them how you feel. You understand me, sport?" Ethel crossed her arms, her legs stretched out in front her.

"You poked me in the back to tell me that?" Kit tried to glare, but she wasn't sure it landed.

"Nah, that was for fun. I threw the wisdom in for free."

"You know, you're even more of a pain in the ass since you relapsed."

"Keep it down," Ethel said. "Someone might hear you. What if there's someone in here who didn't see it for themselves? I have a reputation to tarnish. Meeting's starting."

Kit turned in her seat and met Thea's quizzical stare. She shrugged. Ethel was solid, straight-up, and her dark humor made the world make sense, sometimes.

The familiarity of the start of the meeting soothed Kit's nerves. The routine and repetition were a comfort. Once the start of the meeting was complete, the leader opened the floor to anyone who wanted to speak. Kit sucked in a deep breath. She rolled her one-year sobriety chip in her pocket, which she'd gotten almost a year ago and meant as much to her as almost any other possession. She stood.

She'd never spoken a word at a meeting aside from greeting those who introduced themselves and when she was saying the serenity prayer. Her legs felt wobbly as she made her way to the front of the room. The day's leader smiled at her warmly and patted her shoulder encouragingly. When she turned to face the group she was vaguely aware of the supportive faces of her NA brethren. The only face that came fully into focus was Thea's.

"Hello." Kit shifted her weight from foot to foot and gripped the podium hard enough she thought she might break off a piece. "My name is Kit. I'm a heroin addict."

Kit composed herself as the group greeted her. She didn't want to screw this up. The stakes were too high.

"Since I got clean, I've run far and fast away from anything that labeled me as an addict. I was at war with myself since, you know, I used heroin for a long time. I didn't understand why I couldn't shove my past neatly in a box along with old pictures I was embarrassed about and stow it all under the bed or on the top shelf of a closet. I knew I'd have to pack it up and haul it around wherever I moved, but surely, it never needed to be revisited."

There were knowing smiles and a few chuckles around the room.

"Most dangerously, I wasn't willing to let myself live with my past. I came to meetings but didn't speak. I worked on my sobriety but didn't talk about why I needed to. I never mentioned or discussed the time before sobriety with anyone outside of a very select few. And if it came up, I was ill equipped to handle it. If I was faced with my time using or the threat of returning there, I did what I have always done. I ran to avoid facing it. One of my former drug dealers used to call me Kilo and I was convinced I was fast enough to leave Kilo in my past, but that proved impossible because I am her and she is me."

Kit stopped for a few beats. She scrubbed her face with her hands before continuing. She was in it now, but the hard part was about to begin. She saw Josh give her a little thumbs-up.

"When I ran, I ended up hurting people, even when my intention was just the opposite. I hurt my sponsor, Ethel. I hurt my cousin, Josh. I hurt my new friend, Frankie. And I hurt the woman that I love, Thea. I'm sorry to all of you. Especially to Thea. All of them saw what I considered the ugly parts of me, the Kilo of it all, and in different ways showed me love and support while never judging me or making me feel shame. I was the only one who did that. And because of that, I hurt each of them, Thea more than any."

Kit could see tears in Thea's eyes. She hoped that was a good thing. There was no taking back what she said. She didn't want to. She was in love with Thea.

"But all this running eventually led me to a place of understanding. What helped me get there was something we recite every week. Grant me the serenity to accept the things I cannot change. I cannot change my drug use, but I can accept it. That's the next step in my journey. I'm still very much a work in progress, but I hope to keep learning from everyone in this room. I thank you now for all you've already taught me and all I still have to learn."

Kit made her way back to her seat at ease. She had said what she wanted to say, and Thea had heard it.

When she sat back down the nerves returned. She didn't dare look at Thea for fear of what she'd see. Ethel poked her in the back again, but this time she ignored her. Frankie leaned over and patted her on the back. Josh bumped her shoulder with his. Thea was sitting ramrod straight next to her with her hands on her knees.

*I wish I had mind reading superpowers.* She looked at Thea's hands, pressed tightly to her legs. *Or maybe I don't.* Kit wiped her own hands on her pants. The nervous sweat was back.

After thirty seconds or two hundred years, Kit stole a glance at Thea. Tears were running down her cheeks, leaving little rivulets on her smooth skin before falling onto her collar.

Kit couldn't stand seeing Thea like that. She couldn't stand seeing Thea so heartbroken. Especially since it was her fault. She didn't know how to make it better. She reached out and gently put her hand over Thea's. She didn't do more than offer connection.

Thea turned her hand over and entwined their fingers. She pulled their joined hands to her chest and held them to her heart before lowering them again to Kit's lap. Kit squeezed Thea's hand softly. She hoped she was conveying all she was feeling with that small gesture. Thea squeezed back.

Everything happening in the meeting faded as Kit's entire focus turned to Thea. She reached with her free hand and wiped the tears that still streaked her face. Thea laid her head on Kit's shoulder. If they weren't in the middle of a meeting and if Thea hadn't just settled so comfortably on Kit, she might have jumped up and hollered triumphantly. Kit didn't know what this meant for them long-term, but she was holding Thea's hand, Thea's head was on her shoulder, and for the first time in weeks, Kit's heart felt at peace.

## CHAPTER TWENTY-EIGHT

Thea held tightly to Kit's hand as the meeting ended. She wasn't sure she ever wanted to let go. She'd finally come to the conclusion that living without Kit was making her miserable and she wasn't willing to let her parents and her shitty childhood steal the future she wanted. She wanted a life with Kit, whatever it looked like. And then today, Kit had walked in and given her even more.

Kit didn't let go of Thea's hand as they left the community room. Frankie and Josh trailed behind. Kit looked unsure now that they were out of the meeting. Thea knew the next step was hers. Kit had laid her heart bare and Thea knew it was her turn to take a leap of faith. She let go of Kit's hand to talk to Josh.

"Josh, I'm trusting you can find your own way home?" It wasn't subtle, but it was clear. Thea wasn't about to let Kit leave.

"I know the way," Josh said.

He had a cartoon grin on his face and Thea patted his cheek. The bond between the cousins was never more pronounced than right now, and she was glad she'd have time in the future to get to know him.

Thea turned around and found Kit in an embrace with Frankie. She pulled away from the hug and said something to Frankie that Thea couldn't hear. Frankie pulled her back for one more hug then threw her arm around Josh's shoulders and walked away.

"Josh and Frankie hit it off after she interviewed him for her project. She's been hanging around learning a few things from him." Kit watched them go.

"How does that kid have time for anything else?" Thea knew that, as Frankie had mentioned it a few times, but it was still nice to hear Kit's take on it.

"She's remarkable." Kit looked back at Thea and smiled. "Just like her mentor and personal hero."

Thea knew she was blushing. She looked away. In doing so she realized they were the only ones still outside the community room.

"Looks like we're the only ones left. Where to now?"

"I'll go wherever you lead," Kit said.

Thea was sure she meant more than their next physical destination. She was turning control over to Thea, and there was no question how special that was. "Walk with me."

Kit followed her as Thea stopped by her office to grab her things, then followed her out of the library. Thea high-fived Daisy on the way out. Kit tried to do the same, but Daisy rolled her eyes and motioned her out.

Once they were out of the library, Kit took Thea's bag. She really liked that Kit did that. It made her feel cared for. She slipped her hand back into Kit's and let the words flow. "Thank you for inviting me to the meeting, Kit."

"I meant what I said." Kit squeezed her hand. "All of it."

Thea could see the love in Kit's eyes. She didn't question Kit's love for her. It was right in front of her.

"I can see you still have questions. That's okay. I know you don't trust me. I probably wouldn't either. Ask me whatever you need to know." Kit gently squeezed Thea's hand.

"It's not that, Kit." Thea considered whether that was true. Maybe it was. "I want you to let me in, all the way in, so the next time you get scared, it's not so easy to shut me out. I also need you to be patient with me. I've never had the most exciting, bright, bold thing in my life also be where I retreat when I need shelter from the world. It's a lot to get used to for someone like me."

"I'll do whatever you want." Kit pulled Thea's hand to her lips and kissed it. "I miss you so much. I miss us so much."

"Kit," Thea said. "It's what we need. I'm part of us, but so are you. It can't always be about what I want, or what you want. And for God's sake, you have to stop assuming you know what I need or want."

"I do have a bad habit of doing that, don't I?"

"The worst. And it keeps leading you out the door, which quite honestly is unacceptable, as much as I do enjoy looking at your ass."

Kit looked like Thea had just thrown her a lifeline. They walked, hand in hand, in comfortable silence. Thea had missed this. She'd missed so much about Kit, but just being comfortable and safe in the presence of someone else was a unique experience. Kit was her safe space and now it was back.

Thea hadn't realized she was leading them to her place until they arrived on her front steps.

"One of the best nights of my life was sitting out here with you, after our first date, just talking," Kit said, her smile soft.

"Have a seat." Thea pointed to the same spot they'd shared after the baseball game. "Maybe we can have a second first date."

Kit laughed and sat down. She opened her arms for Thea like she had the first time. Thea wanted to sit down and let Kit wrap her up tightly, but she was also hungry.

"Snacks first, then snuggling."

"I feel like I should be offended at your order of priorities." Kit was pouting.

"Absolutely not." Thea opened the front door and headed inside. "Everyone knows you need snuggle snacks."

Thea ran into the house and hurriedly grabbed some food and drinks. The night was tilting toward chilly, so she pulled a blanket off the back of the couch, too.

When she got back out to the porch, Kit was resting her head back, eyes closed, one leg up casually. She looked at peace and sexy as hell. Thea considered dropping the snacks and dragging Kit inside by her belt buckle. But she wanted to talk. They needed to talk. There would be time for belt buckles later.

"You are so incredibly beautiful. How are you more beautiful every time I see you?"

Thea knew she was blushing. "You've got your eyes closed, what do you know?"

"I watched you walk out, and now I'm saving the image to memory. You have to close your eyes for that."

"Sweet talker. That might have just earned you a pretzel stick."

"What else you got? I can keep going." Kit patted the space in front of her.

Thea settled into Kit's arms and leaned back against her chest, and Kit wrapped her arms around her and held her close. Thea took a deep breath, inhaling the unique scent that was all Kit. The sweet combination of sawdust and sunshine.

"Why did you wait so long to come back to me?" Thea needed to know.

"I was trying to only give you half of me," Kit said. "That wasn't going to work for either of us."

"But I saw all of you. And I loved all of you," Thea said.

She felt Kit tense when she said loved. She wondered if it was the word or the past tense.

"I know you did." Kit kissed her hair, then her neck. "But I didn't. And it's hard to make rational decisions when you're at war with yourself. I had to figure out who I am, so I can feel like I'm giving you everything. I had this discussion with my mentee the other day. Hopefully, she'll catch on faster than I did. And I wanted you to take the time you needed. You said yourself you needed it."

"Can you back up to the mentee part?

"I told you, you can ask me anything. But I also have questions I need answers to. Like what's up with Daisy? And who was sitting outside the bathroom at the library tonight?"

"Me first." Thea turned a little in Kit's arms so she could see her face.

"Of course." Kit nodded. "I'm volunteering as a peer-mentor at Star Recovery. I've wanted to since you helped me get the part-time job there, but I was too scared. But, Kit 2.0 can do anything, including this."

Thea turned fully so she was kneeling facing Kit and threw her arms around Kit's neck. This had nothing to do with them. She was just happy for Kit and the nameless person lucky enough to be matched with Kit.

"Is it weird to say I'm proud of you?"

"Nope." Kit hugged Thea tightly. "I'm damn proud of me too. I decided against the flashing neon sign telling the world all my secrets, but maybe I've got some experience I can use to help someone else. It feels selfish not to try."

Thea grabbed handfuls of Kit's shirt and pulled her forward. She paused for a second just before she dipped her head to kiss her. She wanted one more second of anticipation.

The kiss wasn't fiery or wanton. This one was about emotion and reconnection. It was slow. Thea took her time reacquainting herself with Kit's lips. She didn't deepen the kiss for fear of losing herself. She wanted to keep talking, but she'd needed to kiss her, to reestablish their connection.

Thea pulled away and Kit tried to follow, but she let go of Kit's shirt and gently pushed her back. Kit let out a dramatic sigh but did as Thea asked.

"You're going to live." Thea patted her cheek.

"I might not. You might have just killed me."

"Resuscitate yourself." Thea trailed her finger up the inseam of Kit's jeans. "I have plans for you later."

"Fit as a fiddle. Clean bill of health." Kit flexed her muscles dramatically.

Thea knew what those muscles looked like when she made Kit come and the image was vivid. Thea shook her head to clear it. Kit gave her a look.

*Busted.*

Thea settled back in Kit's arms. They ate their snuggle snacks in silence for a while. Thea was working up the courage to ask Kit what she really needed to know.

"Kit, what happens the next time you get scared?"

She felt Kit sigh. She pulled her close and kissed the top of her head.

"I'm never going to lie to you. My first instinct will always be to protect you and my second instinct will probably always be to run."

Thea stiffened and started to pull away. Kit held on.

"But. I'm learning when I do that, the one who hurts you most, is me. I'm not a perfect woman, and I'll keep making mistakes. But you're the one I want to run to, not away from. I'm sorry I took so long to see that. I said it in the meeting, but I'll say it as many times as you need to believe me. I love you, Thea. That's worth fighting for and figuring out new ways to deal with tough things. You're worth whatever it takes."

Thea felt tears welling. She didn't try to control them. She let them fall. For the first time it felt okay to not know what came next. She and Kit would figure it out together.

"I love you too."

Kit shifted so she could see Thea's face.

"Really? After everything I did?"

"Kit, you weren't the only one who made mistakes. I'm sorry I wasn't there for you, too."

"But I ran. After you asked me not to."

"You did. And I was pissed off and hurt, but I had my own things to process. My dad's overdose came roaring back in a way I didn't expect after I revived Ethel. Being with you felt risky in a way it never had before. I've never had anyone looking out just for me. My parents, my ex-wife, everyone who signed up for the job failed. I got scared you might too, even without trying. But you are you and you are different. I knew you were scared. I knew that and I didn't chase after you. I should've chased you."

This time when they kissed there was nothing held back. Thea scraped her fingers along the short hairs at the back of Kit's head. She ran her tongue over Kit's lower lip and deepened their kiss. She's missed the feel of Kit's tongue on hers.

Kit's kiss was demanding and heated Thea through. Her hands, which had been holding her, now started to wander. Thea's skin felt exquisitely sensitive everywhere Kit's hands moved, and then she spread her hands flat over Thea's stomach and moved upward, brushing her breasts. Thea gasped at the electricity of it and pushed against her.

Kit moved her hands higher and Thea felt like it was the last opportunity to get off the porch and out of public before she ripped Kit's clothes off. She pulled away and out of her arms.

"I'm sorry," Kit said. "Was it too much? I shouldn't have assumed."

"You made the right assumption." Thea was breathing hard. "I just don't want to share your incredible ass with my neighbors, so get it inside. Now."

Kit must have been as eager as she was because she jumped to her feet and scooped up the food in record time. As soon as they were inside, Thea pulled Kit to her. Kit dropped the food and slipped her hands under Thea's shirt.

Thea let Kit explore. When she ran her hands over Thea's breasts, it felt like all pleasure signals fired at once and quite a few headed south. She didn't remember ever being so wet.

"Bedroom please." Thea pointed in the direction of her room.

"Lead the way."

Thea looked at Kit's belt buckle. *Not a tool belt but working for me just fine.*

Kit saw her looking. Thea could see the desire in her eyes. Thea grabbed the buckle and tugged. Kit followed her down the hall. In front of the bed, Thea turned Kit by the buckle and gave her a gentle push. Kit landed on her back and Thea quickly straddled her.

"You always seem to end up here." Kit rested her hands on Thea's hips.

"I like what you do to me when I'm here," Thea said.

Kit sat up, holding Thea to her, and kissed her deeply. She broke the kiss long enough to slip off her shirt and unclasp her bra. Kit's mouth was on her immediately, sucking in her nipple, hard, just like Thea liked. Thea dug her fingers into Kit's shoulders.

Kit flipped their position and was on top of Thea before she realized what had happened. Kit settled her weight on her and Thea moaned. Kit felt so good pressed between her legs. She yanked Kit's shirt off and her bra along with it.

"Why do you still have pants on?" Thea yanked on Kit's belt buckle. "Why do I still have pants on?"

"I can take care of that."

Thea shivered when the cool air hit her naked skin. She didn't shiver long. Kit covered her again and pressed her thigh to Thea's center. She wanted more but Kit pulled back. She grabbed Kit's ass and tried to pull her closer. Kit smiled down at her.

"Impatient."

"You haven't done anything yet. Wipe that grin off your face," Thea said.

Kit took Thea's nipple in her mouth and she arched off the bed. Kit didn't let her get used to the sensation before moving down her body. Her mouth was on Thea's clit, bringing her close to the edge and then it was gone.

Thea arched again, looking for Kit's mouth. She needed more.

"Less teasing Kit, more fucking."

Kit hesitated only a moment before taking Thea's clit fully in her mouth and slipping two fingers inside her.

"Fuck, yes." She held Kit's head in place and bucked her hips in rhythm with Kit's fingers. She felt her orgasm building but tried to hold it off. She wanted Kit's mouth on her and her inside a little longer. Finally, she gave in and let the orgasm crest over her. "Now you deserve that goofy grin."

Kit pulled out and leaned over her.

"Is that right? Maybe I should try again, just to be sure?"

Thea kissed her and could taste herself on Kit's lips.

"We have a lifetime for practice. Right now, you need to get on your back. I have plans for you."

"I love my woman with a plan." Kit rolled onto her back and pulled Thea on top of her.

"I love you." Thea kissed her softly. "Thank you for coming home."

# EPILOGUE—ONE YEAR LATER

Kit checked the burgers on her grill, and Josh looked at her from his grill next to her.

"You sure you don't want to be out there? Someone else can do the grilling," Josh said.

"Nowhere I'd rather be." Kit pressed the burger and let it sizzle.

Josh gave her a look. He pointed down the library steps, partway across the park. "We both know that's not true."

Kit's heart leapt when she caught sight of Thea. Nothing could make Kit's heart race like one look at her. She acknowledged Josh's point. The party was supposed to be on the library property, but it had spilled well into the park. Frankie had wanted a BBQ for her high school graduation. Of course, the whole neighborhood turned up. It was Frankie, after all.

Kit looked back to Thea. Daisy was walking with her toward the group of musicians, and it looked like Daisy was Thea's very own, extra-large, security detail.

"Ms. Marsden, your burgers appear to be aflame."

Kit looked down at her grill. Thea had completely distracted her. It was a good thing she didn't stop by the job sites. Kit would be dangerous with power tools if Thea were nearby.

"Walter, for God's sake, call me Kit."

Walter considered her for longer than Kit found comfortable.

"Did you stop by for something?"

"Only to thank you for throwing this party for Frankie," Walter said.

"You don't have to thank me for that." Kit stared him down. She wanted to make her point clear. "I love her too."

"I know you do." Walter shifted from foot to foot. "And it's obvious how much you love Thea. I guess the true purpose for my visit is to say, welcome to the family…Kit."

Walter walked away before Kit could gather herself enough to respond.

"That felt like a moment," Josh said. "Did I just witness a moment?"

"You have no idea." Why did someone using her name feel so good?

Kit was so caught off guard by Walter finally addressing her like a normal person she didn't see Thea approach. It wasn't until she wrapped her arms around her from behind that she was even aware she was there.

"Hi, sexy." Thea nuzzled into Kit's neck. "We know how to throw a party. Any chance you can sneak away from this grill?"

Kit handed her spatula to Josh and threw off her grill apron. "All yours."

"You sure are." Thea pulled her away from the grill and down the library steps. "Come dance with me."

Kit wasn't at all sure about the dancing part, but she'd go wherever Thea led.

They passed the Zookeeper and Parrot Master as they made their way through the crowd. It had been declared a holiday, and no business was being conducted in the park today, although there was a prominent table staffed with Star Recovery volunteers should anyone feel like making a change in their life. The same went for the family dinners Frankie had instigated. On community nights, everyone was welcome, and Parrot Master and the Zookeeper took the night off of work. It worked beautifully. It wasn't perfect, but it was headway, and that was something.

They both patted her on the shoulder and gave Thea and Kit a genuine hello. Frankie ran over and hugged both of them tightly. She was taking a gap year and working at Star Recovery and the library to get some more experience with the type of clients she eventually wanted to help as a lawyer. Next year she was off to college.

When they got close to the music, Thea slipped into Kit's arms. Kit's dancing skills consisted solely of swaying slowly with Thea in her arms, but Thea didn't seem to mind.

"Are you having a good time?" Thea pressed closer.

"I'm with you. That's all I ever need," Kit said. "But there's one thing I'm curious about. You told me once I'm not a Batman. Did you ever decide who I am?"

Thea put her hand on Kit's cheek while they danced. It was enough to raise Kit's blood pressure, but not enough to scandalize the crowd.

"No," Thea said. "I realized I don't need a masked superhero. I have you. And you are all I ever need, now and forever. Move in with me. I want to wake up with you every morning."

"Wherever you are is home. That's where I want to be. And I'll be sure the tool belt is the first thing I pack."

Kit saw Thea blush and laughed. "I feel like I should send Carrie flowers for letting slip I should bring that home with me each night."

"Speaking of Carrie, she and Josh seem awfully cozy." Thea looked over her shoulder in the direction of the grill.

Kit leaned in so she could whisper in Thea's ear. "Turns out, he has a tool belt too."

"You and Josh are nothing but trouble." Thea shook her head and laughed. "It's a good thing I love you. And your tool belt."

"I'll get a bigger, fancier one once I finish my general contractor licensing requirements and Josh and I start building the business together."

"Is that true?" Thea licked her lips. It didn't look voluntary.

"No. But I'll take you shopping and you can pick out any one you want."

"I've already got everything I want," Thea said.

Kit pulled Thea closer. This woman, this place, was where she was meant to be. It took her a while to find her way, but now she was finally at peace. She'd never imagined happiness like this, love like this. Kit looked around at the party, her friends, her family, blood and found, and Thea, the woman she loved. She sighed happily. For the first time, she felt like she truly understood the definition of serenity.

# About the Author

Jesse Thoma wishes that Swiss Army Knife were an official job title because she would use it.

Jesse grew up in Northern California but headed east for college. She never looked back, although her baseball allegiance is still loyally with the San Francisco Giants. She has lived in New England long enough to leave extra time in the morning to scrape snow off the car and use the letter "r" inappropriately.

Jesse is blissfully married and is happiest when she is spending time with her family or working on her next novel.

*Serenity* is Jesse's fifth novel. *Seneca Falls* was a Finalist for a Lambda Literary Award in romance. *Data Capture* was a Finalist for a Golden Crown Literary Society "Goldie" Award.

## Books Available from Bold Strokes Books

**A Love that Leads to Home** by Ronica Black. For Carla Sims and Janice Carpenter, home isn't about location, it's where your heart is. (978-1-63555-675-9)

**Blades of Bluegrass** by D. Jackson Leigh. A US Army occupational therapist must rehab a bitter veteran who is a ticking political time bomb the military is desperate to disarm. (978-1-63555-637-7)

**Guarding Hearts** by Jaycie Morrison. As treachery and temptation threaten the women of the Women's Army Corps, who will risk it all for love? (978-1-63555-806-7)

**Hopeless Romantic** by Georgia Beers. Can a jaded wedding planner and an optimistic divorce attorney possibly find a future together? (978-1-63555-650-6)

**Hopes and Dreams** by PJ Trebelhorn. Movie theater manager Riley Warren is forced to face her high school crush and tormentor, wealthy socialite Victoria Thayer, at their twentieth reunion. (978-1-63555-670-4)

**In the Cards** by Kimberly Cooper Griffin. Daria and Phaedra are about to discover that love finds a way, especially when powers outside their control are at play. (978-1-63555-717-6)

**Moon Fever** by Ileandra Young. SPEAR agent Danika Karson must clear her werewolf friend of multiple false charges while teaching her vampire girlfriend to resist the blood mania brought on by a full moon. (978-1-63555-603-2)

**Quake City** by St John Karp. Can Andre find his best friend Amy before the night devolves into a nightmare of broken hearts, malevolent drag queens, and spontaneous human combustion? Or has it always happened this way, every night, at Aunty Bob's Quake City Club? (978-1-63555-723-7)

**Serenity** by Jesse J. Thoma. For Kit Marsden, there are many things in life she cannot change. Serenity is in the acceptance. (978-1-63555-713-8)

**Sylver and Gold** by Michelle Larkin. Working feverishly to find a killer before he strikes again, Boston Homicide Detective Reid Sylver and rookie cop London Gold are blindsided by their chemistry and developing attraction. (978-1-63555-611-7)

**Trade Secrets** by Kathleen Knowles. In Silicon Valley, love and business are a volatile mix for clinical lab scientist Tony Leung and venture capitalist Sheila Garrison. (978-1-63555-642-1)

**Death Overdue** by David S. Pederson. Did Heath turn to murder in an alcohol induced haze to solve the problem of his blackmailer, or was it someone else who brought about a death overdue? (978-1-63555-711-4)

**Entangled** by Melissa Brayden. Becca Crawford is the perfect person to head up the Jade Hotel, if only the captivating owner of the local vineyard would get on board with her plan and stop badmouthing the hotel to everyone in town. (978-1-63555-709-1)

**First Do No Harm** by Emily Smith. Pierce and Cassidy are about to discover that when it comes to love, sometimes you have to risk it all to have it all. (978-1-63555-699-5)

**Kiss Me Every Day** by Dena Blake. For Wynn Evans, wishing for a do-over with Carly Jamison was a long shot, actually getting one was a game changer. (978-1-63555-551-6)

**Olivia** by Genevieve McCluer. In this lesbian Shakespeare adaption with vampires, Olivia is a centuries old vampire who must fight a strange figure from her past if she wants a chance at happiness. (978-1-63555-701-5)

**One Woman's Treasure** by Jean Copeland. Daphne's search for discarded antiques and treasures leads to an embarrassing misunderstanding, and ultimately, the opportunity for the romance of a lifetime with Nina. (978-1-63555-652-0)

**Silver Ravens** by Jane Fletcher. Lori has lost her girlfriend, her home, and her job. Things don't improve when she's kidnapped and taken to fairyland. (978-1-63555-631-5)

**Still Not Over You** by Jenny Frame, Carsen Taite, Ali Vali. Old flames die hard in these tales of a second chance at love with the ex you're still not over. Stories by award winning authors Jenny Frame, Carsen Taite, and Ali Vali. (978-1-63555-516-5)

**Storm Lines** by Jessica L. Webb. Devon is a psychologist who likes rules. Marley is a cop who doesn't. They don't always agree, but both fight to protect a girl immersed in a street drug ring. (978-1-63555-626-1)

**The Politics of Love** by Jen Jensen. Is it possible to love across the political divide in a hostile world? Conservative Shelley Whitmore and liberal Rand Thomas are about to find out. (978-1-63555-693-3)

**All the Paths to You** by Morgan Lee Miller. High school sweethearts Quinn Hughes and Kennedy Reed reconnect five years after they break up and realize that their chemistry is all but over. (978-1-63555-662-9)

**Arrested Pleasures** by Nanisi Barrett D'Arnuck. When charged with a crime she didn't commit Katherine Lowe faces the question: Which is harder, going to prison or falling in love? (978-1-63555-684-1)

**Bonded Love** by Renee Roman. Carpenter Blaze Carter suffers an injury that shatters her dreams, and ER nurse Trinity Greene hopes to show her that sometimes love is worth fighting for. (978-1-63555-530-1)

**Convergence** by Jane C. Esther. With life as they know it on the line, can Aerin McLeary and Olivia Ando's love survive an otherworldly threat to humankind? (978-1-63555-488-5)

**Coyote Blues** by Karen F. Williams. Riley Dawson, psychotherapist and shape-shifter, has her world turned upside down when Fiona Bell, her one true love, returns. (978-1-63555-558-5)

**Drawn** by Carsen Taite. Will the clues lead Detective Claire Hanlon to the killer terrorizing Dallas, or will she merely lose her heart to person of interest, urban artist Riley Flynn? (978-1-63555-644-5)

**Every Summer Day** by Lee Patton. Meant to celebrate every summer day, Luke's journal instead chronicles a love affair as fast-moving and possibly as fatal as his brother's brain tumor. (978-1-63555-706-0)

**Lucky** by Kris Bryant. Was Serena Evans's luck really about winning the lottery, or is she about to get even luckier in love? (978-1-63555-510-3)

**The Last Days of Autumn** by Donna K. Ford. Autumn and Caroline question the fairness of life, the cruelty of loss, and what it means to love as they navigate the complicated minefield of relationships, grief, and life-altering illness. (978-1-63555-672-8)

**Three Alarm Response** by Erin Dutton. In the midst of tragedy, can these first responders find love and healing? Three stories of courage, bravery, and passion. (978-1-63555-592-9)

**Veterinary Partner** by Nancy Wheelton. Callie and Lauren are determined to keep their hearts safe but find that taking a chance on love is the safest option of all. (978-1-63555-666-7)

**Everyday People** by Louis Barr. When film star Diana Danning hires private eye Clint Steele to find her son, Clint turns to his former West Point barracks mate, and ex-buddy with benefits, Mars Hauser to lend his cyber espionage and digital black ops skills to the case. (978-1-63555-698-8)

**Forging a Desire Line** by Mary P. Burns. When Charley's ex-wife, Tricia, is diagnosed with inoperable cancer, the private duty nurse Tricia hires turns out to be the handsome and aloof Joanna, who ignites something inside Charley she isn't ready to face. (978-1-63555-665-0)

**Love on the Night Shift** by Radclyffe. Between ruling the night shift in the ER at the Rivers and raising her teenage daughter, Blaise Richilieu has all the drama she needs in her life, until a dashing young attending appears on the scene and relentlessly pursues her. (978-1-63555-668-1)

**Olivia's Awakening** by Ronica Black. When the daring and dangerously gorgeous Eve Monroe is hired to get Olivia Savage into shape, a fierce passion ignites, causing both to question everything they've ever known about love. (978-1-63555-613-1)

**The Duchess and the Dreamer** by Jenny Frame. Clementine Fitzroy has lost her faith and love of life. Can dreamer Evan Fox make her believe in life and dream again? (978-1-63555-601-8)

**The Road Home** by Erin Zak. Hollywood actress Gwendolyn Carter is about to discover that losing someone you love sometimes means gaining someone to fall for. (978-1-63555-633-9)

**Waiting for You** by Elle Spencer. When passionate past-life lovers meet again in the present day, one remembers it vividly and the other isn't so sure. (978-1-63555-635-3)

**While My Heart Beats** by Erin McKenzie. Can a love born amidst the horrors of the Great War survive? (978-1-63555-589-9)

**Face the Music** by Ali Vali. Sweet music is the last thing that happens when Nashville music producer Mason Liner, and daughter of country royalty Victoria Roddy are thrown together in an effort to save country star Sophie Roddy's career. (978-1-63555-532-5)

**Flavor of the Month** by Georgia Beers. What happens when baker Charlie and chef Emma realize their differing paths have led them right back to each other? (978-1-63555-616-2)

**Mending Fences** by Angie Williams. Rancher Bobbie Del Rey and veterinarian Grace Hammond are about to discover if heartbreaks of the past can ever truly be mended. (978-1-63555-708-4)

**Silk and Leather: Lesbian Erotica with an Edge** edited by Victoria Villasenor. This collection of stories by award winning authors offers fantasies as soft as silk and tough as leather. The only question is: How far will you go to make your deepest desires come true? (978-1-63555-587-5)

**The Last Place You Look** by Aurora Rey. Dumped by her wife and looking for anything but love, Julia Pierce retreats to her hometown, only to rediscover high school friend Taylor Winslow, who's secretly crushed on her for years. (978-1-63555-574-5)

**The Mortician's Daughter** by Nan Higgins. A singer on the verge of stardom discovers she must give up her dreams to live a life in service to ghosts. (978-1-63555-594-3)

**The Real Thing** by Laney Webber. When passion flares between actress Virginia Green and masseuse Allison McDonald, can they be sure it's the real thing? (978-1-63555-478-6)

**What the Heart Remembers Most** by M. Ullrich. For college sweethearts Jax Levine and Gretchen Mills, could an accident be the second chance neither knew they wanted? (978-1-63555-401-4)

**White Horse Point** by Andrews & Austin. Mystery writer Taylor James finds herself falling for the mysterious woman on White Horse Point who lives alone, protecting a secret she can't share about a murderer who walks among them. (978-1-63555-695-7)